I0614045

A Secret Network of Specialists Must Prevent a
Global Terrorist Plot

THE
SHADOW
EXPERTS

ANOTHER THRILLER BY
ANDREW B. LOUIS

This is a work of fiction. All characters, organizations, and events portrayed in this novel are either products of the author's imagination or are used fictitiously.

Copyright © 2021 by Andrew B. Louis

All rights reserved. No part of this publication may be reproduced in whole or in part, or stored in a retrieval system, or transmitted in any form or by any means, electronic, mechanical, photocopying, recording, or otherwise, without written permission of the author, except for the inclusion of brief quotations in a review.

For information regarding permission, please write to:
info@barringerpublishing.com
Barringer Publishing, Naples, Florida
www.barringerpublishing.com

Cover, graphics, and layout by Linda S. Duider
Cape Coral, Florida

ISBN: 978-1-954396-06-7
Library of Congress Cataloging-in-Publication Data
The Shadow Experts / Andrew B. Louis

Printed in U.S.A.

DEDICATION

To family and close friends . . .
around the world.

OTHER BOOKS BY THE AUTHOR

Other novels by Andrew B. Louis include:

Operation Kovesh and *Seven Miracles To Save The World*
available at Amazon.com.

www.AndrewBLouis.com

SYNOPSIS

"The Shadow Experts" tells a story that brings together the world of spying and a group of experts whose goal it is to help "just causes." The heroine, a very secretive individual with a European aristocratic cover, founded a network of specialists whose expertise encompasses a vast swath of current scientific knowledge. It ranges from highly technical fields such as nuclear physics or bio-medical research to others, more qualitative, such as psychology, art and criminology. Each of the members of the network is sworn to secrecy and only rarely meets either the heroine or other members. This network is known as "The Shadow Experts." They all have their own known and public activities, allowing them to stay at the leading edge of their specialty. Here, The Shadow Experts are hired by the *Mossad* to help trace a deadly virus which seems to have hit a few geographical pockets with, on the surface, no apparent relationship with one another.

Using novel and at times even experimental equipment, the heroine, with the help of colleagues from "The Shadow Experts" and *Mossad* agents, works to find the source of the virus, the reasons for its introduction in selective geographies and the best approach to contain its spread. The hunt for the source takes her and members of her informal team around the world. In the process, she discovers a parallel network of criminals linked to a large and dangerous organization and at least one, possibly two countries and their secret services. Will the project prevent the catastrophe that is being planned?

Preface: All the parties to this story are totally fictitious and if there was some resemblance with individuals or institutions, it would be purely coincidental.

PROLOGUE

APPROACHING TENZING-HILLARY AIRPORT, NEPAL

Prince Philip of Austria and his wife, Uta, were quite excited. They were in their private jet on their way to Nepal. They were bringing medicine to a local, makeshift field hospital which Malteser International had set up to deal with the victims of an earthquake which had struck the area a few days earlier.

A secondary-line heir to the family crown, Prince Philip had never really been involved in the affairs of the Court. In fact, the crown had really become purely ceremonial, since the establishment of the Austrian Republic on September 10, 1919, when the emperor had to abdicate, losing his family's succession rights in the process. The family was allowed to keep its aristocratic title, though it really did not mean much any longer.

Prince Philip had understood that his future would never involve ruling over the family's empire. Rather, he had dedicated himself to business. In fact, over time, he had made a fortune in a variety of businesses, all perfectly legitimate and with everything always above board. He often reminded his friends and business associates:

"Whiter than white is my vision of what the French call 'Noblesse Oblige.'"

The family had a strong tradition of deep religious faith, and Philip was no exception. He had no compulsion against making money but would never even countenance anything that smacked of illegality, impropriety or even the potential for impropriety to be suspected. Further, considering his successes partly as divine gifts, he felt a need to share them with others. He and his wife had decided to dedicate a part of their time and treasure to serve those that were down on their luck. As a Knight and a Dame of the Order of Malta, their idea of "doing good" naturally drove them to participating in the philanthropic activities of the Order's worldwide humanitarian relief agency: Malteser International which provides help during and following conflicts and disasters.

"Fasten your seat belts . . . We're told the weather on approach is particularly choppy today. Shouldn't be a problem, but I'm afraid it's going to shake us all up quite a bit . . . Sorry."

Neither Prince Philip nor Princess Uta were particularly surprised by their pilot's, Franz, announcement. After all, they knew the reputation of Tenzing-Hillary Airport, in Lukla, Nepal, as one of the world's most dangerous fields. It is named after Sir Edmund Percival Hillary, a New Zealand mountaineer, explorer and philanthropist who, on 29 May 1953, became the first climber confirmed to have reached the summit of Mount Everest, with his Sherpa mountaineer, Tenzing Norgay. So, the prince and princess dutifully tightened their seat belts and smiled at each other, across the aisle of the plane.

"My God! Franz isn't kidding. Don't think I've ever felt such a tough approach here or anywhere else . . ."

Those were the last words ever to come out of Prince Philip's mouth. A second later, he felt the plane banking sharply to the right, and then to the left, before it hit the ground and exploded, killing all aboard.

Princess Alexandra, their only daughter, suddenly found herself a very, very rich but quite sad orphan.

CHAPTER.01

OTTAWA, CANADA, TEL AVIV, ISRAEL, SINGAPORE AND SOMEWHERE IN THE AUSTRIAN ALPS

"Colonel Threadsome?"

"We have a situation . . ."

"What?"

"I see files disappearing from the server."

"What?"

"The server is being hacked . . . Someone is erasing files."

"Damn it! Can you switch the server off?"

"Not without switching off most of our security apparatus."

The conversation was taking place at the headquarters of the Canadian Security Intelligence Services in Ottawa. Though most Ottawa residents would be able to point to its actual address, the service is still sufficiently discreet that its only official address is a Post Office box. Lieutenant Francis Kroll had just picked up the first bit of evidence that someone had intruded into their computer systems. A few files seemed to be disappearing and access to other files was much slower than usual. Lieutenant Kroll had therefore called Colonel William Threadsome to report the problem. He considered himself too junior to take it any farther up in the hierarchy.

Colonel Threadsome also felt that this had to be escalated to his ultimate boss, General Michael "Mike" Marceau, right away. He wanted both to bring him up to speed and, more importantly, to ask for instructions. These came back like the rattle of an automatic weapon: "Switch off the whole system . . . Move to the backup . . . I know this won't give us the same protection, but . . . No choice . . . Make sure I'm kept fully informed . . . Let's do it."

Lieutenant Kroll eventually carried out all the instructions he and Colonel Threadsome had received. Yet, that did not do the trick. Files were still being erased, though possibly at a marginally slower rate. The news was still unacceptably bad. Lieutenant Kroll had to call his boss again:

"Colonel Threadsome?"

"Yes . . ."

"Looks like they're now attacking the backup as well."

"Dammit! Stay the course . . . Everything but the backup is switched off, correct?"

"Correct, sir."

"Well, keep it that way. Keep monitoring. Let me know if anything seems to change. Anything: faster or slower progress; any new sign of intrusion; any change of target; whatever . . . OK?"

"Yes, sir."

"I believe the steps we've taken should slow them down a lot. Maybe stop them. It may just take more time than I thought. Stay on top of it and keep me in the loop."

■ ■ ■ ■ ■

General Marceau was the Head of the Internal Security of Canada. A genial, career military man, General Mike Marceau had climbed the hierarchy of Canadian security step by step. His education was excellent, and his skills as good as anyone's. Yet, he did not follow the classical "royal way" which permits certain officers to rise faster in the ranks.

He was not flashy, but, somehow, always managed to get things done. The lack of flashiness could be seen to have hurt him, as he was not one to toot his own horn. In fact, he suspected, in his rare moments of minor depression, that others may have moved up by taking credit for stuff he had done. He was the quintessential example of the career officer who shows discipline and efficiency and does not make waves. Today, he was at his wits' end. Some group of hackers had gotten into the state's computers. Though Canada has an exceptionally strong counter-espionage apparatus, very often working in very close contact with the U.S. Central Intelligence Agency, they were now seemingly totally unable to trace the intruders. More importantly, the hackers were making fast progress. Something radical needed to be done . . . And fast.

General Marceau called his friend in *Mossad*, the Israeli security service, Colonel Simon Rabinowitz. He was responsible for a particularly secret group, within an already very secretive organization. They were in charge of activities which many would consider illegal, but these activities still needed to be carried out in the interest of the state of Israel. His group did not appear on any organization chart that anyone could procure. The phone rang on Simon's desk:

"Simon?"

"Yes . . ."

"Mike Marceau here."

"Hey. Great to hear from you, Mike . . . What's up?"

"We have hacker activity. They've penetrated our systems . . . Both the principal and the back-up."

"An inside job?"

"Don't know . . . But we must act fast . . . They're deleting files. Don't want them to access the really critical stuff . . . You know, agents' names and all the rest."

"Got it . . . My friend, that's a job for Countess Renate."

■ ■ ■ ■ ■

Princess Alexandra was no ordinary member of the old European aristocracy. After she inherited her parents' financial fortune, she lived a variation on the classical life of a rich aristocrat, but that was only a cover.

Below the surface, Princess Alexandra, a.k.a. Countess Renate, was the head of a global network, which she called "The Shadow Experts." That network was as secret as its leader. It consisted of specialists across a wide variety of disciplines that cooperated with "clients" and were directed by Countess Renate to defend "good causes." They ranged from microbiologists to advanced material engineers, to art experts, to cyber engineers, to electronics experts and to many other specialties, each as esoteric as the others. All members knew they were members of the network, but most did not know who the others were. They all knew Renate; most if not all had seen her on some video conference call; but few had met her in person, after the initial contact when they joined the group. Renate had no board of directors. Her only employees were a handful of individuals who worked for her at the "Castle," her residence in the Austrian Alps. They were the only ones who knew of her twin identities.

Whenever a "problem" was brought to her attention, usually directly or indirectly through a contact she had helped earlier, she recruited a team among her members according to the disciplines and specific areas of knowledge she would need for that "project." Once the mission was accomplished, the team disbanded and returned to the shadows. Though everything is possible, members rarely found themselves involved in a project more than twice a year, although certain specialties were more in demand than others. Virtually all team members had a "real" or "official" life directly connected to their area of specialty.

She received a hefty fee for her services, which she shared with the team members who participated. After it was paid, she routinely sent a thank you note to the client, with an additional request that a charitable contribution might be considered, often on behalf of some local not-for-profit organization and frequently in the realm of health or humanitarian causes. She remained staunchly non-political, though she had never been invited to help by any totalitarian regime. It's quite doubtful that she would have accepted even if the invitation had been extended.

■ ■ ■ ■ ■

Mike Marceau called Countess Renate on an unlisted phone number which Simon had provided him. She picked up after a few rings. In fact, she actually had picked up as soon as she heard a ring in her "office." However, nobody needed to know that the phone call bounced across nearly a dozen other numbers around the world, to make any call totally untraceable. Mike introduced himself and gave her Simon's name as a recommendation.

She told him that she knew and had a lot of respect for Simon. With his introduction, which she would still check, as Mike was warned, she said she would be happy to help. Mike gave her some initial information, emphasizing the fact that the hackers had seemingly penetrated both the principal and the backup system. His main message:

"Countess, this is serious. Time is of the essence. There is risk to the identity and safety of a wide swath of secret agents, Canadian and from other countries. They could be discovered and revealed."

Countess Renate did not express any strong reaction. She just asked Mike for a secure phone line on which she could call back.

Countess Renate immediately contacted Wong Hai Chock, her top cyber security expert. He resided in Singapore. He was normally employed as a professor/researcher at the National University of Singapore. Though he was as honest and straightforward as they come, he had a passion for puzzles. To him, dealing with hackers and all that was broadly known as the "dark web" was of utmost interest, just like solving a puzzle. Wikipedia offers a useful definition of the dark web: "The dark web refers to encrypted online content that is not indexed by conventional search engines. Sometimes, the dark web is also called the dark net. The dark web is a component of the deep web that describes the wider breadth of content that does not appear through regular Internet browsing activities."

To Hai Chock, the dark web was a devil that allowed a variety of more or less criminal activities to be carried out behind the scenes. It had to be put out of business, though he recognized that his goal was probably not achievable. As he often said to himself, *criminal minds can be equally smart as honest ones.*

Hai Chock had never in the past seen a hack that he had not been able to crack and disrupt. Countess Renate had used one of her several satellite phones to call him. They were virtually impossible to detect, all the more so, as she quickly went from one to the other when away from the Castle. She conferenced General Marceau in and introduced Hai Chock. She then asked Mike to explain the issue. He went into some more depth but had to admit that he had very few more specific details:

"Would need to connect you with my people on the ground . . ."

He could only emphasize the fact that it appeared untraceable. So far, the intruders had not managed to get into the secret services files, but as he added:

"Given the speed at which they're working, it's a matter of days, if not less."

Hai Chock paused for a few seconds, gathering his wits as the call had come in what was for him the middle of the night. He asked Mike for a contact person in Canada, as well as for an introduction to him or her, adding:

"Under no circumstance can my real name come out. I shall be Jim Ng. Also, no need to mention Singapore. I'm an Asian cybersecurity consultant." Hai Chock was in contact will Bill Threadsome in a matter of minutes, with Renate and Mike conferenced in. He asked Bill to reboot the system he had shut down, and allow him in. Bill gave him all the appropriate credentials so that he could see on his own screens in his home office what they saw in Ottawa.

Hai Chock went silent for a short while and then muttered:

"Sophisticated little buggers."

Bill asked:

"What do you see, Jim?"

"They're using bouncing addresses. Just like us . . . But they don't know that I've figured out how to trace them . . . Nobody knows that . . . Let's see . . . Well, looks like the culprit is working from . . . Darn it . . . Ottawa."

"What do you mean?"

"They're trying to disguise themselves as coming from China, but your hackers are home grown, my friend."

"Can't believe it."

"In fact, Bill, I'll bet you it's an inside job . . . I can't tell you who he is yet, but the intrusion into the backup system is a giveaway. Why would external hackers know how to get into it?"

Jim, aka Hai Chock, kept everyone on the line for a while, as he was working. Soon, however, he realized that it would take him too much time to solve the problem with them on the line. He feared he could not maintain the security of the line with so many people potentially subject to hacking themselves; he said:

"Can't stay on the line . . . Risk of detection . . . Just too high . . . Countess Renate, may I call you back as soon as I have something to report."

"Sure . . . Staying in the shadows is key. Avoid all risk of detection. Mike, I'll conference you in when Hai Chock calls me back."

"Fine. Thank you."

They all hung up. Jim went back to work on the problem at hand.

It was a hallmark of The Shadow Experts that they had no business hours or days off. They worked when they were needed. Jim's first effort focused on shutting down access to the most sensitive part of the system. It involved creating gates with different and incremental security that in effect would prevent a hacker from penetrating. But that was not quite enough. His strategy had him force any additional hacker activity through one of his own servers which he interposed between the ultra-sensitive part of the Canadian system and the rest. Any hacker who tried to penetrate into the ultra-sensitive section of the system would now have to reveal more than he or she should or would want to. Jim could then identify the culprit and disable their computers.

Hai Chock had developed what he called a "computer bomb." Clearly, it involved no explosives. How could one insert explosives from afar? But, just as a human body can have activity that exhausts it to the point of near-death or even death, he could force the enemy computer into a series of maneuvers which would lead to it blowing itself up. He could indeed surreptitiously introduce himself into the hacker's computer and remotely "detonate" it. He would trick the system into working above capacity at high speed. Eventually this would produce too much heat, drawing too much electricity from the battery, for instance, and disable most of its functions. It would also keep the computer so busy that all other activity was frozen; it could no longer do any harm. The cherry on top of the cake is that the attacking computer would reveal its coordinates just before blowing up.

Within a few hours, Jim was back on the phone to Renate and then Mike Marceau, who would relay the information to Bill Threadsome:

"Problem solved . . . The hacker's computer has blown up . . . He's lost access. And I added two layers of security to your system, Mike. At this point, I would prefer not to disclose them to anyone; at least until you all have identified the culprit. I've sent the coordinates of the offending computer to Bill Threadsome; it sent me a signal when the "bomb went off!" Bill's looking into it. They should have no difficulty identifying him or her. Then, I'll let you back into your own system."

Mike was bluffed. He could not believe his ears:

"How could our own security fail to detect an insider?" Renate simply replied:

"It's often the most obvious that escapes us . . ."

Hai Chock hung up as he was no longer needed on the call. Renate and Mike Marceau would then be discussing the payment of The Shadow Experts' fees. Jim, aka Hai Chock, would eventually receive his share, which he would credit to the cyber consultancy which he maintained officially. It would be booked as a job for the Canadian government. Renate and her team would never appear anywhere.

One does not cheat on one's taxes in Singapore as Hai Chock always thought. The Republic was indeed a wonderful place, created and nurtured by a visionary leader, Lee Kwan Yew. But, in order to keep his country safe, he could be ruthless with anyone flaunting the law. He was known to have been all his life above any form of suspicion and many people who lived in Singapore, permanently or as expatriates, would agree that the place is as free of corruption as humanly feasible. But every coin has another side. People should be prepared to accept modest limitations on their freedom so that they were able to enjoy their freedom. A bit like the classical refrain which argues that personal freedom should end whenever it infringed on someone else's freedom. . . .

Another few hours later, Mike Marceau called Renate:

"The money has been wired."

"Wonderful . . . Thank you . . . Happy to have been of help. As we always ask our clients, but you are under no obligation, I would appreciate a gift to the Red Cross. No attribution to us, please."

"I understand."

The next day, Hai Chock and Renate received word that the culprit had been apprehended. He was using a new computer to try to enter the system through the new gateway created by Jim. Mike could not believe that Bill Threadsome's deputy could possibly be the man. Yet, he confessed after his arrest that he was working for a foreign power. His intrusion into the Canadian security computer systems was but a dry run ahead of a much larger operation.

CHAPTER.02

SOMEWHERE IN THE AUSTRIAN ALPS

After she inherited the family's fortune, Princess Alexandra had completed her studies in biology, all the way to her PhD. She had then decided to remain at university as a researcher, though she was conducting most of her work in the field and from her home.

Her life suddenly changed on that fateful day her parents' plane crashed, in more than one way. Obviously, becoming an orphan at a young age and in a very tightly united family had to constitute a dramatic, emotional shock. It would surely take some time for mourning to ease the pain away, which it eventually did. But now, she also controlled the fortune. She could no longer remain practically anonymous. She was a very wealthy aristocrat.

Yet, she had elected to remain in the shadows. She could have easily afforded the kind of lifestyle that would land her smack in the middle of the jet set. But this was just not who she was. Her family had brought her up in a strict, Roman Catholic environment and she had found it quite comfortable. She did not feel guilty because of her wealth but, just as her parents did, she felt she needed to use it, or at least a part of it, in a way that could help others. Ostentation was simply not in her blood. The downside of her somewhat solitary living was obvious.

Princess Alexandra had married an heir to the Danish crown a few years after her parents' death. In many ways, they were a perfect match. Prince Karl, her husband, was known to be a scientist who disliked any form of public life. He was sufficiently down the pecking order in term of royal succession that there were little or no expectations of him ever having to fulfill an official role. They both appeared to lead very quiet and ordinary lives; people assumed that Karl was continuing his research into ever more esoteric topics, while Princess Alexandra was assumed to serve as manager of her family's business interests. In fact, when he was not working with his wife as her trusted pilot, Prince Karl was the one managing and growing the family's businesses. Karl and Alexandra never had children. Occasionally, she would feel a pinch in her heart; she missed playing a motherly role, but she was not prepared to let it bring her down. Nature apparently was not going to allow her to be a mother; so be it. She had always thought, it *might be nice to have children but, after all, the family fortune can always go to some charity.*

She and her husband lived in the family castle. For some unknown reason, that part of the family fortune had not been confiscated when the Emperor had abdicated. Most likely, it was because her branch of the family was not sufficiently high in the order of potential succession to the throne. Some disagreed with that conclusion. They went as far as opining that her father might have been a traitor, suggesting that he might have paid some "ransom" to keep the beloved castle. But, to those who knew them the family, most probably, escaped confiscation because the castle, at that time, did not own much land other than the immediate surrounding forests; moreover, it did not seem to be in particularly good condition. In fact, Renate could remember her father repeatedly argue that the castle was more a liability than an asset: *Costs a lot to maintain . . . Would cost a fortune to restore.*

Her father's business successes over time, at least a generation after the end of the first world war, provided him with exactly what the doctor ordered—a large fortune. He never was directly involved in manufacturing, nor could he point to some specific invention that had led to the fortune. But he simply seemed to be unusually good at perceiving opportunities. He could hear of a product which was successful somewhere but that, in his view, could be equally successful in some other place. He would approach the manufacturer together with some local connection and offer a joint venture to expand the market. It rarely failed. He had thus brought a number of well-known European or American brands to parts of the world that were "dying" to have them, but where the original owner of the brand was not willing to commit the attention or the capital. Often indeed, his successes were in the less-developed world, though numbers of them were among smaller developed countries, where markets were too small to catch the eye of large businesses. As the saying goes: *small streams eventually aggregate to large rivers.*

He had used some of the fortune to restore the castle to what had been its ancient beauty, though he was always careful to avoid attracting attention. Whether this was because of an instinctive discretion or as a precautionary move against confiscation, nobody knows; most likely, a bit of both. Truth be told, Alexandra did not realize the kind of wealth her parents had until after she inherited it. She knew they were quite well off, but her parents had been careful to teach her the value rather than the price of everything. Additionally, a substantial portion of the wealth was outside of Austria, as her father's business successes had been mostly in foreign countries.

After her inheritance, she was known to be wealthy, but nobody really knew how wealthy she was. Her father's discretion in the deployment and investment of his assets created a useful screen. However, she was proud of the fact that everything which her father ever had and which she now had was dutifully disclosed to the appropriate authorities. At the same time, there were still a number of elements of the wealth that were located in places that allowed taxes to be deferred. Her relatively low-key appearance and lifestyle had not provided any incentive for an investigative journalist to chart her father's business empire or her current wealth.

She was regularly invited to all events that involved old, European royalty. She attended most of the time, but, in truth, never really enjoyed many of these occasions. However, she always believed that her heritage was an important part of her public persona; it had to be nurtured. Her name and physical appearance were well known, as was her address. However, paparazzi had eventually stopped virtually camping on her doorsteps, after they realized that there was no "scoop" to be had. She and Karl were seemingly not going to do anything worth reporting.

She held an annual party in memory of her parents, with members of royalty and the jet set invited to the castle for the occasion. The party was wonderful, but not excessive—good beverages, good food, nice classical, mostly Austrian music, but no unnecessary fireworks or ostentatious display of wealth. Karl was always in attendance, typically dressed in a military uniform he had earned in his bachelor years, with his light, blond hair kept a bit longer than many of his contemporaries. It was probably the only occasion when the media was interested in Princess Alexandra and when there was anything to report at the castle. Guests could admire heavy draperies, antique furnishing, numerous important pieces of art, portraits tracing back the genealogy of the family several centuries, magnificent European tapestries and Persian carpets, as well as occasional modern items, such as a few plushy sofas and chairs, flat television screens in several of the reception rooms and glass covered side or coffee tables. One could tell that the castle was not a museum, but a place which people actually inhabited.

Over time, she found a second vocation that became the most fascinating part of her life, though it was to remain completely hidden from view. The idea came about from an unexpected experience. Once, she had been given the opportunity to help an industrialist resolve a thorny issue, thanks to her background in biology. Though remaining in the shadows, she had been able to find a way to test a competing product which its manufacturer claimed to offer an equivalent result to the medicine produced by the industrialist. The pharmaceutical industrialist suspected that the competing drug was imperfect. Testing them both alongside each other produced results which proved the industrialist correct. The competitor was somewhat of a phony. He went out of business. She was royally paid for her efforts and it gave her an idea:

Why shouldn't I create a network of specialists in most major sciences and offer our discrete and behind the scenes help to anyone who needs it?

■ ■ ■ ■ ■

Thus the "The Shadow Experts" were born. She had initially toyed with a different name: "*The Gemeinschaft,*" a German word that conveys both the sense of association and community. She also considered the idea of somehow adding the term "Just" to the group's name, because of the focus on dealing with "just causes." Yet, in the end, she had opted for a simpler English name, "The Shadow Experts;" it was friendlier and easily understandable to a world where English is the *lingua franca*. Though not quite a modern Robin Hood or equivalent comic strip heroine, she imagined that there was no way anyone, even the most powerful government, could maintain absolute preeminence in so many specialties. Governments could try, but without the spark of private enterprise and the potential financial gain, many scientists would not take the final step separating smarts from genius. She was fully aware that idealists existed worldwide but was always leery that idealism could breed ideological rigidity as well.

She was originally convinced that there were people who were determined to do what is right and prevent what is wrong from occurring. She had been proven right: each person she contacted had agreed to join her effort. She had used some of her considerable fortune to build *The Shadow Experts* into a formidable force. She had also needed to develop and provide the most sophisticated communication capabilities to each member of her network.

Though both she and the members of her network were royally compensated when a mission was completed, it would have been profoundly inaccurate to call any of them a mercenary. In her case, for instance, the money which she was earning was routinely used to develop her capabilities further. At most, one could argue that they were in part financially incentivized idealists, or mad scientists that refused to let knowledge be used to hurt others, however that was defined. Yet, they never fell into the trap that she identified as "becoming ideologues."

Her teammates were all at the top of their professions; they remained officially employed in and contributing to their respective environments. No one would imagine that they all led a double life. Yet, they would occasionally be called upon, at most once or twice a year, to help someone deal with something they could not handle on their own.

Over the prior fifteen years, The Shadow Experts had therefore gradually assumed a considerably greater role, though the group's leader, Countess Renate, remained unknown to most people. Each of her and her team's successes raised her profile with potential clients or references. Yet, somehow, there was never any public acknowledgement of the participation of someone "special." At best, as had been the case recently in Canada, certain newspaper articles alluded to a particularly gifted cyber-consultant in Southeast Asia.

Only a few previous clients knew of the existence of Countess Renate, though no one knew that she and Princess Alexandra were one and the same. Ostensibly, they had the same general build. But where Princess Alexandra had flowing, dark, blond hair and blue eyes, Countess Renate wore her brown hair short and had deep brown eyes. Captain Frederik, aka Prince Karl, also experienced a hair color change, and had a short, neatly cropped beard. Yet, though broadly unknown to the public, it was generally thought that several heads of security apparatuses had some knowledge of The Shadow Experts, but few had any direct experience with it.

Renate had indeed worked for and with many of the intelligence services of the non-communist world. The most senior figures in them knew of her existence and how to get in touch with Countess Renate. They would have seen her, though not always in person but they had no idea where she lived or even where the nervous center of her group was located. When called, she seemed to appear out of nowhere and to disappear as rapidly as she appeared when the mission was over.

A major physical testimony of her efforts was found in the hidden features of her ancestral castle and in the equipment that was at her disposal. Yet, none of this was visible to the uninitiated. The castle was well-known, but it was known as the property of Princess Alexandra, who lived a very discrete life, with her princely husband. She had initially been rumored to have had a few amorous adventures in one or the other of the famous places frequented by the jet set. But all of that came to an abrupt stop, after she met and eventually married Prince Karl. No one who knew Princess Alexandra could remotely consider that this younger woman might morph into a secret agent whenever needed.

The castle, which sat in the alps on a meadow the size of six or seven football fields, surrounded by thick forest, actually comprised a completely, hidden infrastructure, all below ground. The main feature of the large esplanade in front of the castle was an underground lair which was accessed both via a secret passage from the inside of the castle and through an external hidden "elevator." A ten thousand square foot part of the esplanade stood on a massive, steel plate. Five hydraulic jacks, one at each corner, and a larger one in the center moved it up or down. When in its "up position," it would normally be an indistinguishable part of the esplanade, with shrubs around its periphery hiding any visible seam. Cars would drive through it and never know what laid underneath. It is highly probable that it had been photographed several times from the air, by planes or satellites, without anyone being able to guess that it was anything other than what it appeared to be.

When lowered, it provided access to a massive complex, with technology to rival any of those displayed in spy novels or similar adventure books. The centerpiece was a landing pad from which one could take off with a helicopter or with Renate's "slightly modified" private jet. Though appearing totally "standard" from the outside, her CJ-4 jet had several secret features, the most important of which were a vertical takeoff and landing capability and the ability to fold the wings up when not in use as jets used on aircraft carriers. The vertical take-off capabilities were provided by three additional jets which normally disappeared within the body of the aircraft, near the landing gear wells, but could protrude and then be switched on when needed. Combined with the ability to direct the thrust of the two turbofan jets down, rather than horizontally, it allowed the aircraft to hover briefly before touching down. The folding wings allowed the jet to be lowered below ground when not needed. Who would ever suspect the presence of a jet in a place that had no runway for it to either land or take off? The fuel carrying capacity of the plane had been tripled, and the power output of its engines increased fifty percent, with great care to keep its centers of gravity and of lift on the same vertical axis so that the plane would not start to pitch. That had dictated the location of the extra fuel reservoirs, which intruded, yet in a discrete way, into the cabin, along the floor and on each side of the center aisle. While this reduced the space available in the cabin, nobody would likely know about it. First, it simply meant that seats were anchored higher up than normal, with the reservoirs dipping in front of each seat to allow for leg space. The downward recessed center aisle might look odd, but Countess Renate would easily explain it away as an element of decoration. Also, in truth, few people were ever invited to climb aboard other than her pilot, her husband. She usually served as the co-pilot to minimize the need for employees, though she might occasionally hire one if a flight was going to be "plain vanilla" and not require the use of any of the plane's unusual capabilities. The markings on the planes could be changed at will; depending upon where she was traveling, each of them was appropriately registered with the respective aviation authorities. The only point of this feature was to avoid having an identification number show up too often around the world. It increased registration costs, but that was well worth the increased discretion.

Renate's underground complex comprised a massive communication center which allowed her both oral and visual access to any and all members of her network. Antennas were cleverly disguised into the trees on the property, except for a large, rotating, satellite dish which would emerge from the ground when needed and return to its hiding place when not in use. It was typically triggered by Renate when she wanted to call someone, but could be raised if someone called her, provided she was there to receive the call and allowed the antenna to deploy.

Renate's lair also had significant defensive capabilities, if required. Her *modus operandi* did not normally involve the need to use any form of traditional weapon. Confrontations were left for her clients to handle. As she had in the Canadian case, her team had identified the offending computer, but the agency was left with the task of identifying its owner and of dealing with his arrest. Yet, she had a few classical weapons, including a small ceramic handgun she carried with her all the time. One never knows who a beautiful, young woman might run into . . .

Small manufacturing facilities, extending to 3-D printing and a well-equipped laboratory, were included in the underground space.

This made it possible, as needed, to develop prototype equipment that was required and not readily available, or that a member of the network did not want to assemble in a "public space." The biological laboratory served mostly for any experiment that could not be done remotely by a specialist.

There were a number of additional features to the subterranean castle, and Renate had, in fact, quite a list of additional capabilities which she would like to install. She did not want to eat more into her wealth and was therefore just waiting for each assignment to provide her with some of the funds needed. An outside observer might have concluded that there was virtually no limit to her imagination; if she had overheard such a thought, she would probably have replied that there was virtually no limit as well to what criminal minds could conceive.

In many ways, the adventure she was about to live would surely draw on all of these current capabilities and stretch them to the breaking point.

CHAPTER.03

TEL AVIV, ISRAEL AND SOMEWHERE IN THE AUSTRIAN ALPS

Simon Rabinowitz was quietly eating his lunch in the *Mossad*'s cafeteria when the cell phone he had placed next to his dish started to vibrate:

"Simon?"

"Need to see you . . . Very urgent."

Simon recognized the voice; David Heller was calling him:

"David . . . What's wrong?"

Without waiting for a reply, Simon added:

"I'm leaving the cafeteria now. See you in my office in a minute . . ." Simon Rabinowitz was responsible for one of the most secret departments within the *Mossad*. Though now effectively holding an office job, he established a very successful career in the field as a covert operative. Yet, he did not fit the classical image of the secret agent stereotyped by novelists, ranging from Ian Fleming's James Bond to Jean Bruce's OSS 117 and many others. He was neither suave nor debonair, and looked at times more like an accountant or a lawyer rather than someone about to shoot to kill or fight with a villain. He had become an expert at *Krav Magra*. It is a self-defense system developed for the military in Israel. It had taught him that the key was never brute strength or technique alone; it was also having the right attitude, both toward training and life balance. This gave him that sort of calm assurance he needed when facing down some opposition. He had a deep voice which could alternatively sound quite stern or charming, depending on the circumstances.

David Heller was one of Simon's closest associates. Simon had once selected him to lead a major disruption operation against a regional power, which had proven quite successful, though its execution was extremely complex. He was one of the people Simon trusted the most. He was efficient and discrete. No flashiness, but sheer competence. Though a good family man, David took his job very seriously. When on a mission, whether it involved travel or it was conducted within Israel, David had only one focus—the mission. He had fortunately never been tested with a major family issue occurring while he was on a mission. He would probably agree that it would be a terribly difficult choice, except if he had total confidence in his closest associate.

Simon was surprised that David should call him, and more importantly call him with a message like the one he had just communicated. First, it was not in his makeup to allow himself to become flustered. And second, he would most normally have walked to Simon's office from his and popped his head in the always at least half-opened door; that is unless Simon's assistant had told him that Simon was not to be disturbed. *After all*, Simon thought, *he may just have walked to my office and not found me . . . So, he called . . . Keep things simple, Simon.*

They almost bumped into each other as they reached the door to Simon's office about the same time. David was indeed flustered . . . David liked having fun but would never allow it to come out when on a mission. Also, he was a true athlete. This was obvious even if he wore a suit, which he hardly ever did. He was six feet tall and broad-shouldered. David was elegant and well-proportioned, tipping the scales at around 195 pounds. He had come to Simon's office wearing grey slacks and a dark blue blazer, with an open neck shirt in a light shade of blue.

He started speaking even before Simon had motioned him to the sofa in the corner of his office:

"We may just have had a huge bit of luck . . . But I hate to think what would have happened if we hadn't."

His voice was a bit higher than normal and his delivery more rapid. Simon wanted to help him calm down:

"Sit down, my friend . . . Slow down . . . Calm down . . . I hate to tell you, but I'm confused."

Simon's colleagues knew that Simon rarely lost his cool and would never directly attack someone. He was smooth and relished his ability to be so. More to the point, they knew of his habit, whenever something was said that did not make sense to him. He would use his seemingly patented *"I'm confused."* One did not hear anything like *"I don't understand"* or *"You aren't making any sense . . ."* Just *"I'm confused."*

David picked up on the clue. He proceeded to tell the story in a few more words. *Mossad* had just caught a terrorist as he was setting up a bomb. The man was known to the Secret Service to be most likely of Arab origins, though certain people believed that he was in fact a Persian. In practice, he was picked up *because* he was under surveillance. They believed he was a Shiite Muslim, and thus probably affiliated with Syria, Iraq or Iran. He was also known to be associated with at least one foreign power, but there had been contradictory rumors. Certain people thought he worked for the Chinese. Others thought he worked for the Russians. In short, the only real evidence they had was that he was an Arab terrorist, worked for a foreign power and generally was an enemy of Israel and most likely of the West as well. Anything beyond that was probably just conjecture.

Mossad agents were following the man, whom they suspected of planning something against Israel. They saw him walk into the locker hall at Ben Gurion Airport, in Tel Aviv. They were surprised as he had not come in on a flight but by car from Tel Aviv itself. He had a small briefcase as he left his car in the parking lot. Was he going to retrieve something or to deposit his suitcase? And, if so, why would he do that? The agents followed him as closely as they could without being noticed. He opened one of the lockers and placed something inside—his black leather briefcase. They were not able to see what the briefcase contained. They kept looking as carefully as they could and saw that he seemed to be fiddling with the briefcase inside the locker, before starting to close the door. He was about to lock it when he heard someone yell:

"Hands up. Turn slowly toward me."

He did not respond immediately. Rather, he seemed to be looking for something in his pocket. One agent fired his gun, which was equipped with a silencer. When the "pop" rang out, the man dropped to his knees; the bullet had hit his left thigh, as intended. They saw him put his right hand to his mouth. It looked like he was swallowing something. It turned out to have been a cyanide pill. He died almost instantly, without saying a word.

The agents took the soft-sided, leather briefcase out of the locker. They saw that the flap that closed it was not secured into its slot; it fact, if slid down as they pulled the briefcase out. Upon initial examination, they saw it contained a contraption comprised of a latest generation computer tablet, with an extra, external battery and a remote-controlled switch with a small keypad, which seemed to be intended to turn the computer tablet, a Surface Pro, on or off.

The agents immediately realized that the contraption had to be a bomb. They assumed that the electronic part had to mean that the bomb was remote controlled, probably through Wi-Fi. This made it less daunting for them to examine it, without the fear that it might explode on them. With the terrorist dead, who would trigger the bomb now? They asked themselves why the terrorist would use a computer tablet rather than a simple smart phone. A fair question, though the answer simply reflected the fact that smart phones, or even iPads, typically do not allow for a sufficient number of external connections to satisfy the needs of the terrorist for this mission. A Surface Pro had two USB ports next to each other on the right-hand side of the tablet. This allowed the terrorist to connect to the tablet the few devices they needed without having to create complex connectors, which, typically, require special manufacturing facilities.

The underside of the tablet seemed to be covered with a sheet of explosives, probably C-4, but that had to be confirmed; a detonator clearly stuck out of the side of the sheet. Finally, attached to the tablet was a glass flask that contained a clear liquid. However, the whole thing still had to be examined in the lab with the highest secrecy. The initial guess was that the tablet would first be switched on to be able to get some Wi-Fi signal. Then, upon receiving that signal, it would explode. The explosion would break up the glass flask, with the apparent goal of releasing the vaporized liquid into the air. It was assumed that the explosion would be powerful enough to blow open the door to the locker.

Simon jumped up from his chair and grabbed the phone on his desk. He called his boss, Ariel Landau, to bring him up to speed. Ariel was the overall head of *Mossad*, and it was an open secret that he viewed Simon as his protégé. Many expected Simon, Colonel Simon Rabinowitz, to succeed General Ariel Landau, in due course. David could only hear Simon's side of the conversation, but certainly could see Simon's facial expressions. He was concerned, but certainly not panicked. Yet, two messages clearly came out. The first was a reference to Countess Renate whom Simon wanted to alert immediately, a step which Ariel seemed to support. The second was a request from Simon that the lab should immediately make sure the tablet was disconnected from its external triggering mechanism.

After hanging up, he asked, turning to David: "Any idea what the liquid is?"

"Haven't heard anything yet. I'm not even sure they have even opened the flask. The normal instructions are clear: you do not investigate before the higher ups know about the whole thing. After all, it could be a nerve gas or something equivalent . . ."

"Or some bacterial agent . . ."

"Or several other things, Simon. The only thing that looks unlikely is some other explosive: why combine two explosives in a bomb like that?"

"Makes sense, although, who knows? Have them ship the whole thing to me here, but make sure everything remains secret. Other than ensuring that the tablet cannot be remotely detonated, ask them not to touch anything. The two things we want to hide at all costs are first that we've got the contraption, whatever it is, and second that their agent is dead. By the way, on that, any lead?"

David repeated that the terrorist had died too quickly to say anything. Yet, with a wink of his eye, he explained that he had a mobile phone with him, which David's team took. That should give them some information about his past, adding:

"And, with any luck, about the future."

Simon smiled. David further explained that the cell phone was plugged into a charger at a discrete location away from headquarters and on a continuous basis so that it could be maintained at full charge by *Mossad*. Also, an agent speaking both Arabic and Farsi, and with a passable resemblance to the deceased terrorist, was on 24/7 duty to answer if it rang. They intended to move him into one of the Mossad's service apartments, equipped with all sorts of listening and observing devices. So far, nothing had happened, but, as David observed, the enemy agent had been dead less than nine hours. He reasoned: "Our guess is that, at some point, our guy, Mark Levi, will receive a call. Possibly, the dead man was supposed to call someone to report that the job was done. Since he surely did not do it, someone is bound to contact him to find out why he had not called. Alternatively, he was supposed to stay put and under the radar until someone called; that's the call that they would be receiving. Either way, it's a good bet that a call should come."

"Don't disagree . . . Now, let's hope that he wasn't supposed to reply with a code word, because we sure don't have it. You might want to get your people to start brainstorming on possible code words."

"Let's also hope that the terrorist had a voice that was truly not out of the ordinary, or that he did not speak with some funky accent. Mark's voice is as "normal" as possible, but he wouldn't know about the accent. Anyway, we'll create static on the line the first time around; it'll make it harder to pick up differences in the voice."

"Absolutely, whatever! Make sure I'm in the loop as soon as there is a development. In the meantime, I must call my friend, Countess Renate . . ."

"Countess Renate? Who is she?"

Simon smiled and paused for a second. Then, looking David straight in the eyes, he calmly said:

"If you think we're operating in secret here, take it, triple it and raise it to the highest power you can think of. She runs a super-secret, global operation. She has resources we don't have. I'd love to have her working with us on this one."

David walked out of Simon's office to implement the instructions he had received. The words "Countess Renate" were still resonating in his ears. He had never heard of her. He wondered who she was and what she could do that *Mossad* could not. He was one of these agents whose loyalty could never be in doubt. In fact, he probably believed that *Mossad*, as an organization, nearly walked on water. He would get a chance to work with her sooner than he could ever imagine. Simon dialed the same number he had given General Mike Marceau:

"Countess Renate?"

"Yes, who is this?"

"Simon Rabinowitz . . ."

"Simon . . . Great to hear from you. Anything I can do for you?"

"Pretty sure you can. Have you ever worked in a Secret Service team?"

"Not yet. Typically, we work solo and deliver the results to whomever hires us. However, I can't see why not? What do you have in mind?"

Simon went on to describe the case which David Heller had just brought to him. He could see, but wanted to check if Countess Renate agreed, that there were at least two aspects to the effort. The first, probably the least important and time sensitive, involved following up the footprints they had uncovered to understand who was behind the attempt. To him, as he said to Renate:

"This is typical *Mossad* work. I doubt that you're equipped with secret agents around the world . . ."

"Depends what you mean by secret agents. But I think I know where you're going. You're gonna need covert work in several countries. We can do some of that, but it's not our specialty, you're right . . ."

"Exactly as I thought."

"But what you said about where they found the bomb makes me think you might well like to try out a new toy which one of my associates developed in a recent mission . . . A pure, miniature marvel."

Simon nodded, with a broad smile. He went on to explain that the second element was highly time sensitive and required levels of sophistication he did not have access to:

"We need your help to uncover what it is that we found, what the liquid is and whether there is a way of having the equipment talk to lead us to others like it, if there are others . . ."

"We can certainly do that." Thinking out loud, she said that it would take explosive experts, computer and cyber communication experts, as well as biology and chemistry experts. She added:

"If the liquid is a biological agent, we may well need an expert in infectious diseases or whatever medical condition the agent is expected to trigger."

Simon told Renate that he would like to go ahead with the assignment and asked:

"What should our next step be?"

"Is there anything already processed that you can send me?"

"No, not really . . . Whatever we have is unique. It's here under heavy guard. I wouldn't want any of it to leave this building, until we know more."

"OK. Tell you what. I'll see you tomorrow morning at your offices. Can you have a car pick me up at the private terminal at Ben Gurion?"

"I'll do better than that. I'll be there to welcome you myself. It'll expedite all administrative matters. Still use the same secure email address?"

"Sure do . . ."

She confirmed her email address, which Simon correctly assumed was probably one of several. Simon said that he would reply immediately and then asked:

"Please, have your pilot send me a flight plan and details as soon as you have them . . ."

"Good try, Simon . . . Good try. Can't do that, but I'll send you the last hour of the flight plan."

She paused for a minute . . . And added:

"Say, I'll call you as we pass abeam Cyprus. That should give you plenty of time to get to the airport. I'll also give you the call sign and the markings on the airplane. See you tomorrow. By the way, I hope you can have all the stuff that was in the briefcase at your office."

"Count on it . . . Safe flight . . . Will you need a hotel?"

"No, I'll fly out in the late afternoon . . . Hate to spend many nights away from home if I can help it."

CHAPTER.04

Mark Levi, a *Mossad* agent, was assigned the duty of monitoring the terrorist's cell phone for incoming calls. He had been selected entirely for his physique. Though not a perfect double, he looked a lot like the dead terrorist, both in terms of facial features and physical build, although he was a couple of inches taller. He did not normally wear a beard, but he immediately started to grow one. Like many of his compatriots, he would manage to have a believable beard in a matter of less than a week, though nothing like the beards of Abu Bakr al-Baghdadi, the legendary leader of ISIS at the peak of its popularity, or of many of the Shiite Imams. He was fluent in both Arabic and Farsi, in addition to Hebrew and English.

■ ■ ■ ■ ■

Mark was in his mid- to late thirties. A few months earlier, he had met a wonderful woman, of French and Iranian origins. She was a professor of nuclear physics at the University of Tel Aviv. She had had to live through a major personal turmoil which she promised she would one day reveal, but currently simply argued:

"It's still too raw for me to discuss it."

Mark respected her feelings, not from personal experience but out of sincere compassion. She was at the same time exceptionally beautiful, but never thoroughly happy. At times, she was even sad to tears. Mark guessed she had lost her mate and remembered how he felt when Joan, his wife, died. The wounds are deeper than one might think, even if in Joan's case, the ultimate outcome had become inevitable for at least a few months.

Minoo Rakhsha, as this was her original name, had immigrated to Israel under a *Mossad* resettlement agreement. She was, or at least had been a *Mossad* agent in Qom, Iran, where she dated and eventually was engaged to an Iranian scientist. Unfortunately, he ended up committing suicide when, torn between his love for Minoo and his love for his country and at least some of the work he was doing, he revealed to the Iranian authorities an impending operation against Iranian uranium enrichment plants. The saddest part of it all, from his point of view, was that his change of mind had come too late. He never knew it, but the effort to which Minoo had contributed was quite successful.

Minoo, who had chosen with Farid, her fiancée, and her father, Cyrus, to resettle in Israel, was inconsolable for several months. Her mourning was particularly difficult as she had to deal with the love she had for Farid and the pain he had imposed on her by choosing Iran over her. His suicide letter was a model of confusion, and Minoo always regretted that he had not talked about his intentions. She was convinced that she could have helped him stay true to her, given all the conversations they had shared and the misgivings which he had with the military nature of Iran's nuclear activities.

Yet, she had recently begun to date again, pushed in that direction by her father:

"You're still so young, Minoo. You owe it to yourself. I'm still ready for grandchildren, you know?"

"Papa!"

"I know. I know. May be, may be?"

Thankfully, the decision to relocate them had included the choice of two apartments in the same building, one for her father, and the other for Minoo and Farid. While it might have appeared a bit odd in the very early days, which were quite few as Farid's betrayal occurred less than a week after they were back in Israel, it proved a godsend to her as she had to deal with her loss. Her relationship with her father had always been quite close, growing closer after the death of her mother, and even closer yet after Farid's demise. He gave her the support she needed to overcome the pain and return to a normal life. Mark and Debbie, as she was now known as Miss Deborah Massler, met through a common friend who knew that Mark was ready to date again, after the loss of his wife to a virulent, breast cancer. The friend thought that Mark and Debbie were both too nice to finish their lives single, looking back and living what was or could have been. They needed to move on, and they were perceived to be kindred souls.

■ ■ ■ ■ ■

The initial plan with respect to Anwar's, the dead terrorist, cell phone had involved downloading everything that could be recorded so that others could work on all the leads that were thus available. This was tedious work, but that is often, unfortunately, the lot of many secret service officers that outside observers do not see. Here, one is thinking of looking at the record of all incoming or outgoing calls, tracing the correspondents and trying to learn more about the network that they may constitute. It also involves looking at all contacts saved on the phone and cross-referencing them with all known databases.

But there was still the hope that someone would call. That would be the main payoff from having recovered the phone. Mark's mission was, if possible, to play the role of the terrorist and attempt to penetrate his network as much as feasible. He had relocated to a *Mossad* apartment in Jaffa, which is where the large majority of Arabs living in the Tel

Aviv district are located. In fact, it is the southern and oldest part of Tel Aviv-Yafo. It is an ancient port city in Israel and is only about a mile-and-a-half south of Tel Aviv proper.

Suddenly, the phone rang. The call was coming on WhatsApp. It had been three days since the terrorist was intercepted. The long, somewhat boring wait was about to be rewarded. Or was it all going to come crashing down? Mark could not afford a single misstep; he switched on the white noise machine next to him to provide some background distortion. The challenge started very early:

"Hello . . . Ismail here. What do we all dream of?"

The voice at the other end of the line was speaking Syrian-accented Arabic. It added:

"Anwar, why can't I see you?"

"One question at a time, my friend . . . One question at a time," Mark replied casually.

Though arguing "one question at a time," Mark was delighted that Ismail, whoever he was, had asked two questions. He would thus initially ignore the part of the question that dealt with the password and focus on the second. He replied that he had not turned his camera on. Ismail's face appeared to relax, though there were problems still. Ismail then asked:

"What's the background noise? I can't hear you well, Anwar."

"Oh. I know, I dropped the phone in water, and it has not dried up fully yet. I'm sure it'll improve by tomorrow. Sorry for being clumsy . . ."

Mark had turned on the phone's camera. Ismail then asked: "What happened to your beard?"

"I had to shave it. I worried that someone would take a picture of me. You know. When I placed the package in the locker. Before going on my errand, on an earlier run, I had noticed I had picked up a tail. So, I shaved my beard before the mission. I think it worked, as the tail no longer followed me. If they took a picture of me without it, all would have to be done over again. I am growing it back."

"You know what the Prophet says about shaving . . ."

"I know, I know. But I am more useful to the organization alive than captured by the Israelis and even possibly dead. Agreed?"

"Maybe . . . But shouldn't we have discussed it before. I might not have recognized you."

"Ismail, you're such a stickler for detail. For me, that's just what it was, a detail. Now, come to think of it, you guys might have shot me if I came close to the office, and you didn't recognize me. So, sorry. Anyway, water under the bridge. So, what is the problem? You were only supposed to call if there was a problem, or you had another package for me to drop off . . ."

Suddenly, Ismail changed his tone of voice. Mark could see that his face was a bit contorted as well as he said:

"Wait a minute, Anwar. You have not given me the password."

"Ah. That. We were talking of other things my friend. Simply lost track."

Mark swallowed hard, realizing that there was no realistic escape route. Either he had or he did not have the correct password. He paused for a few seconds and, tentatively, said:

"I dream of the Caliphate."

■ ■ ■ ■ ■

As initially suggested by Simon, Mark had anticipated the fact that some password of some form would somehow be required. He had discussed it at length with colleagues, as well as David Heller, the person who was in charge of the mission. It seemed to them that a group which had been badly defeated on the battlefield, but which called itself ISIS was the most likely culprit. Secondary alternatives included Hezbollah and Hamas, both Palestinian archenemies of Israel, and even remnants of Al-Qaeda. Yet, they were considered secondary because the planting of the kind of device that *Mossad* had found was out of character. Admittedly, it could always be a completely different avenue which they were starting to employ; yet the safe bet was that each terrorist group stuck to its *modus operandi*. The fact that the liquid contained in the flask was conclusively determined to be a sarin gas pointed to Syria and ISIS, in the views of the team. Now, whether the origin of whatever was in the flask was actually Syria, rather than Russia or China was yet another issue. With ISIS's official goal to re-establish the ancient Caliphate, and its head being called a Caliph, the answer Mark gave to the first question asked on the phone appeared the least dangerous.

Ismail seemed satisfied with the password that Mark had given. Mark worked really hard to disguise the glee he felt. He did not dare think of what would have happened had he come back with the wrong answer. He added:

"Ismail, should we change the password at some point?"

"I don't see why we should. You know it, I know it, and everything is fine. Plus, if you had been under duress, you would have added "but is it a dream or a nightmare?" and I would have known to call you back."

Mark could not believe his luck. Ismail was not only confirming the password, but also giving him a variation in different circumstances. He thought, *good to know!* Ismail might be a senior figure or not, but he did not seem to be really versed in security.

Ismail then explained that there was a problem with the package. Anwar, aka Mark, did not display the worry that he felt inside. He simply asked:

"A problem? What is it?"

"Well, I haven't been able to connect with the switch on the bomb."

The bomb indeed comprised both a tablet and a switch, which turned it on. The tablet had a good battery that was fully charged, but it would have eventually run out of power if it had been permanently on—thus, the idea of the switch. It was permanently connected to the web via Wi-Fi and used a minimal amount of electricity, which was provided by the extra battery which the team discovered in the leather briefcase. The switch was used to turn the tablet on and off. When it was on, the tablet would be accessed also by Wi-Fi and would surely be using some power. When it was off, it was like in sleep mode and drew virtually no power. It would have been nice to build that functionality—remote activation—into the tablet, but ostensibly the terror group had not been able to engineer it.

With both the switch and the tablet connected to the web via Wi-Fi, they both had an IP address. This allowed the terrorist group both to multiply by two the number of IP addresses that had to be discovered by the enemy, and to verify that both units were still together. Indeed, they both could be located through geolocation and satellite navigation systems. If anyone disconnected one from the other, they would appear apart. That would tell them that someone had penetrated their plan. All other similar units could, if thought necessary or appropriate, be detonated at once.

Fortunately, one of the first things which the *Mossad* team had guessed was precisely that potential trick. They had just ensured that, though disconnected one from the other, both units were still physically so close to each other that they appeared to be in the same place. The one thing they had not anticipated was that the terror group would monitor their locations at regular intervals. So, in some ways, it was fortunate that Simon had wanted everything disconnected. He did not want them switched on because he did not want to run the risk that the terror group might trigger the explosion. Beside the risk of explosion, had they kept them both powered up and connected, the terror group would have been able to see that its contraption was in the offices of the Mossad in Tel Aviv rather than at the airport.

■ ■ ■ ■ ■

Mark asked Ismail what he wanted done. Ismail looked a bit surprised, replying:

"Anwar, you're the boss on things like that."

"I know Ismail, I know. But what do we need done next?"

Ismail told Anwar that he was concerned that all units in place did not appear on his screen. Mark asked:

"What do you see?"

"Well, as you know, I can only see what we've placed in the region. Tel Aviv, Jeddah, Riyadh, Abu Dhabi, Bahrain, Cairo. You know, the places which we want either destroyed or staying friendly. You know that Tel Aviv was the one before the last. You're still supposed to deal with Jerusalem. We'll have a package for you within twenty-four hours. The ones for Europe or the U.S. have not been placed yet . . ."

"Fine . . . By the way, I don't want to go back to the same place to collect the package for Jerusalem. Find another location. If we're not careful, we'll be uncovered . . ."

"But . . . Anwar . . . That's not the plan is it?"

"No, it isn't. But by changing the plan now, we make sure that anyone who might have wanted to betray us will be surprised."

"I see, Anwar . . . Smart . . . But who would want to betray us?"

"Don't know. But, never too careful. OK, tell you what. Let me go back to the airport to check on the package. And for the next one, let me know where to meet on this same number. By the way, keep trying if I don't answer the first time. I may be in a place where I can't take a call."

He told him also to expect some sort of heavy disguise if anyone was attempting to monitor his movements. He explained that he did not want to appear twice looking the same way at the airport . . .

"Why wouldn't you?"

"Security cameras, Ismail . . . Security cameras . . . Unless I was there to remove the package, why would I be back? If I look different, they may not even notice it's the same locker."

Ismail bought the line and assured Anwar that he was not being monitored. After all, he was a senior member of the group. If anybody was going to monitor anyone, it would probably be him doing it. They agreed that Anwar would call back as soon as he had something to report.

Mark deduced from their conversation that Anwar probably was the key explosive or bomb expert, while Ismail was in charge of logistics. He still did not know whether he was senior to Ismail or the other way around. But, at that point, it did not seem to matter much.

■ ■ ■ ■ ■

Mark immediately picked up his own phone. He called David. "Good and bad news . . ."

"What? The phone rang, I guess?"

"It did. The good news is that the password I punted worked."

"What was it?"

"He asked what is it that we all dream of and I replied Caliphate."

"Smart, very smart."

"Not so sure it's smart, but I'd rather be lucky than smart any time. Note that there may well be other passwords, corresponding to other questions . . . I also found out that I would have added "but is it a dream or a nightmare?" if I had been under some duress."

"How interesting. I'll get the team to come up with other possible passwords . . . So, what's up?"

"Well. First, it does look as if Anwar . . ."

"Anwar?"

"Yes, that the name of the guy who killed himself when we got to him . . ."

"Interesting. Sorry to interrupt."

"No problem. So, Anwar looks like he is somehow related to ISIS. Ismail, at the other end of the phone line, is definitely Syrian, or at least speaks like a Syrian. Anwar was apparently a senior member of the terror network."

"Great intelligence."

"The bad news is that they have a central monitoring system where they keep track of their bombs. It looks like the terror group powers them up at some interval and records their location on a Satnav system of some sort."

"So? I'm afraid to ask."

"As you'd expect, they don't understand why the unit we've got our hands on went dead. I said I would go back to the airport to check the unit. I also said I would be disguised. So, I'm gonna do it next. In the meantime, we need to find a way to reactivate the two units, "

"Two units?"

"Yes, the bomb and the switch."

"I get it. Sorry again. Slow on the uptick today."

"Don't worry. We need the units to look like they're on. More important, we must make sure they appear to be at Ben Gurion airport rather than at *Mossad* headquarters."

"Understood. Great work, Mark. I've got to touch base with Simon. Stay put until we talk again."

"One last thing, David. There are other bombs out there. I know a few of the locations. Also, they're planning on planting more . . . In Europe and the U.S. The last one in the region is for Jerusalem. I managed to convince them to deliver it to me in a "different place" so that they won't know that I don't know what the usual place is."

"This is super, Mark. Thinking on your feet . . . Let's keep playing the game, until they find us out."

"Which hopefully they won't. I'm looking forward to a new life with Debbie and I don't want to end up dead."

CHAPTER.05

"Nice to see you in person, Countess Renate."

"A pleasure, Simon."

Renate's plane had taxied to the hangar to which it was directed. The plane was rolled into the hangar and would thus remain "hidden" while Renate was in Tel Aviv. Captain Frederik, her pilot, would stay with the jet the whole time, and made it clear that no one was welcome to come onboard, though he was happy to accept the services provided by the airport, such as the flushing of the toilets and refueling, or the use of a GPU–a Ground Power Unit–which is a vehicle supplying power to an aircraft while it is parked on the ground. Renate was pleased to see that even someone as observant as Simon could not tell that anything was special about the airplane. The truth is that he was not carefully looking. He might still detect something if he put his mind to it.

Simon and Renate climbed in the back of a *Mossad* limousine, a modest, gray Mercedes E 300. Simon wanted to start the briefing in the car, but Renate made it crystal clear to him that she would have none of it. Everything had to take place in his office, away from any prying ear. Simon smiled and thought to himself: *She is definitely extremely careful; I guess that explains why she's so successful.*

In the conference room next to Simon's office, Renate listened attentively to his presentation. He incorporated the latest developments following Mark Levi's progress. In truth, she was impressed by the amount of work which had been done in such a relatively short period of time. She offered a simple summary:

"Let me get this straight. I see three issues that require our attention. The first is to keep going along the current lines with respect to penetrating the terror network, whether it is ISIS or some variant of it. You're already doing very well. I would offer this "toy" to which I alluded earlier, Simon; it could speed up your work."

"Should we discuss it now, or do you want to go through your conclusions first, Countess?"

"Let's go through the conclusions. The second involves working on what I'll call the cyber issues. There, I would offer to bring my associate Wong Hai Chock into the loop; he's the guy who did all the work on the Canadian problem. Note that his "public" name is Jim Ng. The third has to involve the identification of the liquid in the glass flask. You say it's plain sarin, but we may want to check further; I assume you will want our help. We have someone in France who's second to none."

Simon agreed with Renate, though he had a couple of additional questions that he shared with her. Remembering the comment made by Mark Levi, he argued that there was going to be a need to broaden the project to deal with the bombs already placed, adding:

"We don't know where they are, though Mark knows a few broad locations. But we're sure they're not all in Israel. We'll need to connect with diplomatic channels, one way or another. We can't go in other countries to do this kind of work."

Renate nodded. She observed that this was in fact where the new toy she wanted to introduce could help, although it could not be used without someone on the ground attending to it.

"What are you talking about?"

"Oh, it's at the same time so simple and yet so great. We have a small drone which is equipped with an x-ray camera. It can take picture of lockers or closets and show us the rough outline of what is inside."

Simon initially was quite excited, but his face suddenly betrayed doubts:

"How do you see through metal?"

"Excellent point, Simon. You don't miss many, do you? Well, we use a variant on the classical x-ray. One of our members is a physics specialist, a professor in Zurich and also working at the CERN in Geneva. You know, the nuclear research center . . ."

"I know it well . . . It was involved in one of our relatively recent projects."

"Well, it turns out that by projecting an ultrasound wave beyond the audible spectrum on a very specific wavelength, you can initiate a vibration in metallic atoms. The photons emitted by the x-ray generator can then pass through that vibrating layer of metal both going in and coming out. We can get a decent image of what is in any locker or metallic closet, provided we're not talking of an armor-like plate; the metallic layer has to be relatively thin. We can bend physics, but we cannot invalidate fundamental laws. So, when you look at the pictures, you still see the heavy metallic parts like the frame and the hinges of the door, but you can also see what's inside."

Simon marveled at the invention and asked how they used it. Renate explained with an example. They needed to see through a relatively thin layer of metal in a case a year ago or so. They were able to bring in the drone through a window and take multiple pictures of the two cases that were involved. Seeing through the metal allowed them first to know which case to try to open and which one to leave alone. Second, it allowed them to verify ahead of time that the case they needed to open had not been booby-trapped. She added:

"In this case, we could follow pretty much the same model. We'd fly the drone into a hall where the lockers are, take enough pictures to cover all of them and retrieve the drone."

"And what?"

"Well, the pictures would reveal whether there is or is not something in one of the lockers."

"Just like that?"

"Well, almost. It takes a trained eye to detect anything on the small screen that the handler has, but it becomes clearer to all when the pictures are downloaded."

"Amazing, Countess, amazing."

"Thanks, Simon. Now, you've still got to be careful. You want the handler far enough away from the drone that he or she does not risk being hit by radiation. Here, the handler could be outside the hall and therefore unseen, provided obviously that there is no one who can see the drone at work. We can do many things, but we haven't yet managed to make the drone, its operator and its equipment invisible to the human eye. In fact, I should say both the human eye and any surveillance photographic setup."

Simon smiled and then asked:

"How big is the toy as you call it?"

"A big, flying toy. In its widest dimension, it's less than two feet . . . The body, chiefly the x-ray generator and the electronics, is the heavy part; it's about a square foot by six inches thick. Then, at each corner, you have four horizontal propellers."

Simon agreed that this looked like a wonderful solution, both currently and in the future. He rattled off a number of potential commercial applications, but Renate interrupted:

"Our associate is working on the development of many of these. The system is patented. Note as an aside that whether or not it is in the public domain will not change its usefulness to us. The only thing is this: if it is in the public domain, criminals will eventually plan around it. It's simple, for instance, for the bomb planted by your terrorist in this case, to be in a metallic box rather than in a leather briefcase. We could manage to see through the door of the locker, but we couldn't see through the box."

"I see."

"We'll always need to stay at least a couple of steps ahead of criminal minds. In the end, when you think of it that's the reason behind our association. Have the best technology and the people who are at the leading edge in as many disciplines as we need. Always stay at least a half a step ahead of the potential enemy."

Simon returned to the issue of bombs that were already in place:

"We'll need to deactivate them while still allowing the terrorists to see them located where they expect them to be."

Renate argued that Hai Chock, her computer expert, should be able to help. She conceded that she was not sure what exact step he might take. She saw the two obvious options, disconnecting the dangerous part of the bomb and keeping it in the same location or removing it from its location and tricking the system to have it "see" it in the wrong place. Simon mentioned that the team at the lab believes that the flasks are not booby-trapped:

"We could easily remove the flasks and be done with it."

"Wouldn't that expose people to potential collateral damage, if the C-4 still exploded?"

"It would. Yet, again, at this point, we don't know for sure whether that would trigger something nasty. Probably not an explosion, but possibly a signal. We've got quite a way to go before we fully understand these little demons."

Simon and Countess Renate agreed that Wong Hai Chock would be a welcome member of the team. Renate then asked Simon if he would need the help of her computer hardware specialist. His answer was a classic:

"Never too many bright eyes and smart minds."

Renate asked Simon for an hour or so to think through what she could do and to contact the associates she needed for this mission, adding:

"Let's regroup in an hour or so and sign off on our deal."

CHAPTER.06

TEL AVIV, ISRAEL, SINGAPORE, AND BANGALORE, INDIA

The first member of The Shadow Experts to come to the rescue was thus Wong Hai Chock, Renate's cyber-specialist. Renate immediately connected him to the team by Wi-Fi, in the conference room next to Simon's office She explained to him:

"We need two things, Hai Chock. First, we need to make sure that the tablet cannot trigger the bomb once switched on; second, we need it to broadcast a location which is different from where it is."

Hai Chock asked where the team was with respect to the liquid in the flask. He corrected himself immediately and asked:

"Can you disconnect the flask from the computer without exploding?"

"We really don't know, Hai Chock."

"I see, Simon, so it's going to be a bit more complicated. Let me think."

Hai Chock first guided the team through a series of steps they should take to ensure that, booby trapped or not, the flask could be detached. All the while, he muttered that he would feel more comfortable if his colleague Raj Agarwal was on the call. Raj was the best computer hardware specialist in Countess Renate's network. He lived in Bangalore, India.

Countess Renate immediately agreed that he should help. She asked everyone to hold for a few minutes. She called Raj, whom she also woke:

"Sorry, Raj, we need your urgent help."

"Guessed that much, Countess. What can I do for you?"

Countess Renate gave him as broad and quick a briefing as she could and then conferenced him with Hai Chock and the team.

Raj had the team in the lab execute a simple electrical bridge, a shunt, so that the computer would not notice that contact with the flask had been lost. In short, a bypass is created around the point at which one eventually wants to cut an electrical cable. The value of modern video conferencing was absolutely evident. The Israeli team was able to bring a macro-camera close enough to the bomb to allow the two specialists to see everything, as if they were in the room. It was after having seen the setup that they decided that a shunt would work. Once the shunt was in place, the bottle was removed.

They then needed to see whether they could also remove the C-4 explosive—again without triggering an explosion. However thin the sheet of C-4 was, it would probably kill most of the people around the table if it should explode. Raj explained:

"We must be super careful. There can be both external and internal connections. Frankly, if I was building a bomb, I would have both. The external one is easy to see. In fact, look, it's here" he said pointing to a small electrical connection between the computer and the sheet of plastic explosive. He added:

"People finding one connection usually forget to look for another one."

"How do we find out, Raj."

"Well, Simon, all I need is a couple of x-ray views of the bottom of the tablet."

Simon and his team were happy to oblige. Though they did not have the equipment in the room, they had scanners that looked and felt like the equipment in use around the world at airports, train stations and even building lobbies. They walked to the elevator and took it to the ground floor. Raj, still on the video conference, was delighted to see that there was only one connection to the detonator. The terrorists had ostensibly not thought of doubling it up:

"This is a sign of arrogance. It's dumb. But thank God for small mercies."

He added:

"Cutting off the electrical cable should not pose a problem, unless a secondary dose of explosive has been added inside the tablet. Can we run the laptop through the x-ray machine again? Let's focus on explosives, not electrical connections."

Raj actually asked the operator to do a third manipulation just to be sure. In the end, it became clear that the explosive could be removed. Simon observed:

"Seems we've been lucky, team."

"The more we practice, the luckier we get," was that all Renate replied, with a wide smile.

Hai Chock worked next on the tablet itself. He asked the team to switch it on. Simon asked everyone to leave the room and brought in a heavily protected bomb disposal expert with a shield to switch it on, adding:

"Never too careful."

Everyone breathed a sigh of relief when the tablet gave signs of life without any related disturbance. Hai Chock guided them until he could "speak" directly to the system. From then on, one could see "the artist at work." He penetrated the system and was able to get it to broadcast a location that was pre-set at the place where the bomb had been placed. He then got the tablet to show the various IP addresses with which it was in contact. They assumed that one related to the switch, which he changed to the same as the tablet, and the other to the computer that governed the remote powering up or down of the tablet. Hai Chock's next tasks would be to learn all that could be learned about that remote computer and to penetrate that system as well.

■ ■ ■ ■ ■

While Hai Chock and Raj were at work, Mark Levi returned to the locker hall at Ben Gurion airport. Clearly, he knew for sure that the bomb was no longer there: the *Mossad* team had removed it and brought it to headquarters. Yet, he wanted to go through the motions anyway. Mark needed that ruse to consolidate his nascent position within the terror network. Getting to the airport, while in radio contact with *Mossad* partners, Mark would open the locker door, seem to fiddle with something inside the locker which was now empty and upon giving the signal to the lab would have them switch the tablet on; this would have the tablet and the switch broadcast their location, with the caveat that Hai Chock would already have instructed them to broadcast the wrong location. Anwar, aka Mark, would seem to have repaired the connection. This would surely impress his peers, if he was what the *Mossad* thought he was and reinforce his image as the terrorist network's technological whiz kid.

But there was a second, possibly substantial benefit to Mark going to the airport. He did not believe that Anwar, the terrorist he "incarnated," was above any form of suspicion by his peers. If, as he anticipated, he was under some terrorist surveillance, his *Mossad* partners would be able to place a tail on anybody following him. This should teach them some more about the terror group, with potential uses both in this mission and later. The key for them, naturally, was to remain well enough hidden both to avoid jeopardizing Mark's position and to ensure that no bomb was triggered in some form of terror retaliation.

On the surface, one might think that the second benefit was critically dependent upon whether Anwar was or was not someone senior and highly trusted member of the terror group. But, in fact,

Mark and the team had concluded that his seniority did not matter. For its own security, the terror group ought to have its operatives following one another to ensure that no one was being followed by some enemy. Thus, following Mark, believed to be Anwar and a member of the terror group, was a more likely course of action that his working solo.

■ ■ ▦ ■ ■

Reflecting upon whether or not Anwar was truly a senior individual, the one element which, with the benefit of hindsight, militated in his favor was the fact that he was not wearing an explosive vest when he was caught at Ben Gurion Airport, on the mission. Junior members usually did, and, when caught or close to being caught, would blow themselves up. More senior members were not as ready to blow themselves up. The fact that he swallowed a cyanide pill could be an indication of seniority; one has to assume that a cyanide-induced death cannot be as painful as blowing oneself to pieces.

Simon hoped that Anwar's role in the current terror campaign was to put together and place the bombs. It did not make sense in Simon's mind that Anwar "the boss" would simply pick up a fully assembled bomb and place it in a locker. Any terrorist, however low on the totem pole, could do that. Yet, introduce the assumption that he had to assemble the various parts and the insight that the job required seniority immediately jumped to mind. The only remaining disconnect was why he would not pass the bomb on to someone else once he had assembled it. Why would he be the one taking the risk of being captured? He kept asking himself:

"*What are we missing here? Are they lacking people on the ground? Is there something special to be done when the bomb is placed in the locker?"*

In the end, he assumed that an important element of the placing of the bomb in its target location was the manipulation which they had seen Anwar do after having inserted the briefcase into the locker.

Keying in some security code would require skills and reliability; reliability not in the sense of keying the code without making mistakes, but in the sense of knowing a highly sensitive piece of data and keeping it secret. But, if the bomb was really controlled by Wi-Fi, why couldn't they input the security code remotely? Simon worried that there was something they were missing and kept turning in his head all the various possibilities. *Where is the trap,* he kept asking himself.

Mark's work at the airport was critically dependent on *Mossad* and Hai Chock completing their manipulations on time. Mark had to appear to "make" the bomb talk again to its handlers. That was the simple part; he just had to fake manipulations in the locker, as the bomb was not in the locker, but at *Mossad* headquarters. Would Hai Chock get the bomb to "revive" and communicate its location on time? Any delay would create doubt in the terrorists' minds. The worse possible outcome would be for the bomb to "revive" before Mark got to the airport.

■ ■ ■ ■ ■

Simon's next step, with the help of Renate, was to organize the search for other devices in Israel. Renate introduced Romain Switzer to the team. They called him on the video conference system to brief him on the problem. He was a Professor of Physics at the Zurich Polytechnic, while occasionally detached to CERN (The European Center for Nuclear Research in Geneva). He asked a few questions, most pointedly on the material of which lockers were normally made in Israel. Simon answered that they usually were a sandwich of cardboard between two thin sheets of metal. Romain replied that he would expect his drone to do the work, provided the thickness of the metal did not exceed three or four millimeters. Simon made a quick phone call and returned to the conference to confirm that, combined, the two layers were probably around two and a half millimeters thick. Romain informed the group that he needed to be on location to help with the work. Apologizing that he had not had the time to train an operator. Renate replied:

"Not sure we want any other pair of eyes on some of our work, Romain."

Simon organized an Israeli Airforce jet to fly him to Israel. While this would take the extra time of flying the jet to Zurich, it would eliminate any unwanted scrutiny in terms of the equipment he carried with him, as Zurich airport has several private terminals. Simon told Romain that he would pick him up at Palmachim Air Force base, about twenty miles south of Tel Aviv. He argued indeed that the need for Romain to carry some equipment made Ben Gurion Airport a less desirable location than an Air Force base. Romain surprised Simon by displaying no particular emotion, one way or another. Simon asked himself: *is he that used to private travel or simply a tough cookie?*

Simon was at Palmachim Air Force base to greet Romain as he stepped down from the jet. He looked exactly the part that Simon was expecting. The perfect stereotype of the savant who is so focused on his work that the world sort of passes him by. He was tall, probably more than six feet and quite lean. He wore a plaid suit and a nice, dark blue bowtie. The dark blue, short-brimmed, felt hat completed the traditional picture.

"Welcome to Israel, Romain. First time in Israel?"

"In Israel, yes, but not in the region."

Simon had the opportunity to see how disciplined and well-trained all members of The Shadow Experts were. Just as had been the case with Renate, Romain declined to discuss anything sensitive while in the car. And this, despite being assured by Simon that the driver was himself a member of *Mossad*. The trip to Simon's offices took hardly more than thirty minutes, in part thanks to the motorcycle police escort.

Though Renate had returned to Austria, she was conferenced in as soon as Romain was in the office. She wanted to participate in the planning meetings. Romain explained in some more detail how his tool functioned, and, interestingly, his emphasis was on making sure that an appropriate distance was maintained between the equipment and the operator while x-rays were being emitted. Romain added:

"We should also minimize the risk of other people being in the vicinity."

"Security reasons?"

"Always an issue, Simon, but, here, I'm focusing on health issues—radiations."

Simon explained that they would clear the immediate surroundings of whichever location they were investigating. They then turned to discussing the list of locations they would investigate. Yet, before taking that next step, they agreed that they should test the equipment. Simon organized for a fake bomb, comprising exactly the same elements as the original one, to be placed in a locker at the central bus station. They would then go and inspect the place this very evening to confirm that the tool had the ability to find the bomb. Romain remained outside of the hall, carefully operating the drone. He was able to follow what it saw on the screen of the tablet he used to control it. Simon could see him smile at one point. He asked:

"Found something?"

"Yep. We'll download the picture when we get to the office, but I'm pretty sure I found the baby."

"We should remove it before leaving."

"Good point. Let me tell you the location of the locker."

He pinpointed the locker based on his screen, whereupon Simon's associate used the universal key he had had made to open it. Simon smiled too as he saw his associate remove a leather briefcase from the locker.

Simon was fascinated as they were looking at all the images that Romain's tool had taken. Though there was lack of crispness, he observed that the location of the offending locker was indeed not in doubt. Romain observed:

"It's a bit like radiology in medicine. You need a trained eye to see certain details, for instance whether the locker is booby trapped or not. But the general picture can be read by anyone."

■ ■ ■ ■ ■

Mark's mission at the airport worked perfectly. The timing, though partly somewhat fortuitous, allowed Mark to appear to revive the bomb when he simulated keying in the code again. The terrorists were suitably impressed, although some doubt had to remain as to why the system had not worked the first time. Was a part defective? Probably not, since Anwar did not appear to need to replace anything. Was Anwar at fault, having set up the wrong code into the switch? Possible, and this could become an issue for Anwar. But the device had responded just before Anwar had been ready to close the locker door. The terrorists were a bit lost and the actual explanation that the system had been switched off totally never came into their calculations.

Anwar, aka Mark, had, as expected, been followed—early on his trip. As he climbed on the bus taking him to the airport, he noticed that two other people stepped in after him; one he recognized; the other he did not know. The one he recognized was a *Mossad* agent. The other was a terrorist whom he had already noticed loitering near his apartment. What the terrorist would not even see is that a second agent was on an earlier bus to the airport, ready to relieve the first agent. From then on, there would be two *Mossad* agents on rotating stakeouts to maintain solid surveillance on the cell which Mark had uncovered. In fact, Simon's instructions were crystal clear; other agents would join if the cell required more than one tail. Mark then returned to his "home," with his "tails," awaiting the call which would tell him that the Jerusalem bomb was ready. He assumed that the call would not come before he had demonstrated he was doing the job as required. Thus, he sent another, longer text message to Ismail to let him know that he had completed the job at Ben Gurion and was awaiting his call for the next job. He thought: *the call should come any time now.*

■ ■ ■ ■ ■

Simon, Romain and Renate, the latter by teleconference, needed to draw up a list of the cities in Israel which they thought were possible targets. They worked simply on the basis of population size. Within each city, they considered the two or three main sites which terrorists might have used. They agreed that airports, train stations and bus depots were the most likely, though they conceded that, in theory at least, terrorists could pick any spot where there was a bank of lockers. The cities on which they agreed were Tel Aviv, Haifa, Ashdod, Rishon LeZivvon, Petah Tikva, Beersheba and Nevanta. They agreed that shuttling between cities by helicopter was probably the most efficient, though not terribly discrete. Yet, helicopter overflights are not at all unusual in Israel.

Three days later, they had completed their inspection and had only discovered two bombs: one in the train station in Haifa and the other at the Ben Gurion University in Beersheba. In both cases, they had organized to have Hai Chock and Raj on the phone as they were removing the bombs, so that the terrorists would not notice that the bombs had changed location. They also immediately deactivated them, as the last thing they needed was for one of these bombs to explode on the way back to Tel Aviv. They were not convinced at all that they had found the lot, but still elected at this point to move to the next step.

CHAPTER.07

TEL AVIV, ISRAEL, RIYADH, SAUDI ARABIA AND PARIS, FRANCE

Mark was delighted when, back at his apartment and after he had sent the second text message, Ismail replied with a short, congratulatory message. Yet, the phone call he expected to follow the message only came two days later; this seemed longer than expected. Mark, and David with him on the safe phone, kept wondering what could possibly have gone wrong. Did they make a mistake in the location of the bomb? Was there too much of a delay between Mark's manipulation and its getting live again? David had whispered in his ear that the bomb was ready, just before he closed the door of the locker. So, that's when he sent a text message to Ismail to tell him the job had been done. Anyone who had followed him could not have sent a message before they saw the door locked. So, Mark kept telling himself that the delay was simply because Ismail and company had to get the various parts of the bomb together so that he might assemble them, before depositing and setting the bomb on location.

Finally, the phone rang. Mark could see that the person at the other end of the line was Ismail, the same individual that had called him first. He breathed a modest sigh of relief, not because another individual would have indicated trouble ahead, but rather because the fewer moving pieces the better.

He asked that the meeting be at the Savidor Central Railway Station. This is where he would later take the direct train to Jerusalem's Yitzhak Navon. Interestingly, Ismail did not seem to have any issue with the place. Mark, aka Anwar, suspected that the package would be in the same style as previously—a leather briefcase. And it turned out to be exactly the correct assumption. Ismail asked:

"When are you going to place it?"

"Tomorrow or the day after tomorrow. All depends on assembly time."

"Still at the fast train station?"

"Yes, at Yitzhak Navon. Should know that I am not the one that chooses the locations; I'm told where to place them. You know, that comes from you with the parts before I assemble the bomb."

He paused for a second and added for Ismail's benefit:

"Should be able to drop the bomb and get back on a train to Tel Aviv within an hour or so."

"Just as planned."

"Exactly."

Mark could not help thinking that he had so far been quite lucky. First, he had been able to take the place of the dead terrorist with virtually no challenge. But now, things were even better; they were asking the questions in such a way that they gave him the answer. Even the idea that he should take the east-end terminus of the Tel Aviv-Jerusalem railway as the place to make the drop worked.

Looking around, Mark could see that there were two other individuals in the vicinity that appeared to be too sharply focused on Ismail and him to be simple, casual observers. He assumed that the individual he did not know was another terrorist. Was he there to observe him or to check on Ismail? Only time and what they did after he left Ismail would tell. The other individual, Mark surely recognized—he knew him to be a *Mossad* agent. He assumed that there would be, somewhere, yet another *Mossad* agent, so that both Ismail and his accomplice could be followed. It would be quite informative if they happened not to go to the same place.

■ ■ ■ ■ ■

Simon was back on a video conference call with Renate. They needed to plan for the work outside of Israel. Given the fact that Israel had only recently signed an agreement that opened the way to diplomatic relations with a couple of Arab countries, Simon did not have any real contact with the security services of the places where they knew at least one bomb had been placed. Renate seemed totally nonplussed:

"I have an excellent contact in Saudi Arabia."

She went on to explain that a couple of years earlier, a senior member of the royal family had bought quite an expensive painting at auction. His expert was in the room and had inspected the painting in every detail before the final bid was placed. Yet, they were surprised, when the painting was delivered to Riyadh that it was not the same, only a poor attempt at a copy. Though they had reached out to the auction house which immediately said it would take care of the problem and return the money if it was not able to locate the original, the royal family had also contacted Countess Renate. They were aware of other work which she had done in the Gulf region. They were more concerned with recovering the painting than being compensated for the money they had paid—typical art collectors after a trophy.

She was able to identify both the individual that made the switch and the collector who had paid him off handsomely. This had required the help of one of her associates who worked full-time for the Louvre in Paris. The painting was returned to Saudi Arabia after the collector who had stolen the painting had a surprise visit from members of the kingdom's security services.

Because of this prior assignment, Saudi's Chief of Security, Abdul el Wahabi, knew her well. He was a direct descendant of Ibn Abdul Al-Wahhab, who is recognized as the founder of Wahabism, the official, state-sponsored form of Sunni Islam in Saudi Arabia. The plan was for her to contact him and tell him as little of the problem as she could and yet enlist his help.

Renate had decided that the call to Abdul would start with a very strong statement. She knew she needed him, but she wanted him to know very quickly that he needed her as well. She dialed his number. He picked up the phone himself and heard:

"Abdul, Countess Renate here."

"Great to hear from you, Countess. How may I help?"

"Well, funny you should ask. I may need your help and I know you need mine."

"Wait a second, I do not understand. Why do I need you again?" Renate went on to explain that she knew for a fact that a very specific kind of bomb had been placed somewhere in Riyadh, though there might be others as well, in the same city or in others, quite possibly Jeddah. In response to a question as to how she knew of that problem, she was relatively direct in how she had gotten the information, though a few facts remained unsaid, as "non-essential."

Yet, her first comment shook Abdul: "*Mossad* intercepted."

"*Mossad*? What does it have to do with us?"

"I know that this is a sensitive topic, Abdul. Believe me when I say that I know something. They intercepted a terrorist who was placing a bomb with a couple of chemical agents, sarin gas and something else, at Ben Gurion Airport in Tel Aviv. They were able to find out that several of these were placed in both friendly and less friendly countries. They believe ISIS is behind this, and that the bombs are intended to serve as punishments for enemy countries and blackmail for friendly countries."

"Where in Riyadh?"

"Wouldn't it be great if we already knew?"

"What do you want to do, then?"

Renate described for Abdul the campaign they had just gone through in Israel, revealing that they had intercepted a few additional bombs, though conceding that they had visited many more locations than those where bombs were found. She discussed the special tool they had developed and used for that work, together with the help she needed from at least two other associates within her network, adding:

"A cyber computer specialist and a hardware specialist. They both work remotely, by the way."

Abdul was still not convinced but seemed to be starting to vacillate. On the one hand, why would he, Abdul, cooperate with Israel, even indirectly? On the other, there could be hell for him to pay if the blackmail came out: *"How come you did not know about it?"* And the like. Worse yet, what if Renate used the direct line which she had to the Crown Prince to tell him at that time that she had talked to Abdul and that he had done nothing because he did not believe her.

"What do you need from me, Countess Renate?"

"I simply need you to engage us to help with this problem. I will add an unusual clause to our agreement."

"What?"

"There will be no fee if we are unable to find any bombs."

Abdul smiled. He knew that Countess Renate was always above board, and she had just proven it. Renate added another point:

"However, if we do find a bomb, I will need you to help make connection with a number of other security services in the region. We've been told that there are at least five bombs, of which two are in Saudi Arabia. But it's entirely possible there are others."

"That seems fair."

"One other point, Abdul."

"Is your list endless, Countess?"

"No. But seriously. We need to be able to remove the bombs,

though we'll make the terrorists believe they are still on location. For that, I will need someone from *Mossad* to help me. Would you be willing to let him land in Saudi Arabia to take away any bomb we find in Saudi Arabia. I can commit, on his behalf, that he would be willing to include you in the full loop of operations. At the same time, I know he will ask you for total secrecy, even within Saudi Arabia, for as long as the problem is not totally solved."

"Will you allow me to chew on this a bit, Countess?"

"I hate to say this, Abdul, but, at this point, it's an 'either or issue,' you're either in or out. I would be very sorry if you were blackmailed or worse if a bomb exploded in your wonderful country. Yet, I have been hired by *Mossad* and this is a condition they absolutely require."

"They're always so black and white."

Renate did not reply to Abdul's latest comment. In truth, what could she say? Yet, she agreed to allow Abdul a few hours to think the issue through. She asked him to keep to himself everything she had told him and concluded with:

"Don't know how many lives depend on it. The first results of our analysis of the liquid which the bomb will release tell us that one is a pretty classical, nerve gas while the other seems to contain a nasty germ or virus which has not yet been identified."

■ ■ ■ ■ ■

A couple of days earlier, Renate had brought Armand Duchemin into the picture. His usual job was as a researcher and a professor at the prestigious French *Institut Pasteur*. Renate had taken the first flask back with her on the plane when she returned to Austria. She made a stop at Villacoublay Air Base, a part of the French Air Force, less than ten miles to the southwest of Paris. Renate knew the commanding officer of the base and had obtained permission, through her connections with the French secret service, to land, meet someone and take off again.

When he opened the flask, Dr. Duchemin had immediately noticed something which had escaped the team in Tel Aviv; the flask had two distinct compartments separated by a false bottom. In truth, he did not see the false bottom initially. The dark brown glass that was used to make the flask made it quite hard to see what was inside. But, upon carefully twisting the top of the flask to open it, he immediately noticed that there was a second opening within the mouth of the bottle. He immediately closed the flask and put it down on the table; he used a disinfectant hand cleaner to make sure that anything he might have touched from the bottle was safely wiped out.

He had concluded indeed that the second opening probably corresponded to a small tube running vertically along the interior side of the flask; it would be used to fill the lower compartment, probably with a funnel or a syringe, or both. He assumed that the top compartment was filled in the classical manner, through the top of the bottle. However, the way the lower compartment was dissimulated had his antennae up; he feared that it might contain a highly volatile or contagious liquid. Simon was somewhat peeved that his services had made such a simple error; the perfectionist was never far away from the surface.

Once in his laboratory, Armand was able to extract the two separate liquids, using the same equipment they would call upon when dealing with the most toxic substances. Prudence was warranted given the origins of the flask and its bizarre structure. It took no more than thirty minutes for him to identify the liquid in the top compartment as Sarin. Though less powerful than VX nerve gas, Sarin has the benefit of being more volatile and thus easier to dissipate as a result of an explosion. The second liquid was harder to identify. It appeared to contain viruses, of an as of yet unknown nature.

In his first report to Renate, Armand theorized that the plan of the terrorists was to contaminate people close to the explosion via the nerve gas and prevent them from interfering with the ability of the bomb to disperse the biological agent. The insidious and more deadly part of the plan was to start a pandemic with the so far unknown virus. Renate observed:

"This is great, Armand. I think it explains their placing bombs in both friendly and unfriendly countries. The blackmail would be a lot more powerful if they were able to point to the risk of a pandemic, if the country's authorities refused to pay."

Cynically, she added:

"They could always protect themselves from any form of retaliation claiming that they had not disclosed the location of all the bombs. They could threaten to detonate another if someone took any action against them. In fact, they might use them to put pressure on other nations as well . . . really nasty and really deadly."

As soon as she had hung up with Armand, Renate called Simon, who could only say:

"Oh, My GOD!"

CHAPTER.08

RIYADH AND JEDDAH, SAUDI ARABIA, AND SINGAPORE

Renate got a call from Abdul El Wahabi. He had decided that he would cooperate on virtually all fronts. Renate was not surprised; in fact, this was exactly what she expected. In the end, what other avenue was available to Abdul? The only thing that Abdul required was permission to inform the Crown Prince. He made it clear that the information would be conveyed in total confidence. Renate thought for a minute. She smiled and told him that was not a problem, if the Crown Prince was made aware of the sensitivity of the situation.

Romain Switzer and his equipment were flown to Riyadh Air Base, where they were met by Countess Renate who had arrived on her own jet. Riyadh Air Base was formerly known as Riyadh International Airport. Then, in 1982, commercial traffic was moved to a new, more grandiose location, King Khalid International Airport, around twenty-two miles north of the city. Riyadh Air Base is itself about four miles east of the city. Abdul El Wahabi was there to pick all his guests up. He collected them at the foot of the stairs to their respective airplanes, ushered them though custom and immigration and drove them to his Saudi Security Headquarters.

The trio planned out their strategy. They listed both the main cities that could be attacked and the installations within these cities that could offer the required infrastructure, i.e. a bank of lockers. They deliberately ignored industrial or energy-related sites, as what lockers they had would routinely be used by current workers, with access severely controlled. While that did not mean that accessing them would be impossible to a terrorist, there were many other areas which would offer softer, easier targets. The final nail in the coffin was that, ostensibly, the goal of the terrorists was seemingly not to inflict physical damage to plant or equipment, but to kill or threaten to kill civilians, and instigate a pandemic.

Distances in Saudi Arabia are much larger than in Israel; travel would have to be by air. The trio decided that they should plan, as Renate and Romain had done with Simon in Israel, to operate as a single team, with no one outside of Abdul, and possibly the Crown Prince, aware of their activity within Saudi Arabia. They went from site to site in an Air Force helicopter, piloted by a member of the security service who was only told of the town where they needed to go and never found out where they actually were going within the town and what they were doing. Abdul had organized a secure van to take the visitors from the helicopter landing pad to the actual target in each location. The only thing that the helicopter pilot possibly noted was that, at the end of each trip upon returning to Riyadh, the trio disembarked with at least one and at times two additional briefcases. How could he possibly know that each briefcase contained a disabled bomb?

Abdul was flabbergasted and in fact somewhat disgusted when he realized that the terrorists had planted as many bombs in Saudi Arabia as had so far been discovered in the whole of Israel. The group found bombs in Riyadh, Jeddah and Dammam, with two bombs each in Riyadh and Jeddah, one at the airport and the other at the central train station, and a sole bomb at the railway station at Dammam, the capital of the Eastern Province—a total of five bombs. Abdul remarked:

"Whether they want to hurt or blackmail us, this seems like overkill."

Nobody disagreed.

Each time they had localized a bomb, they connected to Hai Chock and Raj via a tablet that Countess Renate was carrying with her. This would allow the "Asian contingent" as they came to be called among them, to help go through deactivation of the device. They were delighted to be able to confirm that each device was communicating to the same IP address as the bombs that had been found in Israel. With a larger number of data points, Hai Chock was able to determine that the central computer with which they communicated was in fact located somewhere in Syria. Renate asked:

"Why have we so far thought the computer was in Tel Aviv?" Hai Chock's answer was direct:

"Simple, Countess Renate. The group currently seems to be operating out of Tel Aviv. However, in fact, there is a main computer, I'll call it the master; I believe it is in Syria. The master then bounces off the information to Tel Aviv. My guess is that their Tel Aviv headquarters will close and disappear when the last bomb is placed in Israel. You told me that it was imminent given the information from Mark . . ."

"Can you find out the physical address of the computer in Syria?"

"No and yes . . . Let me explain, Countess. From the IP addresses I have, it is possible, but quite difficult. Now, if you could find a way to get me a name or anything more, I would be able to cross-reference . . ."

"Could you then hack the Syrian computer?"

"No computer has resisted me so far, Countess Renate."

She smiled at his comment. She immediately called Simon to tell him the news and to ask for his team to get more information if possible. Simon confirmed that he was in touch with Mark directly and through David. He told her that Mark, at the time, was actually assembling the bomb to be placed in Jerusalem. He added with a smile:

"One of our guys went and noted the location of the lockers at the Jerusalem train station. Mark will program it in the system. In fact, he wouldn't even have to go to that location, although he'd need to shake his tail to do that. The tail needs to believe that the bomb is in place . . ."

"Any idea how?"

"Shouldn't be rocket science for someone like him. His colleague tailing Mark's shadow will help. The point will be to create some confusion at which point Mark will simply vanish. I'll bet you this will happen at the Hahagana station in Tel Aviv . . . But, knowing how we operate, Mark is prepared to play the game and waste the thirty odd minutes on the fast train, one way, if he has to."

Returning to the question of getting more information on the computer in Syria, Simon indicated that he would ask Mark to try and get the information as soon as "the Easter egg drop" was complete. In the meantime, Renate invited Simon to meet her at the Riyadh Air Base so that she could hand over the five bombs. She added:

"Abdul, the Head of Security, cleared your overflight of Egypt with his Egyptian counterpart and obviously your landing here. He would like to meet you. He wants to express his sincere thanks for the warning and the help."

Simon could only add:

"Hopefully, this will become routine in the future: the reciprocal help, not the thanks . . ."

"Hopefully . . ."

When they shook hand at the airport, Abdul said to Simon:

"Please feel totally free to contact me, if I can be of help . . ."

"Let me extend the same courtesy to you, Colonel . . ."

■ ■ ■ ■ ■

Before leaving for the airport, Renate and Abdul agreed the next steps. Abdul would introduce Renate and Romain to his regional Arab counterparts, except Egypt's whom he had already contacted for the overflight permission. In each instance, the same scenario tended to repeat itself. First, there was an immediate willingness to help. Then, that initial willingness tended to wane when Abdul or Renate disclosed the Israel link. Finally, in the end, Renate and Romain were welcome. The clincher always seemed to be when Abdul became more specific on what his "guests," as he called them, had found—a total of five bombs in Saudi Arabia.

Countess Renate's team's *modus operandi* was the same everywhere. Countess Renate and Romain would be working together with the country's head of security, under a veil of complete secrecy. At the end of the mission in each country, permission would be sought and reluctantly granted for Simon to come and collect the flasks. Despite being one of the two countries that signed a diplomatic agreement with Israel, the United Arab Emirates proved to be the hardest country to convince. The hard part was not the initial mission; it was the permission for Simon to come and collect the flasks. They were very appreciative of the effort when Renate and Romain discovered three bombs, one at Abu Dhabi International Airport, one at Al Ain International Airport and the other at Dubai International Airport. Yet, Simon remained unwelcome, at least for a while. Countess Renate had to fly the flasks to Tel Aviv herself.

While Countess Renate and Romain were unsure that they had recovered all the bombs which had been placed, they felt that they must have recovered the majority of them. Further, they were still hoping, at some point, to be able to penetrate locally or remotely the terrorists' central computer and thus to have a more accurate listing of all the bombs they were monitoring. Comparing that list to the list of the places from which they recovered bombs, which were still broadcasting their original location; they would be able to zero in on whatever was left.

The team was not able to connect with and thus to get to Syria, Iraq or Iran, among the major regional countries. Countess Renate made a note to herself to ask Simon for an introduction to the CIA. She hoped that the CIA could get them into Iraq, which would have no reason to turn them down. She had accepted the geopolitical reality that Syria and Iran would likely remain off-limits. At the same time, she suspected that neither place was really booby-trapped, given the reputed relationship they had with ISIS.

CHAPTER.09

TEL AVIV AND JERUSALEM, ISRAEL

Mark was now back at his "apartment" in Jaffa, with the bomb he was supposed to assemble. He called Simon, as he could not get through to David, to find out what was happening to the individual who had tailed him. Simon replied that one, which they believed to be Ismail and who clearly was not tailing Mark, but who had been followed by *Mossad*, had returned directly to the apartment they already knew about. The other went to another place, but they still did not know for sure whether that was a permanent location for him or some other temporary locale.

"Just a second Mark . . . I've got a call on the other line. Hang on . . ."

Mark could hear Simon chat briefly with the other party. He came quickly back on the line:

"The second chap left the other place and went straight back to the same location as Ismail. We've got to assume that Ismail's apartment is some sort of local headquarters . . . Now, one thing you need to know, Mark. It seems like there's one guy watching your place. We don't know him. So, assume you're still tailed."

"Thanks, Simon. I'm going according to the plan."

Mark left a light on in the living room, just so that any observer located outside of the apartment would believe he was hard at work assembling the bomb. In fact, there was not a lot of work. The plan was for him to place into the leather briefcase a few things which might look and feel like the bomb, but without the really risky stuff. *Mossad* had deposited for him the various pieces of equipment while he was away from the apartment, thankfully using a back entrance so that anyone watching the front door to the building would not see anything. Mark only needed to connect them so that someone knowing how the assembled bomb looked like would still be unable to tell the difference between the fake and the real stuff. A very careful observer would be able to tell the difference because *Mossad* by then did not know that the flask had two separate compartments; so, the glass flask which Mark connected to the fake bomb only had one compartment. Yet, since *Mossad* had missed that detail, it would only be picked up if one knew about it and was looking for it specifically.

He then went to bed, leaving the light on in what would appear to be the living room, where he was supposed to be working. He had set his alarm for three hours later.

He got up and went to switch off the light in the living room. He called Simon again:

"Do we know if the guy who's tailing me is still there?"

"Let me ask."

"Looks like the guy who was there just left . . . But wait . . ."

"What?"

"I'm told a car just drove near the entrance of your building . . . It's parked there. No one is getting out."

"Do we assume they're still in a surveillance mode or is it something nastier?"

"Don't know at this point. Just told our guy to call for reinforcements, just in case . . . Whatever you do, do not open your door if anyone knocks, until I tell you the reinforcements are in place. I expect it'll be in five minutes max."

Mark swallowed hard and went for the gun which he always carried with him. He made sure that the magazine was fully loaded, the silencer installed and waited in the dark with his phone. Simon called Mark back to say that the team was in place. He told him that there were three agents around the place, with one of them having gone into the building and currently located in the stairway, one half floor above him, adding:

"He's in direct audio contact with the others. If anyone goes into the building, one of our guys will follow him inside. The third agent will stay outside to watch for other terrorists. The guy in the staircase will be available to intercept whoever would have gone inside, though there will be no intercept until he gets to your door."

"Good idea because we don't want to scare anyone for the wrong reasons."

"Exactly. We'll intervene only if he pulls his gun while waiting for you to open the door. Keep your two-way radio on. We won't have the time to call on the phone."

"Thanks, Simon. Hopefully, won't need to talk to you before morning."

"Hate to tell you to sleep well . . . But, still, sleep well."

■ ■ ■ ■ ■

All the agents who worked for Simon liked him personally a lot. He was indeed one of those rare individuals who had risen rapidly and quite high in the hierarchy, and yet never forgotten that he was once a field agent too. They liked the fact that Simon always seemed to care for how his people were doing. In fact, many of them felt that Simon cared more about their well-being than they themselves did. Each of them would have indeed argued that when on a mission, particularly when adrenalin is running high, agents do not have the time to worry. They are focused on the task at hand and believe that their training and the design of mission has minimized all the personal risks they run. At that time, it must be a reassuring thought to know that someone at headquarters is worried about their safety; one fewer thing for them to worry about.

As it turned out, the individual in the car in front of the building never got out of the vehicle. His job was to monitor that Anwar, aka Mark, did not leave the premises or that no one would come in to visit with him. In fact, when a *Mossad* agent went into the building, the man in the car paid a lot of attention. He got out of the car and could be seen talking on the phone. The fact that no activity was visible from Mark's apartment was the first sign that he was not visiting Mark. Coincidentally, a light went on in an apartment two floors above Mark's. Though this had absolutely nothing to do with Mark, the mission or the *Mossad* man who went into the building, the man in the car thought that it meant that the individual who had gone into the building was simply someone getting back home. He went back in the car and resumed his routine.

When morning came, Mark prepared himself to make the fake bomb drop in Jerusalem. Given the surveillance that the terrorists kept on him, Mark decided that he would carry out all the motions involved in the drop. He had indeed argued to himself:

Can't forget that there are two elements to the mission: one is to collect and disarm the bombs; the other is for the terrorists to trust that I am doing the job which Anwar was supposed to be doing.

When he shared the thought with David Heller, David agreed that it made sense, though it was a bit of a waste of time. It was also a bit of a waste of resources, as each individual tailing Mark had in turn to be tailed. But they both viewed the risk of being uncovered as unacceptable. David had added:

"When you get to Jerusalem, Mark, it's highly possible that they'll also have someone to check on you there. One of our agents will be on the earlier train. He will be positioned so that he will be able to see you and all the surroundings. So, do not be surprised if you see someone that has a great interest in you; could be him. You probably won't know who is tailing whom, but that's OK. Just go through your motions and return to the apartment. Let me know when you get there. I'll be in constant radio contact with Simon."

Mark was grateful that David and Simon had thought of the eventuality. He himself had not anticipated that contingency. As he would have been expected to behave, he left the apartment and briskly walked to the Hahagana train station. He bought his ticket and took the fast train to Jerusalem. He was surely not surprised when he noticed that at least a couple of people seemed to be following him and sitting in the same railcar as he. He, correctly as it turns out, assumed that one was from the terrorist network and the other from *Mossad*. For some reason, while on the train, he started to have second thoughts: *Wait, if they are tailing me the way they are, why did they not tail the real Anwar? And if they did, how could they have missed the fact that we picked him up right after he had collapsed on the floor?* He composed a text message with these thoughts to David and Simon and waited for the answer.

Simon was not really surprised when the text message arrived, although he began to worry, after he had taken the message to the next logical conclusion: *If they know that Anwar is dead, why are they playing games with Mark. If not, what's changed?* He immediately instructed another four agents to fly to the Yitzhak Rabon train station in Jerusalem by helicopter. He knew that the train's speed is limited to one hundred miles per hour. The Eurocopter X3, the world's fastest helicopter, which the Israeli Air force had purchased precisely for its speed, could reach a top speed of more than two hundred and fifty miles per hour. It was equipped with a central rotor with two additional propellers one on each side of the aircraft. Agents would easily get to Jerusalem before Mark. They would thus be prepared for any eventuality. The *Mossad* trap was set. Mark could do the job

Anwar should have done. And he should be able to return to Tel Aviv on the next train. Any terrorist attempt on Mark would fail. Local logistics had become a bit more complex, but nothing which *Mossad* and the local police could not handle.

■ ■ ■ ■ ■

Simon's mind had focused on a risk which he had so far not integrated in the plan—what if Anwar was viewed as "expendable" after he had placed the last bomb in Israel? The logic assumed that the terrorists had several individuals able and willing to assemble and place the bombs. Each would be responsible for some territory and would be eliminated after he had completed his mission. While that would suggest that Anwar might not be as senior as originally anticipated, it would be consistent with him being viewed as the key man for that part of the mission. Parenthetically, it would also be likely that Ismail would experience the same fate as Anwar.

Simon quickly raised the issue with David. They agreed that, under this hypothesis, Anwar would not have been followed when placing the bomb in Ben Gurion Airport in Tel Aviv, *because* he still had one last mission to carry out. Mark might be followed now, because, as Anwar, this was his last mission.

Simon and David were therefore not necessarily worried that Mark had been uncovered and that the terrorists were planning to eliminate him because of his treachery. Eliminating the bomber after the Jerusalem bomb was placed could have been in the terrorists' plan all along.

Simon started to worry that the most classical strategy for the terrorists at this point might well be the use of a suicide bomber to eliminate Mark. Anyone who walked close enough to Mark could trigger an explosion that would kill them both. Additionally, it would kill anyone within a close enough radius. That would be one more arrow against Israel. David agreed.

David called all agents on their safe communication system. He told them of his new hypothesis, asking them to focus at least as much on the surroundings of the place as on Mark. A variant on the suicide bomber could indeed be a classical bomb that might be placed in an adjoining locker to the one Mark, aka Anwar, was to use. That bomb could be triggered when Mark approached, resulting in his death. David suggested, however, that the risk of an explosion before the fake bomb had been deposited was minimal. They might want to kill Mark and wreak havoc in Jerusalem, but they surely did not want to do that before the other part of their plan, the chemical/biological bomb, had been set.

That led him to conclude that the potentially exploding locker would be close to but not too near the locker in which the bomb would be. They knew from Mark's placement instructions which bank of lockers was involved. David suggested that neither that bank nor any adjoining bank would make sense. With the help of the local police and bomb sniffing dogs, Simon's men were able to verify that there was no explosive device within the area which Simon had delineated. That sent him back to the assumption of a suicide bomber, unless the bomb was somewhere else in the station.

■ ■ ■ ■ ■

Simon formulated a plan based on a simple idea:

"Let's use the risk of some bomb eventually intended for Mark as an excuse to limit entry and egress from the station."

No one objected. It was easy to execute and individuals seeking access to trains could be screened with particular attention. He had the local police clear a path which would allow passengers to get to or from their trains. At the same time, local police would limit anyone's ability to approach the lockers, or anything else within the station if they did not have a valid ticket or reservation. Through David, he had warned Mark of the change in plan. Specifically, Mark was made aware that there would be a couple of agents near the entry he would have to use to get to the locker room. They would clear him but prevent anyone else getting into the area.

This should allow Mark to place the fake bomb, in full view of any terrorist observer, but without any real personal danger. If the terrorists were there to verify that the bomb was placed, they could report that it was and Mark's credibility with the group would be maintained. If, on the other hand, they were only there to eliminate Mark, they would be prevented from doing so and, in all likelihood, would not be in the position to make any report any time soon. Yet, Mark's credibility with the terrorist group would not necessarily be damaged, unless they assumed, he had himself organized the police operation. Yet why would he do that and place the bomb?

Mark therefore proceeded with the plan as revised. Once the bomb was in the locker and activated, Mark contacted Countess Renate, via Simon, to make sure the bomb was connected to Hai Chock. Hai Chock was to stay in contact with *both* the real and the fake bombs, effectively monitoring the two networks. In all earlier instances, Mark had placed a fake bomb in the lockers after removing the real ones. The purpose was to ensure that they could be detonated, either by the terrorists or by The Shadow Experts, but would not trigger any broad casualty as neither sarin gas nor biological agent would be present. Eventually, the plan would change; once all bombs had been placed, the terrorists would be unable to detonate any bomb.

Initially, he did not want to remove terrorist control as they might have a way of testing their communication with the bombs. The point was to make sure that they could not find out that they had been outwitted. Once all the bombs had been positioned, there was no need to hide anything from the terrorists and the priority shifted to preventing any explosion; even without the deadly poison, the mere explosion could indeed prove lethal, if there was someone walking near the exploding locker.

After having placed the bomb and closed the locker door, Mark was, as would be expected, starting to walk in the direction of the platform, ostensibly to catch his train back to Tel Aviv. He was intercepted, in full view of everyone, and prevented from returning to the platform. *Mossad* had been careful, for the benefit of potential observers, to have agents dressed as police officers take him away from the platform. He was not openly arrested. He was just escorted in a different direction. Arresting him would create the need both for Anwar to delay his return to Jerusalem and to explain to Ismail why and how he was eventually released. Not necessarily impossible, but why complicate matters when he did not have to. Just being visibly escorted left open all possibilities from an outright "*arrestation*" to what actually took place.

Anwar was taken to a side entrance to the station. There, he was met by a taxi, manned by *Mossad*. That taxi took him to the helicopter, which would in turn fly him to Tel Aviv. The time of his arrival could easily be made to coincide with the train's expected arrival as well, given the helicopter's speed advantage. When back in Tel Aviv, whether someone was or was not at or near his apartment, he could go there innocuously, as if he had arrived on the train as was planned all along. Simon had indeed thought that the instruction to eliminate Anwar, if it was ever given, may not have been known to everyone in the group. Therefore, there was a distinct possibility that there could be someone waiting and watching when Anwar, aka Mark, returned to Tel Aviv. Thus, though he obviously wanted to eliminate the risk that Anwar would be killed, he gave some serious consideration to the thought that the extra surveillance might just have involved a precautionary stance.

Simon had organized that the taxi that took Mark from the helicopter landing pad to the apartment should stop substantially short of Mark's place. In fact, the taxi dropped Mark at a point that would be on the way he would be expected to take had he come from Hahagana station. To an observer in Tel Aviv, he had come back the way he went. The timing of his arrival was supposed to suggest that he had returned on the fast train. To help make the subterfuge even more believable, someone slipped Mark an appropriately stamped fast train return ticket. He could always show it to Ismail or anybody else if any question was asked.

Simon had located a couple of agents near the apartment to keep an eye on Mark and to find out, from any terrorist behavior, which of his earlier hypotheses was the most likely. He was somehow relieved when David told him that there was a car with someone in it stationed close to Mark's apartment. He thought:

Well, this rules out the theory that he was to be killed and that every member of the group knew it.

Yet, it did not rule out the possibility that Mark was to be eliminated, *at some point*. Thus, Mark should remain quite cautious in his efforts to penetrate the terrorist group further. Simon had in fact suggested that he should stay in the apartment, specifically adding:

"We've stocked the fridge with food. So, stay inside for at least the next couple of days. The key now is whether or not anyone tries to contact you on Anwar's cell phone."

CHAPTER.10

TOKYO, JAPAN

The *Institut Pasteur* maintains a wide system of thirty-two, associated organizations located around the world. Of those, nine are strewn around the Asia-Pacific region, with one notable exception— there is no direct cooperation link between the *Institut* and any organization in Japan. The system's mission is to contribute to the prevention and the fight against infectious diseases worldwide. It focuses on research, public health issues, education and training as well as the development of solutions and transfers of technology.

Armand was well aware of the Covid-19 virus which had caused a pandemic a year earlier. He did not think the virus he detected in the smaller of the two receptacles in the glass flask was a variant of Covid-19. However, the mere fact that it seemed to have evolved from a virus found in the animal kingdom to contaminate humans suggested that it could be of the coronavirus family. Yet, he wanted to have a second opinion. He therefore decided, with Countess Renate's concurrence, that he would travel to Asia to meet with at least a couple of colleagues. He was acutely aware that he would have to be extremely careful not to be the one that caused any sort of leak. Countess Renate and Simon both wanted to be sure that the terrorists would have no inkling that anyone had pierced their secret. He therefore decided that he would make stops in Tokyo, Seoul and Hong Kong. The *Institut Pasteur* had an affiliate at Hong Kong University and another in Seoul, and Armand had an excellent friend in Tokyo.

Though Armand knew that Asia was one of the regions where a lot of virologic research was conducted, he felt somewhat uncomfortable with the fact that the only pure Chinese institute within the Pasteur Group was in Shanghai. While he had always had excellent professional contacts with people there, he was concerned by the fact that the Covid-19 virus which had caused the deadly worldwide pandemic allegedly originated in Wuhan, China. Adding to his discomfort was the fact that the Chinese authorities, for whatever reason which a scientist did not really care too much about, had not been totally forthcoming at least in the early stages of the pandemic. Armand therefore doubted their willingness or even ability to speak openly following the fallout from the pandemic. Equally importantly, he was convinced that he did not want to share with anyone anything that could in any way come back to the ears of the terrorists.

Over the years, despite the lack of a formal link, Armand Duchemin had developed a special relationship with Koichi Oshima, who had become his friend and colleague. Dr. Oshima was one of the leaders at the National Institute of Infectious Diseases. The institute was located in the Toyama district of Tokyo in Japan. The apparent success which Japan had had in containing the Covid-19 pandemic and the special relationship with Dr. Oshima led Armand to decide to start his trip in Tokyo. Oshima-san had booked a room in Armand's name at the Shinjuku Prince hotel, a stone's throw from the Shinjuku station on the Yamanote Line; the broadly circular, elevated, light green subway line which serves commuters and helps divide the "central part" of Tokyo from the rest of the megalopolis.

Armand had elected to fly Japan Air Lines rather than Air France. Japan Airlines offered a very convenient, non-stop flight directly into

Haneda, the one airport closest to the center of the city. Most others flew into Narita, the larger international airport, which can be up to two hours away, particularly if traffic is heavy. It was a long flight, twelve hours, but the comfort of business class, which Japan Air Lines calls a "Sky Suite" was just perfect: solid service, lie-flat seats and a great aircraft—a Boeing 777. Armand left Paris at 7:00 p.m. and arrived in Tokyo just before 2:00 p.m. in the afternoon, the next day—in effect a long night and a short next day for him. Experienced travelers often view that flight as one of the least disturbing from the point of view of jet lag. Pilots disliked the return trip to Europe; the return jet lag is harder to handle.

Though the route from Haneda Airport to Shinjuku is not usually particularly scenic, the fact that early April was just a couple of weeks past the onset of the cherry blossom season provided wonderful views, all the more so as the azalea blossoms were just starting. There were multicolor bushes located in gardens, but also on the sidewalks of major arteries, particularly around Tokyo Tower.

The Shinjuku Prince hotel was less than two miles from the National Institute for Infectious Diseases. Oshima-san picked up Armand there the next morning right after breakfast. Many people in Asia cringe at what they see as the bad American habit of polluting one's breakfast with business conversations. They think that the business day starts after, not before breakfast. Oshima-san greeted Armand:

"Armand-san, how nice to see you . . ."

"Same here, Oshima-san. I can't wait to show you what I've found."

They continued their banter for the ten odd minutes which it took for them to reach the Institute. They then immediately went to Oshima-san's office, though they had planned also eventually to spend time in the laboratory. Armand had brought both a sample of the infectious liquid and a series of slides he had made in Paris, to show the work he had done. He started with a short history of the find, omitting the key details as to how and where it was found. He managed to do it with a straight face, arguing that he knew little as to the background, which in fact was true. Oshima-san did not know that Armand was a part of The Shadow Experts; neither did he know of The Shadow Experts. Yet, Armand had a hidden desire to bring him into the group as an expert with a different experience from his. Countess Renate had agreed to join them for a brief visit that very afternoon. She would use the meeting to gauge whether she should meet Oshima-san again to discuss the broader issue . . .

When they got to his work, Armand started with a general observation:

"I can't remember having seen this virus any time before."

"Well, one good thing to say, my friend, is that it is not the Covid-19."

"That is definitely true. Yet, it looks like it could still be a coronavirus."

"Absolutely."

As Oshima-san looked more and more closely at the various slides, he suddenly exclaimed,

"Wait a minute . . . I think I have seen something like this before . . ."

"Are you sure?"

"Never sure of anything in sciences my friend, but it sure looks like it . . . Let me check."

He went to his credenza and shuffled files in a drawer, until he pulled out a thin folder. He opened it, carefully looked at the contents and, with a broad smile on his face which revealed a gold crown on his upper right pre-molar said, "Here it is. Just as I thought."

Armand could not wait for the explanation and said so to his friend. Oshima-san went on to explain that a Japanese businessman returning from a trip to the Wuhan region of China had recently fallen sick. In fact, the symptoms he was showing were surprising and different from anything they had seen so far. What he was looking at in the file was a sample which had been collected on that businessman. It had several of the features he could see on Armand's. It was different all-right, but there seems to be a *family resemblance,* as he put it. Armand's ears were now really perked up:

"Can you say more?"

"Not now, my friend . . . Let's go to the lab to get a closer look."

"What happened to the businessman?"

"He died quickly. Quite quickly in fact."

Oshima-san's face betrayed some real sadness as he said that.

"Did you know him?"

"No. No. I'm just sad that we weren't able to help him . . ."

"How did he die?"

"Major reaction in the immune system. The virus was getting his body to reject his main organs . . . lungs, liver, kidneys and even some peripheral damage to the heart muscle. Something crazy. Never seen that before."

"Were you able to work on it more?"

"The Institute as a group, yes, though I did not lead the effort. Tomioka-san, one of my peers, led the effort."

"Did they come to a conclusion?"

"Not yet. They have a few hypotheses. But this seems to be a virus that is not known naturally in its current form."

"Biological weapon?"

"Don't know for sure. Could have originated naturally and been altered afterwards. Or, in fairness, it might have mutated spontaneously. But it sure does look possible that the mutation was engineered, you know, that's what we all call a gain-of-function."

"Oh my God! Any thought on the origin?"

"At this point, there are still many variables . . . The best bet seems to be that it is of animal origin, possibly a tropical animal, but it seems to have been modified."

Armand looked pensive for a minute or so, and then blurted out:

"Could my sample be a further variant on the same theme? Another alteration of your virus?"

Oshima-san nodded:

"That's exactly what I'm worried about. And the mutation is too serious to have occurred naturally."

"Well, if that is the case, then someone must have worked to make it more deadly, rather than less, don't you think?"

"Can't imagine someone trying to make a biological weapon less potent . . ."

They both had a quick chortle. Then, they spent the rest of the morning inspecting the sample in all its various details, using a few of the preparations which Armand had brought and adding a few with the help of technicians on Oshima-san's team. Given the possible link to a deadly virus, everyone was working in the most protected environment available in the lab. Armand was marveling at the quality of the manipulators and of the equipment. He was thinking that this group would be a wonderful addition to the *Institut Pasteur's* worldwide association, as well as to Countess Renate's network.

Oshima-san took Armand to the cafeteria of the Institute for a quick lunch. They were handed a *bento*, an open-top, wooden, black-lacquered, rectangular box with several compartments of different sizes, each lacquered in red on the inside. Each compartment contained some part of the meal. A few sashimi pieces in one, barbecued eel on rice in another, two tempura shrimps in a third and a variety of pickles in yet another. The whole meal was, as always in Japan, very artfully arranged. Armand ate virtually everything, though a couple of the pickled vegetables were too salty or too sour for his taste. They drank green tea, first cold and then warm, as is often offered at lunch. Armand, who had been to Japan before, was very impressed by the wonderful orange he was given as desert: a real delicacy in Tokyo, which can cost the price of a decent steak in the U.S.

■ ■ ■ ■ ■

Countess Renate's jet landed at Haneda at about the time Armand

and Oshima-san were having lunch. She had organized a private car to take her from the airport to Oshima-san's office. She smiled when she climbed in the black, Chevrolet SUV, thinking:

Why is it that they need to have cars with the driver sitting on the left-hand side, when all cars drive on the left of the road in Japan? Private cars have the wheel on the right. Why the snobbery of the driver on the left for limousines? I'll never understand that.

She arrived at the Institute as Oshima-san and Armand were returning from the cafeteria.

Armand briefed her on what they had discussed and in effect "discovered" during the morning. The manipulations in the lab made it almost certain that the virus contained in the flask was a further alteration of the virus that Oshima-san and his colleagues had observed in Japan a few months earlier. The implications were ominous. Renate asked:

"Oshima-san, do you have a sense of where the virus was created?"

"Afraid not, Countess Renate. We know that someone likely caught something like it during a trip to China. But, we know that he maintained contact with so many other people . . ."

"And no one else was infected?"

"Again, we're not sure. But no one else came up with it and asked for medical help; that we know about . . . If you allow me a speculation, I'd argue that this might be why the terrorists made a further alteration. The one which Armand-San brought."

"Why?"

"Maybe, the one they had, you know, the one we have collected was not sufficiently contagious."

Countess Renate conceded this was quite an interesting thought. She asked the obvious next question:

"Can we test how much more contagious this one is?"

"Surely can be done."

Oshima-san, discussing the point more for Armand's benefit

than for Renate's, explained that one would use diverse experiments involving the spraying of some of the liquid at various distances into petri dishes. These are shallow-lidded dishes containing a growth media, such as agar, for instance, in which cells can be cultivated. Comparing the extent of the contamination across dishes located at various distances from the spraying outlet would help identify how contagious the virus is. He noted:

"We have cultured some of the virus that killed our compatriot. We can therefore compare it to the one Armand brought."

Turning to Armand, he added:

"You'd be welcome to participate in that work, Armand-San. My colleague Tomioka-san will need to be a part of the experiment, but I'm sure that should not be a problem . . ."

Armand, seeing the nod from Countess Renate, replied that he would be happy to meet Dr. Tomioka and to participate in that work. He still asked:

"Can Tomioka-san participate without knowing the origin of this second virus?"

"I am sure that he can. He will trust me if I tell him that we need to keep that secret for a while. He is a top scientist . . . The scientific challenge should be more than enough."

With a smile and tilting his head slightly to the left, Oshima-san added that the environment in Japan was much more group-oriented than in the West. He therefore argued that Tomioka-San and he would be happy to work together, noting:

"We can always share the credit if and when something can be published. Naturally, we would be happy to include you as one of us, Armand-san . . ."

Armand thanked him. Returning to his schedule, he mentioned that he was planning to fly to Seoul two days hence but argued that he could participate in the initial phase of the experiment and return in time to see the final results. Oshima-san exchanged a few words in

Japanese with one of the technicians, most likely the head of one of his teams. He then said that the experiment could start the next day. He added:

"We would need less than one cubic centimeter of the liquid."

"I can spare that easily, Oshima-san."

Countess Renate added that her client had now collected more than a dozen of these flasks and therefore had plenty of material . . . Armand, always the scientist, noted:

"Provided they all contain the same biological agent . . ."

Renate smiled. She then produced a second flask from her handbag. It was carefully packaged in a container that was hermetically sealed and leak-proof:

"That won't prove that the virus is the same in all flasks, but it will at least hopefully demonstrate that it is not different in each of these two flasks."

Oshima-san nodded vigorously. The three of them returned to Oshima-san's office. Countess Renate wanted to make sure that the experiment would remain secret for a while longer. She needed to find out where the virus was created and how it found its way into the hands of the terrorist *Mossad* had apprehended. The three of them agreed both that the origin of the current virus would not be disclosed and concocted a plausible story that could be shared with anyone should an embarrassing question be asked.

In the car taking Armand back to his hotel, Countess Renate and he discussed the planned next steps, using French as a language less likely to be understood by the driver than English. The main point was that the visit to South Korea was now taking a much greater importance . . . Would it add to their current knowledge?

CHAPTER.11

TEL AVIV, ISRAEL

Mark was awakened by the ringing of Anwar's phone. It was on his night table. Mechanically, he picked up and answered on the third ring:

"Anwar?"

Mark recognized Ismail's voice.

"Yes. What can I do for you, Ismail?"

Ismail started with a series of questions regarding how Anwar was able to deposit the bomb and disappear from the train station in Jerusalem. Mark casually explained that everything went if not according to plan, still close enough:

"Sure, I was surprised by the police activity . . . But I told them I needed to place something in a locker. I was stunned that they did not even look in the briefcase."

"But someone saw you being led into the hall between two policemen."

"That's right. They asked several questions. They just wanted to know what I was doing and why. I told them a story . . . And they believed it. Once inside the locker hall, they let me do what I wanted. In fact, they walked out and left me alone."

"But how did you come back to Tel Aviv?"

"The return fast train, as planned. Why do you ask?"

"Nobody saw you?"

"They did not look in the right place. In fact, come to think of it, I still have the ticket in my coat pocket. Must have forgotten to throw it away as I left the station when I got to Tel Aviv."

"Still does not explain how you got to the train, Anwar."

"Ismail be reasonable. You should be mad at whoever lost me. Not at me. Would you rather have me in an Israeli jail?"

"No, obviously not. How did you manage to get to the train?"

"Simple. I saw another policeman as I was walking out of the locker hall. I could see the blockages and was worried I would miss my train. I told him I absolutely needed to be in Tel Aviv that evening. He showed me a different way to get to the fast train platform . . . In fact, he took me there on one of their electric carts; we went around the suspect area, and I got to the train with a few minutes to spare. By the way, any idea why they had that police activity?"

Ismail mechanically replied that he did not know. Then he paused. Ostensibly, he was pondering Anwar's reply. He could not understand how he escaped surveillance but could not find a flaw in it. So, he simply said:

"That's incredible. But you've got to be telling the truth. You say you have the ticket, and someone saw you walk back to your apartment here that evening."

"Hey. What's that? Are you telling me I'm under surveillance, even here in Tel Aviv?"

"My friend, it's routine in the group for anyone on an important mission to be shadowed. Let me tell you more. I was under instruction to report anything that you would tell me today that looked suspicious. But everything you said was quite plausible. And, how else could you have been back to your apartment on time? Sure enough, you could not have flown . . ."

Smiling interiorly, Mark replied:

"That's for darn sure."

With a giggle in his voice, he added:

"Never took to flying much. My arms were getting too tired."

Ostensibly, Ismail did not get the joke. Mark continued:

"We need to meet today to discuss an important next step."

"Any chance I can meet you at your office?"

Ismail explained that this was not the plan. They were supposed to meet at Anwar's apartment.

"Why does it matter, Ismail?"

"Orders, Anwar . . . Orders."

"Fine. When?"

"How about in two hours, say at 10:00 a.m.?"

"OK with the time. You know where I live, don't you?"

■ ■ ■ ■ ■

Mark called David as soon as he had hung up to apprise him of this new development. David asked:

"Should we have someone with you in the apartment?"

"Probably a good precaution but be careful. I know I am being tailed quite closely."

David explained that he would get someone to enter the building via the back door. He would introduce himself as usual protocol. He added:

"Make sure you are wired. We want to hear all that is said."

David suggested that he would have a couple of additional agents available:

"First, there is the guy that watches over the guy that sits in front of your building. Second, there will be whomever will be tailing Ismail. And I'll have one extra man, in the event there's more opposition there. Make sure you wear your Kevlar jacket under your shirt . . . We want you to stay alive."

The first knock on Mark's door was his colleague Michael Steinberg. They had worked together a number of times and were known to be good friends. Mark immediately recognized his friend's voice, but still demanded the password, which was promptly given. They used Arabic as required, just in case—both Mark and Michael were fluent Arabic speakers. Mark's service apartment for this mission comprised three main rooms: two bedrooms that shared a bathroom and a living/ dining room. It was carefully designed to be a plausible place for an Arab terrorist in terms of both furnishings and decoration, and it was in the "right" part of town, Jaffa. At the same time, it was totally devoid of any form of Palestinian or Islamic propaganda. The risk would have been too high that a casual police inspection could have given the game away.

Mike and Mark discussed the mission and strategy and were fully in agreement when another knock came at the door. Mike went and hid in the smaller of the two bedrooms, close to the door linking it to the bathroom. Another door at the other end of the bathroom opened into the main bedroom, which in turn opened into the living room. Mark walked calmly to the door and inquired who was there. He recognized the voice of Ismail and opened the door:

"Nice to see you Ismail . . ."

"You know, Anwar, it's funny. I would have sworn that you were a couple of inches shorter."

"Well, I doubt that I've grown much in the last few years . . ." Mark said with a smile.

"Sure, that's right . . ."

Mark asked what he could do for Ismail. Ismail replied that the group was ready to begin to work on the European bomb locations. Mark's ears perked up, as did those of his colleagues listening in to the conversation. At the same time, Mike relaxed a bit, rightfully concluding that a visit to inflict some harm to Anwar would not have started that way. Yet, he said to himself . . . *don't trust these guys . . .*

Stay on your guard and be ready to pounce.

Ismail explained that the process had to be a lot more complex, in his words:

"Because we're going to have to worry about a number of border crossings . . ."

"Understood . . . I would surely have recommended that," Mark mused.

Ismail proceeded to draw up the plan for Mark. In short, the tablets required for the bomb would be awaiting Mark at the Syrian consulate in Geneva, while the electrical and explosive elements would be at the Iraqi Embassy, in Bern. Anwar had to ask:

"Hold it here, Ismail. Why not both in the same place?"

"Prudence . . . Divide and conquer, they say . . . As you know, we are in both countries: ISIS means the Islamic State of Iraq and Syria. So, we have sympathizers in both diplomatic delegations. By making sure that each delegation sees only a part of the full picture, we increase our chances of avoiding leaks or detection."

"Maybe. But we multiply by two the risk that someone could betray us."

"Orders, Anwar . . . Orders."

"And why Bern?"

"It's the capital of Switzerland. That's where all the embassies are. I've been told that it is one of the safest cities in Europe. Plus, two of the three embassies we need."

Mark simply shook his head, adding:

"Two of the three embassies? Why the third embassy now?"

"Same reason: prudence . . . Plus, there's a special issue with respect to the flasks."

Anwar, aka Mark, intentionally did not seem to perk up on Ismail's last reply, although anyone listening in certainly did. He might have tried to say something, but Ismail shifted to the logistics of his travel. In the end, Mark was in fact delighted that Ismail was moving forward, thinking *I could easily have said something wrong. I know too much and much too little.*

Ismail explained that Anwar would need to fly to Riyadh, which had recently opened direct flights with Israel, with Saudi Arabia following in the steps of the United Arab Emirates and Bahrain. He was told he should book the commercial flight himself for a date two days hence, with money which Ismail handed to him. There, he would be met by a friend who would pick him up at the airport and help him disguise himself. Anwar had to ask:

"How will he recognize me?"

"He has a picture . . ."

Ismail went on to say that he would need to pretend to be a wealthy Saudi citizen. Anwar frowned and asked:

"Why a Saudi businessman?"

"You're going to fly on a private jet to Geneva, in Switzerland . . ."

"Another city **and** a private jet?"

"Yes, but, as you know, many Saudi tourists go to Geneva for Spring and Summer . . . You'll just be one of several . . . Anonymity in a crowd."

"And why the private jet? Is that not terribly expensive?"

"It's more discrete . . . We have supporters who are willing to help us."

"I get it," Anwar said with some measure of feigned restrained displeasure.

Ismail continued, explaining that he was to rent a car on the Swiss side of the airport. Geneva's airport straddles Swiss and French territory, with the bulk of the land on the French side. The airport has two main entrances, one on the Swiss side and the other on the French side. Thus, flights from Paris to Geneva, for instance, are considered as domestic flights within France, if the traveler leaves the airport from the French side; he would only need to go through custom and immigration into Switzerland, if he or she wanted to get into Geneva and thus Switzerland.

Ismail explained that Anwar should first drive to the Syrian Consulate General in Geneva, adding:

"For some reason, that's the only Syrian diplomatic mission in Switzerland. No embassy in Bern, the Swiss capital. Go figure."

Ismail continued:

"There, you should ask for Jameel Abadi. Jameel will give you a package. It'll contain twelve tablets. By the way, they are totally standard."

Anwar smiled, but, again, had to ask:

"Why can't I simply buy them, myself, as we've done before?"

"Anwar, so many questions, so many questions . . . I'm only here to tell you of the plan. I had nothing to do with its development. Yet, come to think of it, we may need to have certain default language settings which you would not get if you bought the tablets in Geneva yourself."

"Could be. But, since I am flying private, why couldn't we have the tablets with me on that flight and avoid one extra stop?"

"Reasonable question, my friend. I have no good reply, other than that's not the way it has been planned."

Anwar smiled a weak smile. Ismail may or may not have noticed it, but he did not address it. He went on to tell him that he should then leisurely drive to Bern.

"Why Bern?"

"You already asked that, Anwar. I told you. It's the Swiss capital. That's where the embassies are. That's where you're to get the most important components."

"Sorry."

Anwar's apology sounded reasonable. He did not react further other than with a modest shake of his head. Ismail gave him the address of an apartment that was rented on Justingerweg, in the Embassy district of Bern.

"It's reserved for a month in the name of Mohamed Ahmed Al-Saleh. This will be your base. The owners live in the U.K."

Ismail indicated that they have requested special privacy from the owners. Nobody should come in the apartment without first contacting Anwar. He added:

"You'll also get a European cell phone at the Syrian consulate. This is for local communications only. If you need me, make sure to use your regular cell phone."

Anwar was still unconvinced. The local cell phone had triggered him:

"Wait a second, Ismail, I don't speak German or whatever Bernese Swiss-German that they speak in Bern."

"I am sure our colleagues know that. I'd just assume that English should be OK. And remember, as I told you a minute ago, it has to be Bern because of the embassies . . . After all, nobody is asking you to disguise yourself to look like a Swiss national . . . You'll be assumed to be an Arab tourist, with a Saudi nationality as your passport will show. By the way, here it is."

Ismail handed the passport to Anwar, who inspected it. He whistled softly and commented:

"Not a bad picture, but my beard is shorter."

"I know. We've talked about that before. It's growing nicely. Remember, in Saudi Arabia, they tend to trim their beards, so it'll be even better with your beard as it stands."

Anwar would then go pick up the material that awaited him at the Iraqi Embassy and would store the whole thing in the cellar that came with the apartment, on the first underground level. Ismail added that he should always store all material, including any "finished product" in that cellar, to make sure that there's no trace of what he was doing in the flat . . . Do not ever leave the flat with any of the material in the apartment."

"When and where do I get the flasks?"

"I'm coming to it . . . You will not get all of them in one shot. They will come by batch of three. Someone will contact you when you are in Bern to deliver the first batch."

"Yet another loose end."

"No, not really. Plus, we didn't have any choice. The person who will deliver them is with our direct supplier. I am not privy to who he is or even which country he comes from. But I'm sure the supplier did not want a large supply of flasks out in the open at the same time . . . Detection risk."

"And I'll probably again be tailed and under constant surveillance."

"Wouldn't be surprised . . . And maybe by more than one group. The flask supplier could well want to see what you're doing. Just go along. You've got nothing to hide, do you?"

Ismail closed the meeting by telling him he would receive a phone call via WhatsApp, so that the caller can see his face and recognize him, to tell him when and where precisely to drop the bombs. He cautioned Anwar:

"There will be quite a bit of driving involved. They have mapped out ten bombs to cover six countries on the Continent, after which you'll finish with the U.K . . . And, by the way, everyone in Switzerland will be working with the same password; they'll ask about your dream and you'll . . ."

"I'll answer the Califate."

Ismail did not seem to appreciate that Anwar had cut him off but waved it off when Mark signaled by his body language that he was sorry. Mark could not resist adding:

"Will the other reply work if I have a problem?"

"Other reply?"

"Yes, but is it a dream or a nightmare?"

"Good question. Nobody told me. Assume it will unless I tell you otherwise."

Mark was not through with his questions:

"Should we be changing our password for here? Too many people know it now."

"An excellent thought my friend. I'll ask, but, unless you hear something different from me, assume it's unchanged."

Ismail handed to Mark a list of the locations for each of the bombs he was to assemble and then drop. Mark smiled thinking that knowing so much of the logistics ahead of time was bound to help David and Simon organize their troops. Responding to Ismail's last statement, he added:

"I know I shouldn't ask but can't resist. Why finish with the U.K.?"

"You've got to take a ferry or the tunnel under the Channel. They would rather not have you go through it twice . . . There is more security there than at borders within the European Continent; ever since Brexit . . . The two last bombs are meant for the U.K. The last of the first ten is for Belgium. So, on that last trip, they'll have you drive to Belgium, drop the bomb there, and travel over to the U.K. with the car. Then, they'll have you calmly return the car in the U.K., fly back to Geneva on a commercial airline and grab your private jet to Riyadh. From there, you'll come back here, though I suspect that your role in the mission will be over. I guess you and I return to our undercover work here in Tel Aviv or maybe to Syria. Who knows?

CHAPTER.12

After Renate had dropped Armand at his hotel, she returned to the airport and flew straight back to Austria. The next day, Armand worked with his colleagues on the first step of the experiment to determine whether the new virus was as expected more contagious than its earlier incarnation. He then had to fly to Seoul. The two-and-a-half-hour flight was totally uneventful, although, as always, Armand marveled at the quality and level of service on Asian airlines. Korean Air was no exception.

Armand landed at the Inchon International Airport. He went directly from the airport to the *Institut Pasteur Korea,* located in Gyeonggi-do, the province surrounding the capital, Seoul. The forty-mile trip required him to take a taxi, which, though not cheap, was the most practical and speediest way for him to get there.

Though he had already visited the *Institut,* he was again impressed by the modern architecture of the building. From the front, it looked a bit like a three-dimensional inverted trapezoid, with shiny, white frames and greenish windows. The windowed part of the building looked like it was floating within the overall frame, with open spaces on each side. A recessed top floor broke with the geometrical design of the main body. Further in front, across a small plaza, a curvilinear structure, with the same greenish windows but a more discrete external frame, stood two stories down from the main floor of the main building. Two rectangular ponds at the front of that second structure completed the picture.

Armand asked to see Park Byung-Ho, one of the two most senior Korean researchers. He knew that the CEO of the *Institut* had been, for the last two incumbents at least, a non-Korean native. He would pay a courtesy call on the current head of the *Institut Pasteur* but wanted to talk to someone of Korean origins. He was looking as much for rumors within Korea as for actual research output. Who better than a Korean national would be attuned to all the various actual or imagined reports which always circulate in and around Seoul? The *Institut Pasteur Korea* had played a leading role in the Covid-19 pandemic. Korea had earned many favorable comments around the world, as it was among the most sparkling success stories; in fact, it was arguably the country that contained the pandemic the best. This was probably because of a strong and early emphasis on testing and as a result of well-defined medical protocols. Armand was anxious to find out more.

Armand knew that Koreans typically avoid using first or even last names when addressing other people. They prefer to use honorific titles or to resort to expressions which, to a foreigner, might look awkward, such as older brother, which they use even when they are not related to the other party; the "older" part being there to convey respect. Each time he had met Dr. Park, he had called him Doctor, and Dr. Park had called him Professor. He assumed that he should not deviate from that norm.

"Dr. Park. I am so glad to see you . . . face to face for a change."

"Professor Duchemin, it is indeed a pleasure . . ."

As they were entering a conference room, Dr. Park simply asked: "What can I do for you, Professor?"

Armand explained to Park the reason for his whole trip, though he omitted to discuss any of the insights he had gained in Tokyo. It was, in his opinion, quite a bit too early to talk of something that was still so vague and incompletely known. Further, if Dr. Park was privy to something along the same line, being sure that he had two sources rather than one and a second simply parroting the first was crucial. As he had done in Tokyo, he also did not discuss the origin of the virus, nor the non-Pasteur related reason for his involvement. Dr. Park was initially surprised. Armand could see that he was very attentive to each and every word. And that was not a language issue:

"Professor Duchemin, do you have much of a lead yet?"

"Truth is, we don't at this point. We believe that it might be a modified version of a virus naturally occurring in the animal world. In fact, I have asked one of my good friends in France, Dr. Dominique Dubreuil, a professor at Alford, our best veterinary school, to look at my findings. I am hoping that he may point us in the right direction, if it is indeed from the African animal kingdom . . ."

Dr. Park kept digging in his vast memory bank but could not seem to find anything. Then, his eyes suddenly widened. He inhaled a long breath and blurted out:

"Wait a minute . . . Wait a minute . . . There are rumors of a few suspect deaths in North Korea. We don't know a lot about them, but we have heard of symptoms which sound a bit like what you're describing."

"North Korea?"

"Yes. I have a friend in our secret service here. He told me that a scientist that was working in China had suddenly returned to North Korea. Shortly after his return, a few people in the area to which he returned died with symptoms like those you mentioned."

"Do you suspect that he was working with the Chinese on some biological weapon?"

"Maybe, but who knows? Else, he could have been rogue within the Chinese lab and left as soon as he had something which North

Korea could exploit."

"You know, Dr. Park, that second alternative looks even more plausible . . . Sudden return. No word from China . . . Sudden deaths, probably because some people did not know how to handle some of his work."

"We're in agreement."

"Do you have anything you could share?"

"I don't here. But, let me call my friend, Colonel Kim Dae Jung, in the secret service. Let's see if he would agree to a quick dinner together tonight."

■ ■ ■ ■ ■

The three men met for a Korean barbecue and discussed the rumor. It turned out that there was little that could be confirmed. Yet, a couple of points emerged that Armand knew would be of use to Countess Renate and her client. First, there was indeed a North Korean scientist that left a temporary assignment in China at the Wuhan laboratory. He had been there for more than a year, maybe even two. No name yet, but that should be forthcoming soon. He had been known to be working on animal-derived viruses that he would then manipulate. While there was no evidence that he was working to create biological weapons, it was hard to find any logical explanation for his focus, particularly as he was not known to have any relationship with any pharmaceutical company. Second, there were the suspicious deaths around the laboratory where the scientist returned in North Korea. That laboratory was known to be a government front for biological and chemical weapons research. Though the North Korean authorities would not confirm the deaths, there were enough bits of oral evidence here and there to suggest that the rumor probably had substance to it. They had no proof to connect the two elements, other than simple logic. What else would explain the coincidence?

Armand and Dr. Park agreed to stay in close touch, using the internal email system of the *Institut Pasteur*. Armand had suggested that he might soon be able to share a bit more, as he was hoping that some of the top-secret information he had learned would be declassified. Dr. Park committed to monitor all he could with respect to the North Korean scientist. Armand thanked him, urging caution both for Dr. Park's personal safety and because it was crucial that the North Koreans stay unaware that some of their activities might have been uncovered.

Armand took the early morning return flight to Narita and went directly to the National Institute for Infectious Diseases. There, he met with Tomioka-San and Oshima-San in the conference room just outside of the laboratory where the experiments were conducted. Both Japanese scientists were stunned and very interested in the information that Armand brought back. It confirmed their suspicions that the "new" virus was an evolution of the earlier one.

The work which they had done to measure the potency of the new virus had proven that the virus brought by Armand could contaminate about five times further than the incarnation they had collected from the Japanese businessman. Extending the radius within which contamination could occur would be a way to make the virus more powerful. Tomioka-san remarked:

"The one element of our research which still needs additional work is: what is it that makes the virus more powerful? On the surface, they look generally alike, though the mechanism to attach to receptors seemed to be more developed in your type, Armand-san . . . Yet, that does not explain everything. Could it be that it replicates faster? That it lives longer before it decays? Is it simply a question of concentration? We don't know, but we surely want to find out . . ."

Armand thanked Tomioka-san for his cooperation and asked: "Can we work together to identify, and possibly develop antibodies?"

"As you know, Armand-san, we cannot go directly from here to there: long, drawn-out process. It would be faster and better to find antibodies in someone who has been infected." Oshima-san added:

"I'm sure you understand Armand-san, Tomioka-san means that discovering antibodies from scratch is an incredibly tedious task which could take a very, very long time. It's pure trial and error. You can have a lot of errors before stumbling on the correct one. It is indeed much more efficient to use antibodies found on someone who has been infected . . . Or better yet, naturally occurring antibodies."

Tomioka-san nodded his agreement. Oshima-san continued:

"It would be great if your veterinary friend could quickly identify the genus to which the animal that carried the original virus belongs. With that, we could assume that other species within the genus also carries antibodies that neutralize the action of the virus by binding to the virus and thus preventing it from binding with any other cell. Isolating a few of these would get us quickly on the way to finding a vaccine or even a cure . . ."

Armand nodded his understanding. He replied:

"Obviously, I have not had a chance to talk to Professor Dubreuil yet, Oshima-San. But could we sign an agreement between our two organizations that allows us to work together on the topic? We could co-publish any research we develop, but we could also share in the ownership of whatever cure or vaccine we discover."

Both Japanese scientists agreed that a form of cooperation between the two organizations would be desirable. They decided to have a memorandum drafted for their signatures as soon as possible.

❚ ❚ ■ ❚ ❚

Back at the Shinjuku Prince Hotel, where he would be spending the night prior to flying to Hong Kong, Armand placed an internet call to Countess Renate. He brought her up to speed, with a particular emphasis on what he saw were the two most significant findings of the trip so far. The first was that the virus looked like a further engineered version of one which killed a Japanese businessman a few months ago. Second, it looked like the gain-of-function had taken place in Wuhan, China. However, it was totally unclear whether this was a joint venture between China and North Korea or a rogue piece of work by a North Korean scientist who fled, most likely with the virus and the various scientific findings, back to Korea a few weeks ago.

Renate thanked Armand for all that good work and said that she would share it with her client. She asked to be kept informed on a more granular level than usual, as there were two strands to this particular mission:

"I need to keep both sides as well informed as possible . . ."

CHAPTER.13

Mike Steinberg jumped out of the bedroom into the living room as soon as Ismail had left. He seemed positively giddy:

"Never seen a mission where we're we so close to our target . . ."

"Neither have I . . . Let's call David."

David picked up the phone immediately. He was as delighted as his two agents. His next order of business was to plan their counterattack. He asked them to find their way to his office as quickly as possible.

"I'll bring Simon in."

Mark remarked that since he was surely tailed, they would have to be quite careful. David nodded. He told Mike to leave the flat as quickly as possible, using the back door to the building. He then gave Mark a routine which he had planned:

"Mark, give some time for Mike to leave so that we can organize ourselves. We'll have agents tail Mike, if it looks like he is being followed. When I give you the signal, leave the apartment as naturally as you can. Go straight to the Saudi Air office. You're supposed to buy a ticket, and that's what you'll do; after all, you know the date and you don't have too much time to spare . . ."

Mark was nodding. He put David on hold so that Mike could leave right away. He was not needed in the conversation. David continued:

"I don't want to give you more detail than needed. Let me simply say that you will not leave the Saudi Air office."

Mark's heart missed a beat as he asked:

"Come again . . ."

". . . by the front door. You won't leave by the front door . . ."

"Like that much better."

"Sorry. There is a back door. Ask to use their restrooms. They're just outside of the shop, in the common area. Someone who works for us will guide you to a back door. There, someone else will be waiting for you in a car. They'll drive you here. Again, not to our front door, but down to the parking garage. They'll take you up to the office with the service elevator."

Mark was delighted to see that David and Simon were still, as always, totally on the ball. Less than an hour later, the three of them were in Simon's office. They spent the next hour or so planning for every move that would be required while the European Continent operation was in train. Simon had initially observed:

"You've got to give it to them. They are very well organized. Their only real loose end is you, Mark. You must be playing Anwar's role perfectly. Keep that going."

They agreed that there was little that was needed before Mark arrived in Bern. Until then, they only had to provide safety protection to Mark. Simon noted that the surveillance was probably needed more to learn about the terrorist group's contacts in Europe:

"I can't believe they would try to hurt you, Mark, for as long as the mission is ongoing. You only need protection if there was an accidental misstep that broke your cover . . ."

Mark could not disagree. One thing he did point out was the ever-present risk that he might slip up:

"Punishment would come quite quickly."

Simon nodded and remarked that it was the ultimate loose end.

They could not know what they did not know. Ismail ostensibly had swallowed the Anwar switch with minimal difficulty. Who knew which of the other people he might meet might have known Anwar better. Simon, in particular, worried that they truly knew nothing of Anwar's family situation. Mark granted the point and simply conceded that there had not been any opening that would allow a question to appear innocuous enough.

They all agreed that the challenge would become considerably more serious as soon as Mark got to the apartment in Bern. At that time, the number of people with whom Mark might connect would increase. It would become easier to slip up. Simon reiterated that Mark should adopt, within the limits created by his role, somewhat of a taciturn character: the less he said, the less he would risk saying the wrong thing. He added:

"We know our agents tend to do that in the field when pressure mounts. Should be true for a terrorist as well."

As always, focusing on practicalities and execution, Simon suggested that the first crucial step would be for the service to get access to the cellar in the apartment. Mark offered a possible solution:

"I am supposed to get all the keys to the apartment when I get there. I am to call a number they gave me. The individual will meet me at some agreed time there; we'll agree the time when I call him. I could go up to the flat and get myself organized. Then, I'll go down to the cellar to deposit the tablets; I could then plausibly leave the flat to go on a quick tour. I think I'll go to the Iraqi Embassy to see how long of a walk it is. Again, that would be reasonable."

"Absolutely, my friend."

"Well, Simon, just have someone tail whoever is following me. I'll be miked up. So, as soon as I find an appropriate place, I'll casually drop the keys to the cellar in some grassy area. I'll give a signal, with a very simple description. I'll continue on my way. Let me know when you have picked it up. Then, you all can have a duplicate made and return it to me."

Simon conceded that this sounded like a good plan. David nodded. Yet, they were worried about returning the key. David reminded the group that they did not know the topography of the building in which the apartment was located.

"All that we know, from Google Earth, is that it's a low rise, with three or four floors. We don't know how the cellar, which has to be in the basement, can be accessed. For instance, what if we need keys to the flat to get in? I'll get our people in Bern to tell us as much as they can."

Mark suggested that it is not unusual for rentals of this type to provide a couple of keys, adding:

"You could make a duplicate of these too . . . You'll need them to access the flat anyway."

Simon calmly smiled and then said:

"Guys, we're making a lot of assumptions. I think we should simply have two or three versions of our plan, depending upon one or two key assumptions being right or wrong . . ."

David piped in:

"Totally agree. That's what your plans usually look like, Simon . . . I remember Operation Kovesh."

David was referring to a very complex operation which Simon had orchestrated eighteen months earlier and in which David had led Simon's team of agents on the ground.

▌▐▐▌▐▌

The interplay between Simon and David was quite interesting. An outsider might have wondered why Simon, the ultimate boss, would appear to be taking the lead rather than allowing David to run his show subject to Simon's approval. Yet, the degree to which David and Simon worked as a well-oiled pair did not require that level of complexity and delegation. David knew perfectly well that Simon was the ultimate planner. That's how his mind worked. He saw himself as a great associate that would implement Simon's plan, with all the flexibility and discretion needed if something went awry in the field. David knew that he might, one day, succeed Simon, but he also realized that the handover was at best a number of years away. It really depended upon the willingness of General Ariel Landau, the head of *Mossad*, to step down. There was no indication that he wanted to retire any time soon. Thus, he felt comfortable as a de facto deputy to Simon, focused as he was on what would be best for *Mossad*: Simon planning and himself executing.

■ ■ ■ ■ ■

Simon's main focus at that point was twofold. First, he and David needed to organize their agents around Europe and second, he had to contact Countess Renate to coordinate their efforts. He hesitated for a while as to whether he should contact the secret services of the countries in which Mark would be operating. He finally decided that only Ariel Landau, the overall head of *Mossad*, could make the decision.

With Ariel's line busy when first attempting to call, Simon first talked to Countess Renate. There, the news was excellent. Simon was elated to hear of the progress on the scientific front, even though it raised the specter that this was beyond a mere localized terrorist issue. The potential for North Korea being officially involved was quite serious.

As Countess Renate emphasized, they did not know yet whether the North Korean scientist was a rogue or an official operator. However, there were valid reasons to be worried. For instance, could it be that, instead of the terrorists using North Korea's help, it went the other way around? North Korea using the terrorists? Dealing with Islamists had become an unfortunate reality in the prior ten years or so, if not longer. Yet, Simon felt that *Mossad* and many of its equivalent organizations around the world, had a good grip of what Islamists would or would not do. On the other hand, the North Korean dictator was known to be totally unpredictable. While one could imagine the ultimate, religious goal of Islamists, there was no possible way one could see North Korea as a superpower. Finally, one could always imagine that a North Korean blackmail might eventually lead to Armageddon for that country, and raise all sorts of questions as to who would line up with them; the classic: *"the enemy of my enemy is my friend . . ."*

In the end, Simon and Countess Renate agreed to keep going as planned. Yet, they also pledged to work even more closely when it came to North Korea. This was one issue that one could not afford to get wrong.

After hanging up with Renate, Simon connected with Ariel. He elected first to cover the question of the degree of openness vis-à-vis local secret services, reserving the question of North Korea for later:

"On the one hand, we're going to be working with very few agents at a time in one place. We do not expect to apprehend anyone, unless forced to by the need to protect Mark or some other agent. On the other, we will surely be handling a deadly poison which Mark will deliver to us in exchange for innocuous, inert, liquid gases. I can see us doing all this on our own and getting away with it. But if any trouble develops, we could not avoid local involvement . . ."

"Understood, Simon. How much lead time do you think we would have if anything went awry?"

"Well, I think it'll range from a few hours to seconds if we need to defend an agent and kill an opponent."

"But that would in all instances look like legitimate defense, wouldn't it?"

Simon could see where Ariel's mind, at times called "steel trap" by his subordinates, was going. *Stay in the shadows until you can't any longer . . .*

Simon replied:

"I guess it's the old adage: better to apologize afterwards than to ask permission beforehand."

"Exactly, my friend. Plus, frankly, looking at the countries you all will be visiting, there are at least a couple where I would not be sure they are totally on our side . . . By the way, I am not talking of their official policy; there, they all support us. I am talking down in the ranks. That's where a leak could come."

Ariel added that he wanted to think for a while longer as to whether the cover would have to require some political involvement:

"We have to remember what the risk is for each of these countries. So, it may be that we need a contact at the level of the foreign affair ministers, with a request for total secrecy so that we can execute the operation. By the way, what would be the position of Countess Renate on that?"

Simon replied that she typically tried to avoid any exposure, for herself or any member of her team. The only exception she would allow to that general rule is that associates, as she called them, could participate in official activities provided these did not offer any risk that one could trace it back to her. Simon explained:

"I'm sure that, eventually, she'll have no problem with them going public, if the scientists do find something that attacks and kills the virus, or which prevents its contamination. But there would be no way to guess that one of them was one of her associates. They'd be doing it in their official functions."

Simon at that point thought he should emphasize the issue he had discussed with Countess Renate—the potential North Korean connection. Ariel reacted quite vigorously:

"Hold it. That's totally new news, Simon. This whole thing becomes a whole mess if some country is directly involved . . . There's a lot we can do behind the scenes. I'll even vouch for the bet that your team will be able to eliminate or at least minimize any damage caused by the bombs placed by ISIS. Now, imagine we're talking of a biological attack directed in some way by North Korea . . . That's a totally different kettle of fish. By the way, my friend, why stop at North Korea? There could be other tentacles. Watch that like a hawk . . ."

"Sure appreciate it, sir. Whether the scientist is operating solo or not, we must eliminate him, his samples and all his notes to avoid a second wave with an even more powerful variant of the virus."

"And that, we can't do surreptitiously. You're good, Simon, and so is your team. But you'd have to work really hard to get me and the War Cabinet to approve any form of operation in North Korea."

Simon said he understood and painted an even more portentous picture, in the event there was a secret but real collaboration between China and the scientist on this particular project.

"Simon, you're opening Pandora's box."

"I know, sir. Frankly, I am not enjoying this any more than anyone else. Yet, it's got to be a consideration . . ."

They agreed that speculation at this moment was neither needed nor constructive. Ariel would let Simon continue with the current project, but he asked Simon to make sure he was kept closely in the loop. Simon kept to himself the thought he was having at that time: *looks like everyone wants to work more closely . . . This could really be the world's biggest mess . . . World war III, anyone?*

CHAPTER.14

HONG KONG

After a good night's sleep, Armand flew Japan Airlines to Hong Kong. The flight which lasted a bit longer than five hours gave him plenty of time to reflect on what he wanted to discuss with his friend, Lee Han Soon, a senior researcher at the *Institut Pasteur Hong Kong* affiliate. Though he did visit Hong Kong occasionally, he could not stop marveling at the genius behind the now twenty plus years old airport on Lantau Island. It surely was a fabulous replacement for the old Kai Tak airport which, for quite a long time, had the dubious privilege to be listed among the world's most dangerous airports, with its well-known and rightfully feared approach over buildings in Kowloon and its sole runway running from the mountains to the harbor. Touch down there had to be a precise science. In fact, it so happened that this may well have been what led Cathay Pacific, the territory's airline, to buy L1011 airplanes, when its competitors went for DC-10s or Boeing 747s, in 1974. Initially, at least, the L1011 aircrafts were the only ones equipped with automatic-pilot landing features.

Armand was facing a quandary. He had known Han Soon for many years. At the same time, the climate in the territory had changed quite dramatically in the last several years, particularly in the last twelve to eighteen months. China had become considerably more assertive, going as far as, in certain people's minds, the virtual repudiation of the commitments it had made when it signed, on December 19, 1984, the Sino-British Joint Declaration. This had followed the pronouncement by British Prime Minister Margaret Thatcher, on September 27, 1982, that the U.K. would return Hong Kong to Chinese sovereignty on July 1, 1997, when the lease on the New Territories expired. Though the agreement appeared to work according to its principles for some time, there was a gradual shift in China's attitude and an ever-growing assertion of its power on the erstwhile British colony. The first skirmish probably was the introduction of the Fugitive Offenders amendment bill by the Hong Kong government. The passage on June 30, 2020, of the Hong Kong National Security law was the latest nail in the proverbial coffin.

Armand wondered how much weight he could put on anything that Han Soon would say. He could imagine at least a couple of scenarios, neither of which looked very promising. On the one hand, Han Soon could have decided that his future was in Hong Kong. He could in fact have become a supporter of the Chinese regime, by political conviction or simply by default, as a condition of survival. If that was the case, was there not a definite risk he might parrot the official Chinese line? What use would that be, given the misinformation that had circulated widely with respect to the Covid-19 virus? Though there was still no clear smoking gun, revelations by a scientist that had defected certainly appeared to support, but not to prove conclusively, the thesis that the virus was not an accident. On the other hand, Han Soon might have decided that his future did not include Hong Kong. He might therefore work to ingratiate himself so that he might be invited to join another *Institut* within the Pasteur group. If that was the case, would he present a balanced view of events, and treat rumors as such, rather than as facts?

The final straw was that Hong Kong University housed a World Health Organization reference lab, alongside the *Institut Pasteur*. That lab is the top coronavirus lab in the world, and probably in one way or another participated in the work on Covid-19. Numerous accusations have been lodged against the lab, with several individuals directly accusing it of having helped the Chinese authorities hide the issue, at least early in the process. In fact, this is where the senior researcher that eventually defected to the U.S. worked. She had argued that the virus was man-made and deliberately released. Armand therefore would have to be even more cautious. Thankfully, he was himself a very proficient researcher in virology and was hoping that he could separate the wheat from the chaff.

Armand knew he had his work cut out. He elected to use a "straight bat" approach, a cricket term that describes being as direct as possible without taking any risk. Thus, he would position himself as if he did not have an axe to grind. Simultaneously, there was no point, in his view, discussing the developments in Tokyo. The main risk was that Dr. Park would have called Han Soon from Seoul; after all, both labs were part of the International *Institut Pasteur* system. Yet, Han Soon did not know that Armand had been to Seoul before coming to Hong Kong. So, whether he had or had not talked to Dr. Park, Han Soon would not learn about their work from Armand. At any rate, Armand thought that Dr. Park would not have shared anything yet. The conversations with Armand had been tentative, though the conclusions reached at dinner with his friend in the secret service pointed clearly in one direction. On the other, Armand, who did not read too many spy novels, still had enough familiarity with them to know that minuscule coincidences were what usually tipped the plot in one rather than another direction.

In the end, he decided that the defection of a scientist to North Korea and the rumor of a few deaths in that country were sufficiently well-known that he might use them as the lead into his questioning. At the same time, he would not come close to any discussion on Covid-19 as it did seem pretty clear that the virus they were studying was not of the coronavirus family.

Armand went directly to the Dexter H.C. Man building on Sassoon Road within the Hong Kong University campus in Pok Fu Lam, at the northern tip of Hong Kong Island. The building, a small structure, looked a bit lost, in the surrounding forest of medium and tall high-rises. Though "modern," the sandy-white building was quite elegant and almost "traditional." The street was sharply sloping toward the harbor, giving the site an intriguing perspective. The entry portal, at the highest point along Sassoon Road, seemed to be at the same level as midway between the second and third floors of the building. Armand walked through the portal and straight into the reception area. There he asked for Dr. Lee Han Soon. The receptionist smiled at him, called Dr. Lee and eventually motioned Armand to follow the escort whom Dr. Lee had sent. Armand stepped out of the elevator on the top floor of the building. He walked into Dr. Lee's office and marveled at the side view of Hong Kong harbor it afforded, adding:

"I bet you never get tired of such a view . . ."

Han Soon ignored the comment, which had to be a well-worn line by foreign visitors, and replied:

"Armand, it has been a long time . . ."

"Indeed, Han Soon. How have you been?"

Han soon replied that he had been quite busy since the onset of the Covid-19 pandemic, adding:

"As you know, there have been competing claims as to the origin of the virus . . ."

"Did you know the lady researcher who defected to the U.S.?"

"Sure . . . I met her several times. A very nice person. I don't really understand why she is behaving the way she is."

"You're talking of the rumors, right?"

"Absolutely. She is the only one with her claim. Virtually everyone else is on the record saying that the virus was not altered by man, nor was it released intentionally . . . After all, why would China choose to contaminate its own people first? And, in particular, to contaminate the people who work at one of its most secret, but also most advanced labs?"

Armand chose to evade the issue, arguing that he really did not have any insight that he could rely on. Yet, he noted that Han Soon was definitely using the official Chinese line. Though he personally did not have any basis to judge the credibility of the lady defector, he had thought highly of her work until that time. Further, the fact that she had left her husband behind, as he refused to follow her, would seem to him to suggest a deep emotional commitment to her work. His immediate thought was—*How can one be so deeply committed to a lie?*

Yet, returning to his plan, he immediately shifted the conversation to the new virus. He had brought a sample for Han Soon and took him through the same material that he had shared in Tokyo and South Korea. Han Soon was initially quite surprised, and became visibly more and more excited as the presentation went on:

"This is quite interesting, Armand. It's also quite worrisome . . . You didn't say how you got ahold of it?"

"I am not at liberty to disclose that, even to such a good friend as you, Han Soon. In fact, other than to name our client, which wouldn't help, I really don't know much. The only thing I can say is that it was intercepted in transit. The original source, which in all sincerity I do not know, is believed to be in the terrorist world. The main issue is that I don't know which organization they're referring to . . . Finally, we don't know whether they created the virus or bought it from someone. And, if that, from whom?"

Han Soon initially surprised Armand by his candor. He told him that he was aware of at least one deadly infection in Japan. Though he had not seen any hard evidence, he said the virus which was described in the rumor mill looked quite a bit like the one Armand was showing him, adding:

"Judging from pictures, is it possible that the source is the same?"

Armand replied that he did not know. Noting that Han Soon made no reference to Dr. Park, he felt he could open up a bit. He said that he had visited the *Institut* in Seoul where he had heard rumors of a scientist in Wuhan defecting to North Korea. Han Soon did not seem to know much about the topic, other than to say that he had heard the same rumor. Armand asked:

"Could this virus also have originated in Wuhan?"

"Hard to tell . . . I know they're quite advanced in virology there. I also know they carry out a lot of experiments on viruses originating in the animal world. Covid-19 was said to come from bats. This one looks different, but there are a number of viruses that could come from a number of animals . . ."

"Is there any way that you could dig a bit deeper to tell me more about the North Korean connection?"

"If there's one . . ."

Han Soon added that he could make a few phone calls. He suggested that Armand make a courtesy call on the head of the *Institut* in Hong Kong, adding:

"I had told him you were coming, and he said he would love to spend a half hour with you if you can spare the time."

"Is it still Dr. Yeo Yap Chan?"

"Absolutely. Do you know him?"

"I'm sure we've met at some point, somewhere, but that's about it . . ."

■ ■ ■ ■ ■

Han Soon called Dr. Yeo's office, which simply said they would send an assistant to fetch Armand and take him to Dr. Yeo.

Dr. Yeo was a typical Hong Kong academic. He had a lot of charisma. He still dressed quite formally, with a bowtie but without a jacket. He wore a yellow, cashmere sweater draped over his shoulders, probably because the air-conditioning was set at too low a temperature. His dark brown hair had partially receded revealing a wide forehead, but careful combing of the remaining hair made sure that he did not look bald. He said:

"Professor Duchemin . . . It's a pleasure . . ."

Armand was initially surprised by the British accent. He had observed that Hong Kong personalities were now tending more toward the Chinese than the British as was the case when Hong Kong was a British colony. He had noted, in particular, that taxi drivers, who used to speak some broken English ten to twenty years ago, were now only fluent in Cantonese. The Chinese influence was growing; after all, it was now a part of China. Had he in fact looked further around, Armand would have noted that all the clubs or organizations that used to have the word "Royal" in their name, had dropped it.

He recalled a time when, at a party in Hong Kong before the handover, he was talking to an expatriate when he had heard, behind him, a booming, low voice speaking in the Queen's best English. He had turned around and was stunned to find that the voice emanated from a Chinese individual. He was sorry to think that one then had to fake or acquire a British accent to be accepted in expatriate circles. Dr. Yeo, in Armand's judgment, was not faking. One of the diplomas he could see on the wall was telling him that Dr. Yeo had been in part educated in the U.K., and in fact at Oxford . . .

"I think we've already met a few times, here or there, Dr. Yeo, but it's a pleasure indeed to see you again; and this time for more than a few seconds . . ."

"Indeed. What are you looking for Professor Duchemin?"

"Well, I have run into a virus which we do not know. I am pretty sure that it is not related to Covid-19, but really don't know much more.

It looks as if it has evolved or been altered, but I don't know why or by whom if altered. So, in view of last year's pandemic, I thought I would go to Asia to see if anybody could help me."

The story was generally true, although a number of important details were missing. Armand indeed knew even less about Dr. Yeo than he did about Han Soon. He could not afford to reveal anything that could leak; in fact, he had to work on the assumption that whatever he said could be leaked. After all, one did not get to the position that Dr. Yeo occupied without significant support, and inevitably some support in the current environment had to come from the Chinese authorities.

Dr. Yeo seemed quite interested, though he added that he was no specialist. He asked the classic question about the provenance of the virus. Armand lied and said that their client had stumbled onto it and had no idea what it was intended for. He added that he was not even sure how dangerous it was, observing:

"For all I know it could be innocuous . . . But can we afford not to take it seriously?"

"Certainly not. Do we know anything else?"

"At this point, no. Visiting the joint venture in Seoul, on the way to here, I was told of rumors alleging that a scientist defected . . ."

"You mean the lady that went to the U.S., Dr. Li Shen Yee?"

"No. Not her. That was last year, wasn't it? Someone else, more recently . . ."

Dr. Yeo ostensibly preferred to discuss Dr. Li than any other defector story. So, he replied only to Armand's comment that she defected the prior year:

"Yes. She's been making waves for nearly nine months now . . ."

Armand decided to play devil's advocate to draw Dr. Yeo out:

"I've heard, but there are a lot of elements which don't make much sense. Maybe, alleging certain revelations were the price she had to pay to be granted asylum and protection in the U.S."

"You're a cynic, Professor Duchemin . . . But you may be closer to the truth than you know."

"Anyway, the rumor I heard in Seoul was about a male scientist defecting to North Korea."

Dr. Yeo looked surprised but did not allow his demeanor to betray him more than a few seconds. Quickly, he looked totally nonplussed and replied:

"I've heard that one too. Don't know what to make of it. You know, if I had to guess, I would bet that he was a rogue scientist who did some research alongside whatever mission he had. I'd bet that he found something interesting and decided to take it back to North Korea, possibly to get a big promotion . . . If he had wanted to make money, he would either have stayed in China or come to Hong Kong . . ."

Armand thought that the scenario was plausible. At the same time, he noted that this would be the one narrative that China would like the world to believe if the whole thing ever came out, even if it was knee-deep in it. The fact that Dr. Yeo was feeding him that line made him more and more concerned that China might have been working on some biological weapon, possibly with the help of the North Korean scientist. That would be consistent with the accusations of Dr. Li, currently in hiding in the U.S.

■ ■ ■ ■ ■

Armand left Dr. Yeo's office puzzled. Dr. Yeo had confirmed the defection but presented it with a twist that exonerated the Chinese and did not even directly implicate the North Koreans. He had in effect acknowledged some connection, but effectively placed all the blame on the scientist. So, if North Korea was caught using the virus, it could claim that it had fallen into its lap. Armand noted that it would still have been a crime to use it even in these hypothetical circumstances. Yet, it would be much less damaging than an alternative that had North Korea sending a scientist to China, with China's agreement, for the sole purpose of developing a virus-based biological weapon.

Returning to Han Soon's office, he was disappointed that Han Soon did not seem to be able to get any additional information for him . . . He thought: *The long arms of China?*

Back at the hotel awaiting the time to go to the airport for his return flight to Paris, Armand set up a conference call with Countess Renate on a secure line. He gave her as complete a rundown as possible, though, in the end, he emphasized two principal conclusions. The first was that the virus was most likely man-made, from an animal root which he hoped soon to identify. The second was that North Korea was most likely an important element in the scheme, though it was not clear if it was a deliberate plan or an opportunistic move. From his point of view, he said that the practical conclusion had to be:

"The sooner we can find out where the liquid gas comes from the better. But my bet is that North Korea is in the loop somehow. Now, whether it's in it officially or unofficially, who knows?"

He turned to the mystery with respect to China. He told Countess Renate that he had been marginally disappointed by his friend Han Soon, though he did not know if Han Soon was intimidated or a willing participant against him, adding:

"I can't believe that people in Tokyo or Seoul could know more than those who are in Hong Kong. Yet, on virtually every topic, he wanted me to believe he knew less."

The one element of caution in Armand's mind was the role of Dr. Yeo. He had originally thought that he was "genuine" and then changed his view when Dr. Yeo seemed to be peddling a Chinese line. Armand could easily understand why someone in that position would by definition be influenced by his Chinese masters. Yet, there are ways one can turn a sentence to convey confusion rather than simply repeating a line which seemed like Chinese propaganda. After all, Dr. Yeo headed up a group that was a part of the *Institut Pasteur* network. Countess Renate was impressed by Armand's work:

"This is really good, Armand. Thank you. I know that we are still far from having the answer to all our questions. Yet, we've made a great deal of progress. What do you plan to do next?"

"I am going to maintain contact with our colleagues in Tokyo. They're the ones which seem by far the most reliable. In passing, I really believe that Dr. Oshima would be a great addition to The Shadow Experts . . ."

"I did like him too. Leave that one to me . . ."

Armand argued that his next two steps were first to follow up with his friend, Dr. Dominique Dubreuil, the veterinary professor. Knowing where to look in nature for the "raw virus" as he called it would be a huge step forward. Second, he would pursue the work with the two Japanese professors. Renate asked:

"What about Seoul?"

"Well, I'll stay in touch with Dr. Park, but I'm not sure what we can reasonably expect. Remember that I am a biologist, not a criminal investigator . . ."

"Totally understood, Armand. But I'm more optimistic than you. I bet he'll give us more information, with the help of South Korean intelligence."

CHAPTER.15

RIYADH, SAUDI ARABIA AND SWITZERLAND

Mark was now ready to start his own part in the action. He left Tel Aviv as planned on a Saudi Air flight, bound for Riyadh, a novelty given the newness of the reciprocal agreements recently signed between Saudi Arabia and Israel. He landed safely and proceeded through local immigration and custom with no difficulty. He was traveling as an Arab-Israeli businessman who was going to visit a few clients in Riyadh. He had only a limited amount of luggage, just what he would need for the three days that the trip was scheduled to last. In fact, he had purchased a roundtrip ticket from Tel Aviv to Riyadh, as it would have been suspicious for him to have only a one-way ticket, with the trip appearing to stop in Saudi Arabia. And, anyway, his masters wanted him eventually to take that return trip when the mission was complete; he could always change the date on that return ticket. Plus, he really did not care about costs; after all, the terrorists were paying for that ticket.

He was met in the arrival hall by someone who was carrying a tablet displaying the name Mohamed Ahmed al-Saleh, written in Arabic. His "host" was wearing the traditional, local dress: full-length white robe with a white *ghutra*, a large square of cloth they wear on their heads. A black *agal*, the cordon that is worn on top of the head, held the ghutra in place. They exchanged polite greetings and walked together to the black limousine, apparently of U.S. origin, which would take them to the place where Mark would change. The place looked like an elegant apartment building and the apartment was quite comfortable and nicely furnished.

His make-over was relatively quick, the only important changes being for him to wear more expensive clothing, with a couple of last-minute alterations, principally in the length of the pant legs. These same alterations were to be made to the clothing that was packed in the suitcase he was going to carry to Switzerland. Mark found the time to have a grateful thought for Simon who had told him to pack his Kevlar jacket into a double bottom of his carry-on luggage, where he had stuff which he would argue was critical. That included his ceramic handgun, with silencer and ammunition. They went totally undetected.

He was told that he should spend the night at the apartment: "This is all for you. Don't hesitate using anything that's in here . . ." *A golden prison, but a prison nevertheless* was all he could think of.

The corporate jet flight for Geneva was not scheduled to leave until the next morning. The seven odd hours of travel time and the one-hour time difference would have made it awkward for them to leave in the mid-afternoon, which was the earliest flight they could have made and not arrive in Geneva too late. Geneva had a curfew from 22:00 p.m. to 6:00 a.m. for non-commercial flights.

Mark was told that a catered dinner would be brought to him, if he only dialed a number which he took down on a piece of paper. He elected to take a good, long shower when everyone had left, but not before carefully inspecting the apartment. As he fully expected, the apartment was bugged, except, small consolation, for the toilet and the bathroom: *I'm gonna have to do the sensitive stuff there . . .* was all that came to his mind. He was again very grateful for the anti-spying equipment which had been loaded into his own computer tablet. It could detect any microphone, by emitting a sound that was inaudible to the human ear and awaiting any return vibration. It could also point in the direction of any video equipment, working on a similar principle.

The dinner was somewhat basic from Mark's culinary standpoint, as it had to satisfy Muslim dietary restrictions. Yet, it was quite good. Mark was disappointed that no alcoholic beverage was offered, although he could not deny that this was exactly what he expected. He went straight to bed, after having used his own phone, from the bathroom to report to David and contact Debbie. He was happy to hear that she was in great spirits. She seemed to open up more and more as she learned that he was involved in government work that appeared to involve *Mossad.* He thought, *I wonder why she is reacting that way . . . But whatever it is, it's gotta be good news for me . . . And for us, I hope.*

At the appointed time, the next morning, Mark was met at the apartment by his handlers. They took him straight to the airport and drove him directly to the plane. The lone, male flight attendant took his suitcase and placed it in the hold. Mark kept his carry-on with him. As he reached the top of the stairs, he was surprised and very impressed by the luxury in the cabin. Mark had flown on a private aircraft before, but it had always been a plane from the Israeli Air Force. While the interior appointments of those planes were nice and quite comfortable, they looked like abject poverty when compared to this cabin. Though there was space for potentially as many as sixteen passengers, the cabin only offered seating for eight: four seats and two sofas. The seating areas and their immediate surroundings were in cream leather, with dark brown piping. The furniture was all brushed aluminum highlighted with gold, and wood, which looked like burl elm. Later in the flight, he would use the bathroom which offered not only the customary toilet, with fixtures that looked like they were in gold, or at least gold-plated, but also a shower cabinet so that the traveler could arrive refreshed. Mark assumed, correctly as it turned out, that the two sofas transformed into beds, with curtains surrounding them, to ensure a modicum of privacy.

Mark made a mental note that, just opposite the cabin door of the aircraft, there was a framed sign that had, again in gold or gold-plated material, the Arabic characters for "GD Group," which he knew to be a large construction and civil engineering company in the Kingdom. He assumed that the plane must be theirs, though nothing could tell him whether the plane was rented from them or simply provided free of charge. The latter would signal that the company was a hidden supporter of ISIS, while the former would unfortunately not contain a large amount of intelligence value. He would still mention it to Simon or David at the first opportunity.

The plane landed in Geneva, on the single concrete runway, toward the southwest. Mark could see Lake Leman in the final approach, and then a few, largish homes before hitting the runway, with the major terminal on the left. The jet had a short taxi to terminal T3, as it is located at the southwest end of the runway. He was taken by car to the main terminal, about half a mile away, where he went to the car rental counter. A car was reserved in his name, a Mercedes C series, which afforded discrete luxury. He assumed that his handlers knew that he would have to cover substantial mileage and thus wanted him to be comfortable, without excess.

He drove out of the airport and set his pocket GPS to the address of his first destination. Within fifteen minutes, he was right in front of the Syrian Consulate General, rue de Lausanne, down the road from Geneva's main railway station, Cornavin. Using the local phone provided to him by his handlers, he called the number that he had been given:

"I dream of the Califate . . ."

The voice at the end of the phone asked:

"Please turn the camera on . . ." Mark did. The voice replied:

"Where are you parked?"

"A block short of your location, on the left going east, the opposite side of the street from your offices . . . I am driving a metallic grey Mercedes C300 Sedan . . ."

"Pop the trunk in one minute exactly. I will drop the package in it. Do not get out of the car. Drive away immediately . . ."

Mark thought: *Serious security precautions.*

He asked:

"How will I know that the package is what I expect?"

"You won't. If you want to check it, drive at least a couple of miles away, stop, check and call me back if something is missing."

"OK."

The drop was made into the trunk and the stranger closed the lid. Mark drove east until he reached Geneva's Jardin d'Hiver—or Winter Gardens—which are squeezed in between the train tracks and the coastal road along Lake Leman, eventually leading to Lausanne, forty miles away. He chose the place because there was no car that he could see in the parking lot. He stopped, opened the trunk and found not one, but two packages, next to his own suitcase. He opened them both and verified that they contained twelve computer tablets and twelve, extra, external batteries. He was surprised, and happy, to find an envelope in the first suitcase he opened. It contained direction to the apartment that was rented for him in Bern, together with a couple of keys: one had a tag reading main door, in English; the other also had a tag which read, still in English, cellar. Interiorly, he was mad.

He had been told by his handlers to call another number when he got to Bern. He had assumed that this meant that they would provide him with the keys to the apartment when he got to Bern. Having the keys now would make it so much easier for him to give them to someone from *Mossad* for duplication. He knew that *Mossad* had mini 3D printers which they could operate while driving their cars. Plus, they printed with both the usual plastic composite and metal filaments. He closed the trunk and noticed that his car was no longer the only one in the lot. Another was parked at the other end. He correctly assumed that his handlers were watching his moves. This calmed him down a bit, as it would have been very hard to hand the keys for duplication without being noticed. He climbed back into the car. After having checked, again, that there were no bugs in the car with his own tablet, he called *Mossad*. He told them about the keys. They agreed that he would stop at a service station on the way to Bern first to drop off the keys in the toilets and another time closer to Bern to get them back. *Mossad* would send someone ahead to the first stop; he would be in the toilet when Mark arrived. They agreed on the gas station where he would stop first and was told that he would be handed the address of the second in exchange for the keys. Satisfied, Mark hung up and drove away.

He knew that he should get onto the divided highway number 1 which would take him to Lausanne and then to Bern, offering great views of Lake Leman to the right at the outset and of Lake Neuchatel later on the left. With a speed limit of a hundred and twenty kilometers per hour (about eighty miles per hour), it should take him an hour and a half to cover the hundred miles that separated Geneva from Bern, according to the directions on his tablet. The road was mostly flat during the whole trip. He noted that the car that had come into the parking lot with him in Geneva was still behind him. He thought . . . *They don't even seem to want to hide themselves. Arrogant or simply not terribly good.*

He made the stop that he wanted to make as soon as he saw the service station that had been flagged for him. The keys were handed over without a third party coming into the toilet area; the small piece of paper he received told him where to stop next. Nearer Bern, he stopped there and dutifully fueled the car. As he was doing it, a gentleman that was fueling his car on the other side of the pump bumped into him. He apologized. Mark could feel something being slipped in the pocket of his coat that faced toward the front of the car. He smiled. He took advantage of the few extra moments to call Debbie and say Hi. Everything looked great *"at home"* as he said to himself.

Arriving in the Embassy district of Bern, as instructed, he dutifully parked the car about a mile from Justingerweg, where his rental apartment was. There, he called the number he had been told to call:

"Anwar here. I am almost at the apartment."

"Excellent. Go park by the British Embassy, at 50 Thunstrasse, just before you reach Thunplatz. Open your window. Someone will ask you for keys. Give them the keys you received in Geneva and they'll give you the keys to the apartment . . ."

Mark thought, . . . *bastards . . . The first set of keys was a setup. Need to call Mossad and tell them we need to start over . . . Good thing they gave them back to me at the service station . . .*

He did as instructed and received another envelope from the gloved hands of someone wearing a scarf around the lower half of his face. He could not see it, but someone inside the Israeli Embassy, which was a couple of streets away from the British Embassy, on Alpenstrasse, was operating a relatively silent drone, taking plenty of pictures. He could not know it, but another car had also been following him. This one, belonging to *Mossad*, had been careful not to be noticed. As he drove to the front of the British Embassy, the other car kept going, went around Thunplatz and then, after a couple of turns veered right into Alpenstrasse; it had to make these turns because Seminarstrasse which it would have to take was a one-way street in the wrong direction.

He was pleasantly surprised when he opened the door to the apartment. It was spacious, on the second floor of what might at one point have been a large, single-family home. He was surprised to see that the flat did not look like it was bugged. His equipment indeed captured no audio or video signals. Had he looked carefully through the window, he would have seen someone standing across the street, with what was clearly a long-distance microphone.

He decided to call David to check in. Yet, though he had not detected any bug, he called from the toilet, taking care to flush every sixty seconds or so. The phone call was quite quick as it appeared that everything was occurring according to plan. David still injected a note of caution:

"I am pretty sure you are under surveillance. They've not been terribly good at concealing their activity so far, but, maybe, another team will do better. The switcheroo with respect to the keys was quite smart . . . Proceed as planned for the keys. We'll duplicate the cellar's key first. We'll get you a second lock to make sure that your friends cannot get into the cellar during the mission. Let's see if they complain to you . . . If they do, appear surprised and just tell them that you always take extra precautions."

"Thanks a lot for all that, David. Have someone ready to get the cellar key when I go to the Iraqi Embassy. That's my next move."

CHAPTER.16

BERN, SWITZERLAND

Before going to the Iraqi Embassy, Mark decided that he would plan his drop off routes and then call the number he was supposed to reach to get the flasks. He had initially been told that the flasks would come by batch of three. He therefore tried to plan trips involving three drops. He did not have much of a choice in terms of where he was to drop bombs as the locations were preselected. Yet, he had not been given any specific instructions as to the order in which they were to be deposited, except for the last three.

As he started to plan, he quickly realized that the last trip was the easy one. He had been told it had to cover Brussels and London. So, he would start with Brussels North Station, the busiest train station in the country. He thought: *They must want to inflict the maximum amount of damage.* He would then drive to Calais, ride the *Le Shuttle* train which would take the car to Folkestone on the English side using the Chunnel, the tunnel under the Channel which only accommodates trains. There, he would drive to London, where he was to drop the last two bombs, one at Victoria Station in the center of London and the other at London City Airport, which, though smaller than Heathrow, was more densely designed; there is only one terminal there. Again, he noted that they wanted to maximize impact.

The tough part was the rest of the mission. With the exception of the Netherlands, where only one bomb was to be dropped, at Schiphol Airport, every other country required two bombs. Traveling from Bern to each city, all the while covering the minimum number of miles, looked difficult if one was going to follow the initial plan of dropping three bombs per round trip.

Mark chose a different plan, which he would submit to his handlers for their approval. His first trip would just involve Italy and two bombs. He would travel to Milan's Malpensa airport, and then Rome's Fiumicino Airport, sometimes called Leonardo da Vinci Airport. In both cases, he noted, he was shooting for the largest airports, defined as those with the highest density of pedestrian traffic.

The second trip would have to involve four bombs, starting with Gare de Lyon-Perrache in Lyon, France. It was on his way to Barcelona Sants Station which provides train service for the whole of Spain and beyond. Mark would then drive to Madrid's Puerta de Atocha, again the largest train station in that city. He realized that his handlers had chosen train stations rather than airports. He assumed that this reflected the desire to vary the targets and because there was a lot more travel via train in Spain than by air. From there, he would drive north to Paris, placing the bomb in the locker room of Gare to Nord, the busiest train station in Europe. From there, he would drive back to Bern.

For the third trip, he would need to cover North Europe, with bombs dropped in Frankfurt, at the airport, and in Berlin, at Berlin Hauptbahnhof, the German capital's main station located in the heart of the city. From there, he would drive due west to Amsterdam's Schiphol Airport, the third busiest airport in Europe, after London Heathrow and Paris Charles de Gaulle.

‖ ‖ ∎ ‖ ‖

Mark elected to go to the Iraqi Embassy before calling for the flasks, to collect the explosives he needed and to be able to effect the cellar key drop allowing *Mossad* to duplicate the key. Mark was wearing his microphone when he left the apartment, to ensure that his *Mossad* colleagues could follow him. He decided that he would walk through the patch of national forest located just south of the highway and between it and the Aare river, not more than one hundred and fifty yards from the flat. He walked in the direction of St Ursula church and then went due south. The forest provided useful cover for his colleagues who were waiting for him where the trail connects with Kalcheggweg, the only road that crosses the forest from east to west. He was walking on the left-hand side of the road, facing the oncoming traffic. The key drop off worked like a charm; the *Mossad* car was driving east on Kalcheggweg, while Mark walked west. It did seem that someone was tailing Mark, on foot, but he could not have seen the maneuver. Mark thought he could see him walking behind him and on the other side of the road.

Mark walked casually until Kalcheggweg emerged from the forest. He knew that a colleague was tailing him from some distance away, as a small signal emanating from Mark's pocket pinpointed his location on their GPS system.

Soon, he was turning left on Elfenstrasse, going in a northwesterly direction, and expecting to reach the Iraqi Embassy on his left. The three-story structure that housed the Embassy was quite impressive; red-brick walls framed with grey stone quoins. He rang the intercom by the black, wrought iron gate and was told to come in. He walked up the grandiose, covered staircase on the right-hand side of the house, reaching the reception area on the second floor. There, he asked for his contact's name, Ibrahim Alshaibi, and sat down. A female assistant called his name. Mark stood up and dutifully followed her. He was ushered into an office and asked to wait there for a short while. He immediately switched off his personal locator as well as his microphone to ensure that they could not be detected if checking him out was the point of the wait. Alshaibi walked into the room, dressed quite elegantly, with a grey suit, a white shirt and a dark green tie. He greeted Mark:

"Nice to meet you, Anwar."

"Nice to see you again . . ."

Mark had learned that it was always best to claim to have seen someone before and then apologize if it was a first encounter. The opposite, behaving as if one had never met an individual only to learn that the person one impersonated was a known acquaintance, could be deadly. The trick worked perfectly. Ibrahim replied:

"It's been a long time, my friend . . . Funny, I remembered you a bit shorter."

"Time passes so fast . . . As far as my size, sorry, but the only thing that's changed is my waistline . . . I'm growing out, not up."

Again, Mark had avoided the obvious trap. Anwar and Ibrahim had met probably less than one year earlier, in Bagdad. Ibrahim tried to trick Mark for the third time:

"Where was it that we last met?"

"Seems to me, it must have been in the home country, but I could not swear to it. I've been in so many places in the last year, that I've kind of lost track."

Ibrahim seemed satisfied, though he added:

"I keep asking these questions because you look a bit different . . . Not just your height."

"Someone else told me the same thing, in Tel Aviv. As for my height, I bet it's because I am wearing special soles in my shoes. The arches of my feet have weakened, and the soles help correct for that . . . For the rest, you must be confused by my beard. Had to shave it before the drop-off in Tel Aviv."

"Ismail had warned me. Must be it . . . Anyway, what can I do for you?"

"Wait a second . . . You don't know? Now, maybe, I should be questioning you . . . I'm here to collect a package containing twelve components for the job that brings me to Bern . . ."

"We can stop playing this game, Anwar. You've convinced me. The explosives are in this suitcase. How did you get here?"

"I walked, through the forest . . ."

"I'll get an embassy car to drive you to your apartment. This would be too heavy for you to carry any distance . . . Where are you staying?"

"Justingerweg."

"OK. Just hold here. I'll arrange a driver."

"Best wishes."

"*Insha' Allah.*"

Mark's mind was still racing. *What was Ibrahim looking for? Have we missed a crucial step? Even here, is he coming back with a driver or with a gun drawn?* Turns out, there was no gun in Ibrahim's hand when he returned. Ibrahim picked up the suitcase and motioned to Mark to follow him. They exited the embassy by the door on the ground floor, opposite the grand staircase. A black Mercedes Benz was waiting in the garden, trunk opened. *Looks like I was worried for no reason . . . But, better safe than sorry.* Mark thanked Ibrahim who closed the car's door behind him. The wrought-iron gates opened, and the car exited the embassy grounds. The car turned left on Elfenstrasse; Mark noticed a car neatly parked on the other side of the street. He could not turn to see what it was doing but he knew that he would have an opportunity to see whether it was behind, as they would need to turn left on Thunstrasse and eventually make a U-turn to get to the flat. *No surprise . . . They're following. Hopefully someone will take a picture of the car. We need to identify their fleet. I'm sure they'll keep tailing.*

The driver offered to help carry the suitcase up to the flat. Mark thanked him but preferred to do it himself. Once in the flat, Mark knew he now had to get the flasks. He called the number that he had been given. He did not know who he was calling or where that individual worked. He simply knew that he had to call him.

"Anwar here . . ."

The man at the other end of the line replied with an Asian accented English:

"What is your dream?"

"The califate . . ."

"Listen carefully: What kind of car do you drive?"

"A grey Mercedes C300."

"OK. Drive to Kalcheggweg, where it emerges from the forest, to the east . . . Park your car on the side of the road and unlock your trunk. Then walk away from the car at least two to three hundred yards. Someone will come and drop the package. Come back fifteen minutes after you've left the car . . ."

The man at the other end of the line was about to hang up when Mark managed to stop his monologue:

"There has been a small change in plans . . ."

"What? Can't be."

"The first trip will only require two units; the second will need four and then back to three for each of the others . . ."

"No. We don't change plans. Arrange your trip according to the delivery schedule . . ."

Mark realized that the individual at the other end of the line was either unauthorized to make changes or simply not willing to countenance any. He thought that it did not matter anyway, as he would never be out any flask, given that the only trip with four bombs was the second. He thanked his interlocutor and indicated he would be at the agreed upon location in fifteen minutes. The phone line went dead . . .

These guys are really careful . . . Need to make sure that our people can tail whoever drops the stuff in the trunk of my car . . . Better talk to them right away. Should use at least two teams in case the fellow behaves in an odd manner.

CHAPTER.17

PARIS, FRANCE

Armand was quite excited. He had just hung up with Dr. Dominique Dubreuil, the professor at the Alford veterinary school. Dr. Dubreuil had found a virus that resembled that which Armand had shared with him in blood samples of lions. Dominique explained to Armand:

"Usually, we know that when one animal in a genus carries a virus, it is typically found in similar if not exactly comparable forms in the rest of the genus . . . I checked the theory in this case with the blood of leopards . . . And bingo . . . Found something similar . . ."

"That would fit with the initial findings that suggested an African origin . . ."

"Quite possible. But listen . . . This is huge: I also found something quite similar in the blood of simple, regular house cats."

"What does that mean?"

"Well, my friend, it means that cats probably carry an antibody to that virus."

"Why?"

"They don't die from it, so they must be immune to it . . . That means that we don't have to go look for antibodies in esoteric blood, when we can find it in house cats."

Armand realized the incredible potential of Dominique's discovery. It would indeed be a lot easier to procure blood from cats than from lions.

His next phone call was to Countess Renate. He was both reporting his findings and asking for direction. Countess Renate was just as ecstatic as Armand had been:

"We can develop antibody research and eventually start production quickly."

"Do we reveal this publicly or is it something that remains close to the vest?"

"I don't think we should reveal it publicly. That would be a signal to the terrorists and whoever is supporting or, worse, sponsoring them. But we could share the information with the *Institut Pasteur* and your friends at the National Institute of Infectious Diseases in Tokyo. It'd be best if the two of them agreed to do this as a secret joint venture."

"I'll see what I can do . . ."

■ ■ ■ ■ ■

Armand first needed to spend time with the appropriate authorities in the *Institut Pasteur* in Paris. Though, in many ways, he enjoyed his work for The Shadow Experts a lot, he was still first and foremost a senior researcher and a professor at the *Institut*. His initial findings were greeted with a mixture of surprise, excitement and doubt among the two senior colleagues with whom he shared them: Charles Durand and Pierre Morand. He could not tell them where he had found the offending virus and why that had to remain secret. Professor Durand went as far as asking:

"Why should we worry about something which may not exist? We would look silly."

"Charles, I know why you're reacting that way. Worse, I would probably do the same if I stood in your shoes. Yet, I'd like to ask you to trust me that this is a serious menace. I know that the people who provided me with the sample are working very hard at identifying all possible sources and all places where it might be. Believe me when I add that I myself do not know any of the details. The only other thing I know, and this has to remain between us, is that it is linked, somehow, to some terrorist activity."

Armand had decided that he had to disclose that latter detail, although he was not expected to. His rationale was simply that, if he was on the other end of the same conversation, he would not move without that detail. His analysis proved correct, as Charles Durand replied:

"That changes everything. Who knows about this? The DGSI?" Professor Durand was referring to Directorate General for Internal Security, a group closely related to the better known DGSE, the Directorate General for External Security. Both, together, make up France's secret service.

"Truly, Charles, I don't know. My contact operates from outside France. We meet very rarely. I help them in situations like this, by contributing my expertise in infectious diseases. Nothing more, nothing less . . ."

"But, Armand, how do you expect us, and here I mean Pierre and me, to conduct a project which is bound to be expensive without any stronger justification?"

Armand knew he was in a tough spot. He understood how his colleagues felt and sympathized with them. He excused himself from the conference room for a minute and dialed Countess Renate:

"I'm gonna need some funding to get the *Institut* to work on the antibody."

"They won't start without that?"

"Nope. Worse, I understand their stance, as I would react in the same way if the shoe was on the other foot."

Countess Renate paused for a few seconds. Then she offered: "I can commit one million Euros and there may be more . . ."

Countess Renate at that point was thinking that she could either get the money from *Mossad* or finance the project herself, billing her clients for it later.

Armand returned to the conference room with his two colleagues. With a wide smile, he declared:

"I was able to raise one million Euros for a start. Surely, it will cost more eventually, but I suspect that we'll be able to raise more. My only guess, and at this point it's only a guess, is that the more we ask, the more equity in the eventual solution we'll be asked to give up."

Charles and Pierre were, to say the least, very impressed. Research funding in France is not always easy to get. They immediately realized that, for Armand to have been able to raise that amount of money in a matter of less than five minutes, he had to have some strong backing. They agreed to begin the process, asking Armand:

"Will we be the only ones on this?"

Armand replied that the National Institute for Infectious Diseases in Japan would also be involved. Charles bounded:

"Why? They're not even affiliated with us?"

"Understood, my friend. But they were the ones who helped us identify the virus as a mutation of an earlier one. They're helping trace the source of that virus, which, judging from the genome, seems almost undoubtedly man-made. They're partners with me on that and I'm prepared to ask them to partner 50/50 with the *Institut*."

"This is totally irregular Armand . . . We're not supposed to operate like that."

"I know Pierre. I know. Now, put yourself in my shoes please. Imagine you're brought into a process. You are presented with something which can be deadly and is currently unknown. You're told it is of terrorist origin. And then, as part of normal due diligence research, you discover that what you're looking at is not totally new, but in fact has already been found, in Japan, where it has killed at least one person. Now, let me ask you . . . How would you react?"

Pierre and Charles looked at each other. Neither had a good answer to Armand's questions. They still had to ask another question because they were sitting just below the CEO of the *Institut*:

"Are you sure that your secondary activities are totally legitimate?"

"Totally. They do not interfere with my work. They lead me to looking at things which, at times, we have not even thought about . . ."

Armand added:

"And the *Institut* gets its full pound of flesh from me."

Charles and Pierre were only partially convinced, but, looking at each other, they knew very well that they would not get anything more. Armand was the star researcher at the *Institut* and would get any job he wanted outside if he simply asked for one from a solid list of laboratories, whether government-related or privately-owned. They were stuck. The trio agreed to proceed on this effort, with the funding provided by the anonymous donor. The two senior professors also agreed that they would recommend the joint venture with the Japanese, though they said they could not guarantee that the whole board would follow the recommendation. Armand could only reply:

"Let's hope they do. If they don't, we'll have a competitor in the marketplace. The Japanese already worked on this virus, which, as I said earlier, they identified as a boosted variant on another one on which they have been working for more than a year."

"Why would they let us in, then?"

"I am the only one that has the one clue as to how to proceed. I've shared it with you, but not with them yet. I am morally obliged to share it with them, but they would owe me something. Partnership with us is the price I expect them to pay. And the Japanese understanding of honor and commitment will do the rest."

"I'm beginning to wonder why you've never expressed any interest in participating in the management of the *Institut* . . . For a scientist, you seem to have quite a business mind."

Armand smiled. Then he simply said:

"You know, Pierre, there are two reasons. First, because of my additional, honorific activity, I feel that the management of the *Institut* would be a chore which I'm not sure I could really handle. You know that that honorific activity has provided useful grants in the past, still from that anonymous donor . . ."

"Yes, we know. Quite generous I might add . . ."

"Second, though I generally know how to manage myself in a business environment, that's not where my passion is. I don't need to do that to feel content. I much prefer these occasional assignments. I learn more that way, and it remains a true scientific challenge."

"Totally understood. Yet, my friend, this is the first time your ancillary activity is generating a business opportunity for the *Institut Pasteur*. Might you consider a seat on the Board with nothing more than the need to read the material, show up and offer us the benefit of your wisdom?"

"I'll give it some thought . . . if it is ever offered . . ."

■ ■ ■ ■ ■

Armand had to wait until the next morning to have a video conference with Oshima-San and Tomioka-San. Tokyo is indeed seven hours ahead of Paris, and it was already too late to catch his friends before they had gone home. The conversation was a lot simpler than with his French colleagues, and immediately more productive.

"Armand, if you have that information, we are ready to sign a joint venture agreement with the *Institut Pasteur* in Paris. This is too important a project to run the risk of losing that opportunity. After all, why compete when you can cooperate?"

Oshima-San was then reacting in a typical Japanese fashion—seeking cooperation. Armand probably should have been more cynical; the Japanese are known to be formidable competitors when it comes to export markets. Hopefully, the *Institut Pasteur's* legal department would think of all the guarantees that were needed to ensure that the cooperation went truly both ways. Armand replied:

"I knew I could count on you Oshima-San. Can you send me by email a draft agreement to negotiate the formal legal agreement? I know lawyers will take a few days to get there and I do not want us to waste a minute more."

"Let me draft something now, have it reviewed by the Legal Department and sent it to you today. Have your people look at it, request any change if needed and send it back to me."

"Sounds like a great idea, my friend . . ."

CHAPTER.18

ACROSS EUROPE

With his full complement of parts collected, Mark was almost ready to start assembling the bombs. One final detail needed to be resolved: the switch of the deadly flasks for inoffensive ones. For that, Mark had to wait until the *Mossad* delivered the original key to the cellar.

As soon as Mark had told David the address of the flat that he would be occupying in Bern, David briefed Simon who asked the *Mossad* correspondent in the Israeli Embassy in Bern for help. Moshe Schneider had no difficulty in recognizing that 18 Justingerweg corresponded to the Apartments Justingerweg. These units were a well-known location in Bern—a three-story building with Mansard roof in the Hausmann style. Located within ten minutes of Old Town, the Clock Tower, the Cathedral and Bern BärenPark Zoo, the apartments were particularly convenient, especially with a bus stop less than a hundred yards away. Proximity to tourist attractions and public transportation mattered little to Mark and his colleagues; the important thing was that the building was located in the Embassy district, close therefore to places where he might be asked to go. *Mossad* immediately booked another apartment in the same building for a guest of the Embassy; fortunately, one was available. It was smaller, offering only one bedroom, but given its prospective use, one bedroom was acceptable since it had twin beds.

David had the two members of the Tel Aviv team covering Mark take residence in the apartment. Mark contacted them when he returned from his first trip to collect the first three flasks, using his own Israeli phone and speaking from the bathroom of his flat. A knock at the door told him a friend was here. He checked through the peephole and recognizing the person opened the door. Without a word, they exchanged the two packages in a way such that, even if there was a camera in the room no one could see the action. Somehow, the person at the door apologized for what must have been an error:

"Must have knocked at the wrong door . . . Truly sorry."

"No problem. *Auf Wiedersehen,*" using the Swiss-German dialect for goodbye to appear more believable if anybody was listening."

Opening the package on the dining room table. He now had two options to dispose of the deadly flasks. He could use the cellar as originally anticipated or deposit them in the other apartment.

Mark assembled the first three fake bombs on the dining room table. He dutifully used the inoffensive flasks rather than the deadly ones he had exchanged with his colleagues. He was very careful to wipe the table clean afterwards. Theoretically, there was minimum risk. Why would his Arab handlers worry if they detected the presence of C-4 dust on the table? Yet, he wanted to be sure; it would demonstrate professionalism, if his handlers actually checked.

He had not been able to identify the individual who had handed him the first three flasks. Thus, was there a risk of him, or one of his cohorts, entering the flat and checking it out? Mark decided to go grab dinner, looking for something reasonable and plausible for an Arab man in Old Town. He first dropped off all the equipment he needed for the assembly in the other flat, giving strict instructions that no one should get into the cellar or his flat. He then placed the completed bombs in the cellar. He was careful to create a couple of traps in his flat and in the cellar so that he could see whether anyone had entered while he was having dinner. He knew he was tailed. He knew that whoever was following him was tailed as well. But he wanted to know how far his handlers would go to keep him under close surveillance.

He selected a typical Swiss restaurant offering cheese-based dishes. He ordered the classic cheese fondue with thinly sliced air-dried beef, bread and boiled potatoes. He took care of verifying that there was no contact between these and pork products, and was assured that the restaurant was used to serving Muslim customers:

"Everything is *Halal* here, sir . . ."

He took his time and even asked if he could get a couple of extra bottles of water. He said that he was going on a hike the next day and had forgotten to buy the water he would need to keep himself hydrated. He then returned to the flat.

Before going upstairs, he went to the cellar to take back the bombs and bring them upstairs. He was happy to see that his traps were still in place. Walking up the stairs to his flat, he paused in front of the door. The hair that he had placed at heel height covering the door and its frame was no longer there:

Didn't inspect the cellar but came into the flat . . . Good to know. These guys are really cautious.

As he was preparing to go to bed, a thought crossed his mind: what if they had not placed any listening device that broadcasted what he said, but had located a simpler tape recorder of some sort? The dinner time visitor might simply have come to retrieve a tape and replace it with a new one. He had a frightening thought: *What if that listening device is in the bathroom?* He rushed to the bathroom and did a complete, inch by inch inspection. Fortunately, he found nothing. He breathed a sigh of relief but was not ready to abandon the detailed search. He spent the next hour combing the apartment.

Eventually, he found a small tape recorder hidden under the frame of the bed. He was surprised because he could not think of ever having found one hidden there in any prior mission. He looked at it carefully and took a few pictures which he sent to Simon via secure email. The lesson was that his instincts were correct not to have any potentially incriminating conversation other than in the bathroom.

Before going to bed, and despite the fact that it was then past ten p.m., he knocked at the door of the apartment housing his two colleagues. He told them of the listening device and asked them to bug his apartment with both sound and video equipment. The fact that the decoration in all Justingerweg apartments was Art-Nouveau-style made is relatively easy to conceal the equipment.

The next morning, Mark left for Italy. After he left, his colleagues dutifully placed the bugs and, using the Wi-Fi system provided in each apartment, made sure that the bugs would broadcast continuously to recording devices they set up in their own apartment. They were very careful that no sound could be picked up on the terrorists' tape recorder.

Mark took E 62, a divided highway that eventually went through the Simplon Tunnel from Switzerland into Italy. He knew that, just before arriving at the tunnel, in Brig, he would have to wait and load the car onto a train which would take him and the car from Switzerland to Domodossola in Italy. He felt that the risks of something being found in the car were minimal given how well dissimulated the two packages were. At the same time, the ability to rest while on the train would be much appreciated. Five hours later he arrived at the Malpensa Airport in Milan. He parked the car in the short-term parking, despite it being more expensive, and walked quietly with his soft-sided leather briefcase to the locker hall on the arrival level of the main terminal. There, he located an empty locker, opened it, carefully placed the briefcase in it and dialed the six-digit number which would set it up. He immediately called Hai Chock in Singapore to tell him that the baby had been born and that mother and child were doing just fine. Hai Chock understood that he was to add the bomb to the group he already controlled. It would also immediately appear on the map which the terrorists kept.

Mark then drove to Rome's Fiumicino Airport. The trip was expected to take in excess of six hours and a half, as the route would take him via Bologna and Florence on E 35. The coastal road might have been a mile or two shorter, but the risks of congestion if not outright bottlenecks were just too high. Mark knew that he would arrive at the airport in the evening. His plan was to drop the bomb just as he had done in Milan, and then to start the return trip. He doubted that he would be able to drive all the way back to Milan, let alone Bern, without at least a short stop; it was almost six hundred miles and should take nearly ten hours, when counting stops for refueling the car as well as food or bathroom breaks.

However, he had been used to missions that required him to stay awake for long stretches of time; the answer had been to take a quick powernap once in a while. Combined with the medicine provided by Mossad, these usually did the trick. He wanted to exit Italy as soon as he could. He could not imagine how someone could find the bombs but having to explain the mission to Italian policemen would require Simon to ask for help from Agenzia Informazioni e Sicurezza Esterna (AISE), Italy's secret service. Though the risk for him was minimal, the risk to the mission would be quite serious, not to say deadly.

Mark was smiling internally as he was having these thoughts. He was noting in his own mind that those that were tailing him were having the same problems. *Mossad* had, with Mark's accord, made the decision that the risk of him being attacked on the road was not critical. Thus, rather than having him followed during the trip, they had made sure that someone was near the place where he would be placing the bombs. Israeli agents were not extremely numerous, but there were enough of them that sparing a couple of people for a few hours in Milan and in Rome was not arduous.

On the other hand, the handlers who were following him had to deal with the fatigue, as they could only change drivers when Mark made a pit stop. Mark thought that the dark brown BMW 5 series which he had seen several times in his rear-view mirror on the way down was suspect. He became sure of it when he saw the same car on the way back. He refrained from any maneuver which would have allowed him to lose them. First, that might have been viewed as odd. Second, it would not have helped much as the route he was taking was pretty standard. They would have caught up with him at some point anyway: all pain, no gain. He noted that they were careful not to be too obvious, most likely because they also knew that the route did not offer too many realistic alternatives. They could afford to let him take up to a mile advance without worrying too much. In fact, they may have had another way of keeping track of Mark, which he did not know about.

CHAPTER.19

ACROSS EUROPE

Back in Bern, Mark had to repeat the experience in the acquisition of the flasks. He had spoken to David earlier, and they had agreed that they should try again to identify the source of these flasks. However, even if the courier came from an embassy, there were simply too many of them to hazard a wild guess. Speaking to Simon, David was reminded that Countess Renate had offered a crucial piece of information: possible North Korean or Chinese connections. He therefore decided to orchestrate Mark's surveillance starting with a focus on the North Korean and Chinese embassies. The North Korean Embassy was located on Pourtalesstrasse, about a couple of miles southwest of the Chinese Embassy on Kalcheggweg. *Mossad* agents would have to split the monitoring task if, as expected, the drop-off point selected was somewhere in between the two, as the prior one was.

Mark called the same phone number as the prior time.

"Anwar here . . ."

The man at the other end of the line replied with the same Asian accented English:

"What is your dream?"

"The califate . . ."

"Listen carefully: What kind of car do you drive?"

"The same as the last time, A grey Mercedes C300."

"OK. Go park your car outside of the playground called Kinderspielplatz Elfenau, off Elfenauweg. Unlock your trunk and leave the doors unlocked as well. Walk to the coffee shop called Parkcafé Elfenau. Someone will come and drop the package in your car. Someone else will check that you are at the café. There will not be any drop-off, if you do not follow our instructions."

"Did I fail to do that the last time? . . ."

"No matter. Come back fifteen minutes after you've left the car . . ."

Mark noted that the words that were being used were almost exactly the same as the last time. He concluded that the man at the other hand of the line was probably reading from a piece of paper. He was unwilling to entertain anything that differed from the script, as Mark had observed when he had tried to change the number of flasks in the first and second deliveries. David had organized a couple of cars and three agents on foot to cover the area, as well as the full route from the North Korean Embassy. He had also dissimulated a video camera in the trunk of Mark's car to take pictures of the face of the man dropping off the package.

Mark had ordered a coffee at the Parkcafé to pass the time. He drank it with pleasure as he enjoyed the fact that the Swiss always serve coffee with a small chocolate bar on the side. He returned to the car and went straight to the trunk of his car. He opened it and was surprised to see it empty. He thought: *Did I come back too early?* He was ready to go back to the coffee shop when he saw something inside the car, on the passenger seat. He looked at it more carefully and realized that it was what he expected. *How could they have known about the camera?*

He called David on his personal phone:

"They outwitted us . . ."

"Well . . . Not quite. We have a couple of good pictures. There were two of them, one tailing the other. They came by car. Turns out they came from the North Korean Embassy, no action on the Chinese Embassy side. They parked a couple hundred yards away and walked the rest of the way. One went to check on you and the other worked on your car. I'm surprised they picked that place, right next to the green nursery. It's full of trees, but there aren't many places to hide. I've even wondered whether they were looking to be found out . . ."

"That would surprise me . . ."

"I know that . . . But still . . . Anyway, we have good pictures of their faces and one of our agents placed a bug on their car. Maybe, we'll learn some more that way. At any rate, the bug we placed is available in electronics stores in Switzerland—no means of tracing it to Israel. That should get them thinking if they find it, but they have no reason to worry about us. Maybe, they would worry about another ally . . . Who knows? They could suspect the Chinese."

Mark went back to his apartment, though he first stopped at the flat rented by *Mossad* to exchange the deadly flasks for innocuous ones. He assembled the three bombs which, together with the one left from the prior delivery, would give him the four bombs he would need for his second trip. He moved them to the cellar until he needed them, the next morning. He set up a trap again, to see whether someone would inspect his work. He went out to stretch his legs and get a nice dinner, pretty sure that, as usual, he was being followed. When he returned to the flat after dinner, he stopped by the cellar to pick up the bombs and noted with a wry smile that the door had been opened. *Should have used the extra lock . . . These guys really don't trust me. It's a good thing that we were able to replicate the flasks perfectly . . .* He checked all the bombs when he went back up to the flat; they all looked OK. He thought that whoever went into the cellar simply wanted to check that the bombs were ready. *It's a good thing our flasks are now exactly like theirs: no one could tell the difference.*

He spoke to Debbie from the toilet, set his alarm for 7:00 a.m. and went to sleep.

■ ■ ■ ■ ■

Mark took little time to get ready the next morning and left quickly. He knew he had a lot of driving ahead of him. The first leg of the trip was totally uneventful, as it only used divided highways. The drop off at Lyon Perrache, the main train station, did not present a lot of difficulties, though it required Mark to drive into town. He was well aware of the fact that train stations tended to be in the center of town, while airports were usually at the periphery. Train stations were thus less convenient for him, but, as he thought: *what the heck?* Yet, this trip would see him target four distinct train stations.

He exited the A6 autoroute right after crossing the Saone river and found a spot in Q-Park Perrache, one of the several parking garages around the train station. He checked that there was no one around him, removed his suitcase from the trunk, in order to access the other suitcase in which he had placed the four briefcases. He grabbed one of the leather briefcases and put his suitcase back in the trunk. From there, he walked casually to the train station. He selected the largest of the locker halls and placed his briefcase into a locker, near the center of the hall, activating the bomb before closing the locker door. The signal to Hai Chock was sent within seconds. Mark then decided to get a coffee near the station, just in case he had been followed. That might serve to explain why he had used the locker to any third-party onlooker.

Getting back to his car, he drove onto the A7 autoroute initially along the Rhone river, into which the Saone river merges less than a mile away from the train station. That's where the local authorities had built Lyon's Science and Anthropology museum, calling it the *Musée Confluence*, named after the point at which the two rivers become a larger one.

The drive from Lyon to Barcelona was also entirely on autoroutes, which can be tedious with at times low speed limits that are only observed by a fraction of the driving population. Yet, it was both safer and considerably less stressful than taking any of the side roads, however more scenic that might be. The highway eventually brought him along the Mediterranean coastline, in France around Montpellier. He followed it until in Barcelona, where he exited it to use side streets. A sharp left turn at the Columbus Monument, and he was less than a mile from his destination: the Sants train station. He repeated the same steps he followed in Lyon, placed the briefcase in a locker and drove to the Hotel Ibis Barcelona, about two miles away, near the Basilica de la Sagrada Familia, Gaudi's famous unfinished basilica that combines Gothic and Art Nouveau styles. Though its design divides Spaniards almost equally between those who love it and those who hate it, it is a unique piece of architecture and a magnet for tourists from around the world.

After a pleasant dinner and a good night's sleep, Mark was up again early. He now had to drive to Madrid. It was going to take him about six hours to cover the slightly less than four hundred miles between Barcelona and Madrid. He was going to use E90, which would initially take him almost due East until Zaragoza, at which point the autoroute would veer to the southwest and get him to Madrid.

■ ■ ■ ■ ■

He was casually driving when, just after going past Siguenza, an accident exposed the mission to the risk of dramatic failure. The road from Zaragoza to Siguenza rises slowly from about nine hundred feet to thirty-four hundred feet above sea-level. It then slopes gently down to around fifteen hundred feet in Madrid. For some reason he could not later explain, Mark had not properly set his cruise control. He therefore soon found himself exceeding the speed limit as the downward slope of the road helped the car accelerate. He was stopped by a policeman on a motorcycle. Mark, though usually an extremely cautious driver, had not seen him in his rearview mirror until he was too late: *You idiot,* he muttered to himself. The policeman asked him in Spanish:

"Do you know how fast you were going?"

Mark replied mostly in sign language that he did not speak Spanish. The officer repeated the question in somewhat heavily accented English. Mark replied:

"Honestly, I don't. I must have forgotten to switch on my cruise control."

"You were going ninety miles an hour in a seventy-five mile an hour limit. May I see your driver's license and the car's papers?"

"Sure . . . I'm really sorry officer."

"Oh. This is a rental car?"

"Yes, I am driving to Madrid and then to Paris."

"Where do you live?

"Bern, Switzerland. I rented the car there. That's why the license plates are Swiss."

For some unknown reason, the policeman asked Mark to open his trunk. At that point, the two handlers who followed Mark and had stopped their car a couple hundred yards back panicked. They revved up the engine of their car and sideswiped the policeman, sending him up in the air and then down hard on the gravel part of the road that borders the asphalt. He bounced up once and then rolled on the grassy shoulder. Mark ran to him. He was still breathing, but unconscious. Mark thought that the poor fellow had most likely been saved by the helmet which he had not removed.

Mark was furious. He turned his attention to his handlers, as he approached their car that was now stopped less than a hundred feet in front of his. He told them, in Arabic:

"Well, this time you guys have done it . . ."

"We were trying to help you."

"By knocking out a cop. Why?"

"He was going to find the packages."

"Well, who knows? But, for him to find them, he would have had to ask me to take the two suitcases out of the trunk and then would have had to think of asking me to open the correct one. Could have handled it myself if it came to that then. Now, we've got to scramble. I've got to change cars and to hurry out of Spain."

"Why?"

Mark simply shook his head and did not even react to the fact that the two handlers looked sorry. He really did not care. It was time to act and act quickly. He started to drive away and carefully set his cruise control. Then, using the hands-free feature of his European phone, called the car rental agency in Madrid, giving them all the details of his rental contract. Then he said:

"Just found out I'll need a larger car."

"How large, sir?"

"One size up from this one."

"Where are you?"

"On E90, about one hundred miles from Madrid."

He added that he would probably be in Madrid in an hour and a half or so. They confirmed that they had another car available. He asked them to have the contract pre-filled as he really only had a very limited amount of time. They agreed and even offered to waive the need for him to fill up the Mercedes.

He thanked them and drove the remaining miles in a state of stress. Though the policeman was surely "out" when he left him near his motorcycle on the side of the road, someone was bound to see him. Whether another policeman or a civilian, people would start looking for him. Further, he assumed that the policeman would have radioed to his base the license plate number of the car he was about to stop, as is standard practice in Israel. He was thus worried that someone would come after him as soon as the policeman awoke on his own or with some help.

While driving, he called Ismail on his phone:

"Anwar here. What's going on?"

"Well, the handlers that have been tailing me ever since we started this project stupidly knocked out a cop who was going to give me a ticket for speeding."

"Oh. Really? And?"

"Well, I wish you would tell whomever to have them leave me alone."

"They meant well . . . Didn't they?"

"Maybe, but now I'm a marked man. I've got to change my appearance. I'm gonna shave beard and mustache. I'll wear dark brown, rimmed glasses. Also, as soon as I can find one, will get a blond toupee. Warn whoever should know that my appearance will be radically different. I'll also have to change identity. I'll send you a selfie as soon as I have completed the change in appearance."

Mark did not wait for Ismail to reply. He hung up, changed phones and then called David to bring him up to date. David commended him for his quick reaction. He asked if there was a need to alert the *Mossad* representative in Madrid, adding:

"If you need help . . ."

"Don't think so, David, but thank you anyway. I'll let you know if I need help with the local authorities. I'd rather behave as Anwar would have. If we call *Mossad*, I'm done. Obviously better than going to jail for an attempt on the life of a policeman but the mission is over."

David agreed that Mark's logic was right on. He asked whether Mark was going to sleep in Madrid. Mark answered that he wanted to get out of Spain as fast as possible. He added that he would shave all facial hair as soon as he could. He expected to spend the night on the French side of the border, in any small village around Bayonne or Biarritz, on the Atlantic Ocean, about three hundred miles to the north east of Madrid. He added:

"I'll send you a selfie as soon as I look different . . . I'll need new

Israeli papers . . . I've already said the same thing to Ismail."

"Good thinking. I'll be waiting for whatever you send."

Mark drove to the rental car agency, which, as would be true throughout Europe, was quite close to the train station. He was offered and accepted a dark green, Volvo station wagon with Spanish license plates. He paid the extra cost associated with the upgrade and quickly went to the Atocha train station in the center of Madrid. He removed both briefcases from the suitcase that had carried the four bomb assemblies at the outset. He did not want to have a suitcase containing a single briefcase: it would look suspicious. He then deposited the penultimate briefcase in a locker as usual and signaled the drop to Hai Chock who did his magic.

After closing the locker, he looked around. He was hoping that the train station would offer toilets and shower facilities. He found toilets right away but had to ask before he was pointed in the right direction for the toilets with showers. He went in and, making sure he was on his own, proceeded to shave. He then took a shower. He used a *Mossad* shampoo that dyed his hair blond; the shampoo contained both some bleach and some coloring agent. He reserved a small dose of shampoo for his eyebrows, thinking: *the usual give away for people who forget that most blond people also have blond eyebrows.*

He finally gave himself a shot of a mix of Botox-like substance and fat filler which had been developed by *Mossad*. It was meant to accentuate certain features of the face to help agents look as different as they could without having permanent cosmetic surgery. The effect of the drug usually lasted no longer than two weeks, and when applied to zones which absorbed the fat faster, as little as a week. He would use the drug on the face, on his cheekbones, thus looking as if he had more pronounced cheekbones. Other agents could use the substance to make their lips fuller, or to alter the shape of their chin. *Mossad* had packaged the drug in pre-filled syringes; he used two twenty-five milliliters subcutaneous injections, one on each side, and replaced the syringe in his toiletry kit, packaged as it was to look like an insulin injector. He took a selfie and sent it to Ismail first, asking for a new driver's license and passport to be given to him at Gare du Nord in Paris. He then sent it to David and Simon, asking for a new semi-official identity, with driver's license and passport as well, with the new face.

He felt better as soon as he received a text message from Ismail telling him that he had received the mail and the picture, and that all would be arranged. Ismail added that he would send a rendezvous point later when he had been able to organize it, suggesting:

"It should be as close as possible to your next drop-off point." Mark replied with a simple thank you SMS.

The man who exited the toilet area was quite different from the one who entered it. Mark chuckled at the thought that his handlers would probably not recognize him unless they had been warned by Ismail. To test his own assumption, he walked right in front of the handlers who had followed him and "camped" just outside of the bathroom. They did not seem to notice him or look at him in any particular way though he had not changed his clothing. He smiled and returned to his car before starting on his way to Paris, thinking, *I wonder how long they'll wait before they go into the toilets and look for me.*

He proceeded due north on E3, switching to E80 at Burgos, a bit short of halfway to the French border. Mark worried about the border crossing. He assumed that the Spanish authorities would have set up some sort of trap at the border, as well as at airports and train stations. He approached the crossing with his heart beating faster than usual, and his fears were validated when he saw that there were custom agents asking all cars to slow down and looking quite carefully as they drove by. He did not have much of a choice and elected to keep driving as normally as he could, hoping against hope that he would not attract attention. A border agent did motion him to slow down, which he did. He lowered his window ready to ask what was happening.

CHAPTER.20

TEL AVIV, ISRAEL, PARIS, FRANCE, SEOUL, SOUTH KOREA AND AUSTRIA

Simon needed to speak to Countess Renate.

"Countess Renate, Simon here . . ."

"Ah . . . Simon. What's new?"

"Well, we now have solid proof of a North Korean connection."

"Really? How?"

Simon described all the steps they had taken to spy on the second delivery of flasks to Mark in Bern:

"We tailed the two people who delivered them to Mark's car. They outwitted us in a minor way as they did not drop them in the trunk where we had set up a camera, but we were able to take plenty of pictures of them from different points. We also have the details of the car they used; in fact, we bugged it as well. We saw them both come out of the Embassy and return to it . . . We're currently working diplomatic channels with Switzerland to check the identity of the people and to whom the car is registered. Since it had diplomatic plates, I'm ready to believe it's registered to the embassy."

"That's wonderful . . . Well Done. What's next?"

"Well, I need you to work your network to see how much we can find out with respect to the defector. We've got to flush him out and, although harder, destroy the formula and any remaining virus he may have . . ."

"What a program."

Renate thought for a minute and decided that she would immediately contact Armand. He was the one who had the contacts in South Korea. She briefly discussed her plan with Simon and hung up. After Renate gave him a summary rundown of her conversation with Simon, Armand agreed with her that there was at least one easy next step. He should call Dr. Park in Seoul.

"Dr. Park, Armand Duchemin, here . . ."

"Professor Duchemin, what an unexpected pleasure . . . Anything I can help with?"

"Well, Dr. Park, in fact there is news on the North Korean front."

"Uh Ho."

"I am told there is conclusive proof that they are supplying the virus to terrorists. We are not sure how the liquid containing the virus travels, or even where it's manufactured. But we know for a fact that someone posing as a middle eastern terrorist was supplied with three flasks each time, twice, while in Bern."

"Oh. My."

"The suppliers, whom our contact did not see, but which others photographed, came from and returned to the North Korean Embassy . . ."

"This is very serious. Yet, what can I do?"

"First, remember that all the details regarding Bern are top secret. We must make absolutely sure that the terrorists do not get wind of the fact that we have penetrated their network. They would drop their plan or trigger a whole series of bombs or anything in between. Also, the life of our informant would be at serious risk."

He continued:

"What we need now is to find out everything we can about the defector and try to discover where the lethal concoction is manufactured. We also need to find out how much of his activity is shared with others. In other words, if he was eliminated, would there be somebody naturally taking his place?"

"I think it's a job for my friend, Colonel Kim Dae Jung, you know, the one who works in South Korean intelligence. The one with whom we had dinner in Seoul . . ."

"Yeah. I remember. Can he be trusted not to disclose any of the details that I flagged to you?"

"I'm sure he can. After all, your help could bring him an eventual great coup. By the way, would you like me to organize a Zoom meeting between the three of us? You could tell him yourself what he must know and see, by his questions, where he may need more."

"Great idea. Let me know when you've set it up."

"Sure. With the time differences, it will have to be tomorrow in the morning for you; you're behind Seoul. Is that OK?"

"No problem. I will make anything you set up work."

Armand's Zoom conversation, the next morning, went quite well. He was able to shield any detail that might lead to Mark or to the terrorists. Yet, he provided enough that Colonel Kim could start some serious investigations. He said that he was pretty sure where the laboratory was, since, as he had discussed with Armand and Dr. Park earlier, there had been a few reported unexplained deaths, after the defector came back. It had to be the place they identified then. Armand told him that he would have a friend in a country's intelligence service contact him with all the secret information that he could share:

"Do you work for them, Professor Duchemin?"

"No . . . Not at all . . . I am part of a group of people who try to help good causes. That's all I can say, and, by the way, that's about all I know."

"I think I know of your "association" . . . Never had a chance to work with them. But . . . great respect for what they do."

Armand thanked him and clarified the challenge with a couple more details:

"We have been mandated by that intelligence service to help them with the part of the work that they feel they cannot do themselves."

"Excellent. Well, give your contact there my phone number . . . I'll be expecting the call."

■ ■ ■ ■ ■

Within hours, Colonel Kim and Simon had started to talk about some of the issues. It was the first time that South Korean Intelligence, officially known as National Intelligence Service and reporting directly to the President of the country, and *Mossad* would be working on a joint project. They were both cautious about what they should or should not say—being very frank that prudence was the main consideration. They agreed to weekly briefings and hung up with their immediate goals agreed upon.

CHAPTER.21

In the end, Mark was delighted that the border crossing proved uneventful. He breathed a huge sigh of relief. Yet, he kept asking himself, *Is that routine or are they looking for my grey Mercedes C300?* The custom agent he had questioned indeed had nothing to say other than: "routine, sir." Though Paris was still five hundred miles away and it was already 7:00 p.m., he decided to keep driving for as long as he could: *better safe than sorry. Will let David know when I next fill up the car . . .* He finally chose to stop near the autoroute when he reached Bordeaux and booked himself into the Hotel Mercure Bordeaux Aéroport. He was simply too tired.

Mark woke up early the next morning, after a fitful sleep. There was nothing wrong with the bed, although he had certainly not chosen a palace to spend the night. The relatively cheap hotel was the closest to the highway and that was good enough for Mark. During the night, he had tried to convince himself that he looked different and had a different car, but that was not enough. So, on the spur of the moment, he made the decision to go to the rental car agency near Merignac, Bordeaux Airport—*let's change cars again!* He thanked his "good star" for the inspiration to book himself into a hotel at the airport.

He returned the Volvo, arguing that he had changed his plans. He was going to stay in Bordeaux for a few days and did not need a car. He then went straight to another rental company, which, not so coincidentally in an airport, was almost next door. There, he rented a car, a French-made, metallic beige Peugeot 508 with French license plates, which he thought would be more discrete than any foreign car. He said that he would return it in Paris.

His plan was that, once in Paris, he would indeed return the Peugeot. He would walk to yet another car rental agency and take another vehicle to drive back to Bern . . . He had checked on his tablet and found that all major rental car companies had offices near the Gare du Nord, the train station in which he was to place the last briefcase. The successive car changes would not be foolproof, but they would delay anyone who found out he had returned the Mercedes in Madrid. The lady in the car rental agency was surprised by the difference between his passport picture and his current appearance. He had concocted a story about a decision to turn away from Islam and change his appearance, adding:

"It is rather recent. I have not had the time to get my license renewed . . . It's not due to expire for another two years plus, and I hate to spend money uselessly."

She insisted a bit, but Mark's smile and his explanations eventually did the trick, but not before he had to repeat all of them to her supervisor. Driving away with his Peugeot, he was happy that the subterfuge worked, but remained concerned about future instances where he would need to show his driver's license: *the last thing I need is to be stopped again by a policeman.* He sent a message to David, who simply replied:

"Be careful on the drive to Paris. We have everything organized for you. Someone will look for you near the train station and give you your new papers. *Mazel Tov.*"

Arriving in Paris, around 2:00 p.m., things initially did not look great. There was plenty of police milling about near and inside the station. They seemed to be focused on individuals of Arab ethnicity. He thanked God for the fact that he had been forced to alter his appearance, which now looked more North European than Semitic: *sometimes, good things come out from unpleasant events . . .* He noted that they appeared to be focused on the area of the station which served the Eurostar, the very fast train between Paris and London. He wondered whether a terrorist threat had been made with respect to that train; or whether there were rumors of such that were circulating. He did not worry anyway, as he would be nowhere near that area. The locker hall he was going to use was one level down and at the other end of the station; that was where most of the traffic was. He stepped out of the Peugeot having found a convenient parking spot around the corner from the entrance to the station and walked calmly to the trunk of the car, where he retrieved the last, black leather briefcase.

As instructed by Ismail, he met an individual at the entrance to the station on 18 rue de Dunkerque. He received an envelope which he knew contained the documents he had requested. He refrained from looking at them at that time, for fear that would look odd. He proceeded into the station, headed for the locker hall and went through his usual routine. The last briefcase of this trip had now been dropped. It was time to look as normal as he could and to return to Bern. *Two trips done, two to go!* was all he could think about.

He returned the Peugeot to the car rental agency as planned. He went to another company and, with his new identity information, rented a car to be dropped in Bern the next day. He hated the idea that he would potentially have some time without a car in Bern, but there were enough Uber drivers available there that it should not be an issue. If it became one, he would simply rent earlier the car he needed for the trip to Germany and the Netherlands.

The dark, metallic grey Renault Talisman he rented was quite comfortable. A direct competitor to the Peugeot in the French market, it was very similar. Mark noted that German cars, or even Swedish cars, tend to have a higher inside quality fit and finish than their French counterparts, but that was not a problem. Its trunk was large enough to take in Mark's luggage. He chose to take the Autoroute A6 because it tended to be the one where traffic, according to the app on his phone, was the lightest. He would still need to plan for six or seven hours before reaching Bern. *Another day when I'm gonna get to bed late. At least, I'll feel safe at the flat.* When there, he placed another phone call to Debbie from the toilet and went straight to bed.

■ ■ ■ ■ ■

He was in fact fully rested when he woke up the next morning. The series of car changes and the fact that he was back in Bern had relieved the anxieties that beset him since the accident on the road to Madrid. He did not feel particularly rushed, as he knew that his routine would not take him more than two or three hours. From the bathroom, he called David to thank him for the documents he had found on the desk in the apartment, as expected. David did not have a lot of news, other than the fact that Simon was now, thanks to Countess Renate's network, in direct contact with South Korean Intelligence. David asked Mark to have his phone on speaker when he would call his contact for the next three flasks:

"That way, we can hear what the instructions are. I'll connect the rest of the team to the conference . . . Remember not to say anything on that line: walls may have ears . . ."

Again, Mark had to repeat the experience in the acquisition of the flasks. He knew that the dialog would be quite repetitive, but he still had to go through it. Simon had suggested that he be particularly sensitive to any change in the behavior of his correspondent, reminding him that *Mossad* now had pictures, as well as names to attach to him and his confrere.

"Anwar here . . ."

The man at the other end of the line again asked the same question. His English was still Asian accented, and the voice sounded very much the same. Mark thought: *they don't know that they've been unmasked.*

"What is your dream?"

"The califate . . ."

"Listen carefully. What kind of car do you drive?"

"A grey Renault Talisman."

"Why the change?"

"Safety precautions . . ."

"OK. Drive to the corner of Wernerstrasse and Kalcheggweg. Opposite that corner is the Chinese Embassy, and behind it is a park. Park the car behind the embassy and go walk in the park. As usual, do not try to look for me. Give me about fifteen minutes and return to the car. Leave it unlocked . . ."

Mark hung up after agreeing to the details and saying he would be there in about thirty minutes. The man on the line did not seem happy with the delay, but Mark simply told him that he had just awakened, after a long trip through Europe. He needed that time to get ready. The man reluctantly agreed. Mark took his own phone and walked calmly to the bathroom. There, he asked:

"Everything fine, David?"

"We'll have it covered. I wonder whether the use of the Chinese Embassy means anything. We'll have someone watching there as well . . ."

Mark drove to the park that had been indicated to him, parking the car behind the Chinese Embassy as requested. He walked some distance away from the car to a point where he could no longer see it. He saw a bench and decided to take a seat and wait. Less than five minutes later his "terrorist" phone rang:

"What's this? You're not Anwar . . ."

"Sorry to surprise you, but I am. I just shaved my facial hair and dyed my hair blond . . ."

"Why?"

"You can check with the people who have been following me or with Ismail, my main contact in Tel Aviv. We had an incident in Spain that required some serious change."

"What was it?"

"Can't discuss it over the phone but call whomever your contact is. He'll confirm it . . ."

"Don't move until I call you back with further instructions . . ."

After the Asian man had hung up, Mark felt he needed to call David. Yet, he wondered where the person was who had seen him. So, rather than dialing his phone visibly, he first put an earbud with microphone in his right ear, facing furthest away from where he had come and thus from the embassy, pressed his speed dial and got connected to David:

"What's going on?"

"Can't talk much. I know I'm being watched . . . Be careful and try to help . . ."

"Don't worry, we have you covered. Thanks."

David immediately called his lead agent in the field, Nathan Zeiner, and asked him:

"Nate, Mark thinks he's being spied on. Is there anybody there? I'm near the Chinese Embassy myself."

"No, David. No one within at least a hundred yards if not more . . . Oh! Wait a minute. Could it be from the Chinese Embassy?"

"Can you see any window from where you are?"

"Affirmative. I can see two."

"Could they have seen Mark as he left the car and walked to his current location?"

"You bet . . . Plenty of time . . . Great view in fact."

"Super. You know what to do. Stay discrete. We don't want to miss out on the delivery of the flasks."

"Roger."

David immediately asked his man who was closest to the Embassy to get as many pictures of the windows as he could without being seen, adding:

"Feasible?"

"No problem. I'm sitting in a tree; plenty of leaves."

Frank Henning, the agent, shot a number of pictures, using an electronic zoom to get as close as he could. Suddenly, in his view finder, he could see clearly a military man using binoculars. *This has got to be our guy,* he thought . . . He turned a dial on the camera to polarize the filter on the lens; that would attenuate the glare on the window. He spoke to himself: *There you go. Can see you as if you were next to me . . . You won't stay secret for very long, my friend.* He sent the last few pictures to David, who immediately forwarded them to Simon.

Mark's terrorist phone rang:

"Anwar?"

"Yes . . ."

"Your story checks out. Someone should have told us of the mishap."

"To tell you the truth, I am being followed virtually everywhere I go . . . If anybody failed to inform you, blame it on them, not on me. My main concern was to complete the mission and finish it alive."

The Asian man sounded surprised by Mark's forceful language, but he quickly came back:

"Wait where you are for fifteen minutes. Then return to the car. You'll find the package there. No funny trick between now and then . . . Understood?"

"When did I start with funny tricks?"

The man did not bother to reply and simply hung up. Having been warned that he was being observed from the Chinese Embassy, Mark turned his face away from it and smiled broadly: *If you guys only knew . . .*

CHAPTER.22

ACROSS NORTHERN EUROPE

After the fifteen minutes had passed, Mark walked calmly back to his car. He was fully aware that he was likely being observed from the Chinese Embassy, but he decided that he could not care less. First, they probably already had his picture; their "bosses" surely had, since he had sent them a selfie to have them produce the new travel documents. Second, this was not the way he looked in reality, so who cared how many versions of that picture circulated. Thirdly, he hoped that *Mossad* would find a way to identify, get to and possibly eliminate the guilty parties.

He found the car just as he had left it. A thought went through his mind . . . Could they have booby trapped it? He called David on his service phone using his ear bud to ask. David quickly reassured him:

"The only guys that came close to the car are the same as last time. They popped the trunk, dropped a package in it and walked away . . . Just for information, one is still walking back to the North Korean Embassy, but the other, surprise, surprise, went to the Chinese Embassy."

"Very interesting. Thanks."

He checked his trunk and did find a package in it. It looked familiar.

Yet, though he assumed he was still being watched, he opened it to check the contents. The three flasks were there. There was nothing else with them. So, he thought, *the car is not booby trapped and there is no bomb in the trunk. I can safely drive away.* He started driving leisurely back to Justingerweg and his flat. As usual, after having retrieved the flasks from his trunk, he went first to the cellar to get the three incomplete bombs and their respective briefcases. He then went to the *Mossad* flat to exchange the deadly flasks for their inoffensive replacements. Without wasting any time, as he assumed that he was expected to enter the flat quickly, he walked into his apartment.

His next job was to complete the assembly of the fake bomb. He had already done it six times on this part of the mission and felt he could almost do it with his eyes closed. When finished, he placed the briefcases back in the cellar and set up his usual traps to check on any visit which the cellar might receive while he was away. This time, he added two new twists. First, he used the extra lock and second, he placed a hair on the lock of each briefcase. That way, he would not only know if the handlers had visited the cellar, but also if they had inspected the briefcases.

He then went to the car rental agency to return the Renault. That done, he went to yet another rental agency to rent a car to be returned to Bern in two days. The red, Volkswagen Arteon was the only reasonable choice. He surely was not keen on the color, but the only other color available was a goldish yellow which would likely attract even more attention. He drove it back to the flat and decided that it was time for him to have a powernap. He woke up an hour later and went out to the cheese-dish restaurant he had already visited, thinking, . . . *it was excellent the last time. This time I'll go for raclette rather than fondue. Otherwise, no point changing a winning team. But, boy, would I like a glass of red wine with that? But I know I can't.*

The next morning, he started on his way to Frankfurt, Berlin and Amsterdam. He knew that the sixteen-hundred-mile trip would involve at least twenty-five hours at the wheel. He had planned to sleep in Berlin. Most of the trip indeed would be through Germany, and wherever he stayed, it would have to be in that country. Thus, staying in Berlin, after having dropped the briefcase at Berlin Hauptbahnhof, the German capital's main station located in the heart of the city, allowed him access to a wide cross section of hotels.

On the way to Berlin, he stopped briefly at the Frankfurt airport to deposit a briefcase in the locker room of the international terminal. Driving between Frankfurt and Berlin, he observed the contrast that still existed between what was formerly East Germany and West Germany. While the reunification had surely greatly improved the economic conditions in the East, a careful eye could still detect a higher level of poverty or maybe simply a lower level of affluence.

■ ■ ■ ■ ■

The main railway station in Berlin is a sight not to be missed. Opened in 2006, It looks like a modern, glass bridge straddling the multiple railway tracks as they emerge on the east side of the station and cross over a water basin. That basin is a part of the waterworks which surround the entire center of the city. The station seems tightly packed; everything appears to be close to everything else. It is considered virtually comparable to Singapore's Raffles MRT Station or Taipei main station, both of which are just as densely packed. As instructed, Mark went to the locker hall on the above-ground level as it was likely to provide the bigger bang for the buck, obviously assuming that the bombs were going to do what they were intended to do . . . Which they surely were not.

■ ■ ■ ■ ■

The two drop-offs in Germany were thus totally uneventful. Mark thought that he had seen people with physiques that would fit his usual handlers, but he had to concede that, this time, they were quite well hidden. He walked out of the station and chose the nearest hotel, the Meininger Hotel Berlin, which is in the central station. He chose the high end of their offerings, which starts with dorm-style rooms and goes up from there. His room had a double bed and private bathroom and toilet. As he thought—*It's clean, it looks semi-soundproof. That's all I need . . . And that's all Anwar would have booked.* He went to the hotel's cafeteria for a quick dinner, observing how hard it can be, in Germany, to find food that suited Muslim requirements. He finally had to settle for cheese and fruit.

Mark got up quite early the next day, as his hope was to be able to get back to Bern that same day. He knew he would be stretching it a bit, but he was counting on the fact that some of his route was over German divided highways without speed limit. *That should allow me to make some time . . .* Fortunately, getting to Schiphol Airport did not require any complex detour, as his route led directly to it. He parked near the center of the airport, which, as it has stretched further and further away from the original terminal, had become like a city onto itself.

From the parking lot, he was a few hundred yards away from the locker hall he had already targeted. He went through his usual routine and returned to the car in less than fifteen minutes. He jumped back in the car and took the direction of Koln and Frankfurt, and then Manheim. He stayed on the German side of the border as he drove alongside the Alsace region of France and crossed into Switzerland at Basel. From there, the sense that he was close to home overcame any fatigue which was starting to become quite noticeable. He was driving on an adrenaline rush. He arrived in the late evening at the apartment in Bern. He went straight to the bathroom to report his safe arrival and talk to Debbie and then go to bed.

He did not even think of the hassle that awaited him the next day— using this car to get his last contingent of deadly flasks, assembling the bombs, placing them in the cellar, returning the car and booking another one which he would return in London.

■ ■ ■ ■ ■

As it turned out, unfortunately, little progress had been made on the identity of the Chinese gentleman in the embassy, or the reason why one of the North Koreans had chosen to go to the Chinese Embassy. David and Simon were still asking themselves a lot of questions while Mark slept off the exhaustion of the last two days. David, in particular, was worried that not knowing what role the Chinese were playing in the plot was a major loose end. Simon was too, but his major source of worry had to do with whether, as they had announced, the terrorists would implement the last phase of their plan: placing bombs in the U.S. as well. Simon was worried because, should that part of the plan no longer be in effect, then Mark's aka Anwar's role would no longer be needed after the last bomb had been placed in London. He added:

"We've got to protect Mark. They might well elect to dispose of him. David, let's plan to capture Mark discretely."

"Wait. "Capture?" You mean have him disappear from the scene?"

"Yep."

"I assume you still want him to complete his bomb drops. You want us to have him vanish before flying to Geneva and catching his corporate jet to Riyadh?"

"Exactly. With London City Airport his last drop-off, let's have him 'disappear' right after he has placed the last bomb. I'll organize an official Israeli Air Force jet. I know you'll be organizing your team back to Tel Aviv, so I'll fly to London with the jet; that would be normal procedure. I'll book a conference room in the terminal, as many corporate executives do. That I'll be alone in the conference room, nobody needs to know. When Mark has dropped his bomb, let me know. I'll return to the plane. You guys get Mark through customs with his Israeli credentials and have him on the plane, whether I have arrived or not. The pilot will have filed a flight plan for Palmachim

Air Force base. Later, we'll find a way of explaining his disappearance if his contact, Ismail, calls him."

"Consider it done . . ."

■ ■ ■ ■ ■

Unaware of all these machinations, Mark woke up. His phone was ringing, and it was the usual North Korean contact. He was quite surprised when the man dispensed with most of the usual questions, though he did ask him what kind of car he drove. Mark replied:

"A red Volkswagen Arteon . . ."

He was surprised when the rendezvous was set in exactly the same place as the prior time. Mark pleaded for at least forty-five minutes, if not sixty, to get there:

"You just woke me up. I drove almost sixteen hundred miles in the last two days. I was bushed. I needed some sleep. Nobody wants me to mess up on the last trip . . ."

The North Korean agreed to give him the full, sixty minutes he requested and hung up, not before having added:

"Any surprise this time?"

"No, I look just the same as the last time . . ."

From his bathroom, he called David and gave him the full report. David told Mark that the sixty minutes left him plenty of time to get organized. He added, casually, that special monitoring would be provided for the Chinese Embassy:

"We've been quite creative. We will be able to get better pictures. We must find out who the chap is."

Mark thanked him and said that he would plan on leaving the apartment about fifteen minutes before his rendezvous time.

CHAPTER.23

TEL AVIV, ISRAEL AND AUSTRIA

Simon called Countess Renate to brief her on the Chinese developments. She was quite surprised and asked:

"Can you figure out if he is a rogue Chinese or an official of the regime?"

"That's what we'd love to do. But, so far, we haven't been able to put a name on him . . ."

"Why don't you send me what you have? I have ways of finding out. We once did a job for a mainland Chinese businessman and he may be able to help us."

"Can you trust him?"

With a smile, she simply replied

"We know a lot about him."

"I see . . . When will you contact him?"

"As soon as I get the pictures. The time zones still work. I'll get back to you when I have an answer."

Simon hung up and could hardly believe the dialog that he had just had. He was the head of the most secret group within one of the best secret services in the world. They could not put a name on someone whom they believe to be Chinese. Yet, Countess Renate believed that she might be able to do better. *Best of luck, Countess,* was all he could think.

His services had however been able to put a name on the North Korean defector scientist in cooperation with the National Intelligence Service of South Korea: Choi Jae-Jin. His biography was available in the scientific community, and by extension on the Internet. Though North Korean scientists are generally not thought of particularly highly, some of Choi's work, published while he was in China, had been quoted. It must therefore have been respected and thought of as a relevant part of the body of knowledge in his discipline. His quoted work was solely focused on viruses and changes that can be performed to give them different properties, so-called gains-of-function. Published work always seemed to deal with steps to make viruses less dangerous or less prone to contaminate hosts. Yet, Simon had guessed that reverse steps were equally likely to make sense, promoting more dangerous and contagious strains. Of particular interest was one paper which discussed an experiment where he was starting with a virus that occurs normally in lions and lionesses in southern Africa. Simon recalled that the virus in the flasks was supposed to have come from the blood of lions. *Things are starting to come together . . .* he thought.

Simon called Professor Armand Duchemin to find out where his joint work with the Japanese scientists was leading. Armand picked up the phone at the first ring:

"Simon, what a surprise . . . I was expecting a call from Oshima-San, from Tokyo."

"Would you rather I call you later?"

"No, I can talk now. But I may have to hang up suddenly if the other call comes."

"No problem. So, how much progress have you made?"

"Well, quite a lot, but please appreciate this is medical science. We must proceed with great caution. At this point, we believe that we have isolated two possible antibodies in feline blood, from regular house cats. These antibodies seem to have some ability to bind with the virus. What they do, see, is this: they attach to the virus. That effectively prevents the virus from binding with anything else and the virus from replicating itself."

"Isn't that very good?"

"Well, sure. It's in fact very encouraging. But there is a lot more to do. Besides figuring out which of the two does the best job or if we have to use them in pairs, there is the whole issue of possible side effects in humans."

"How far are you on those fronts?"

"Well, that's the phone call I am expecting. We must discuss how we are going to proceed in testing any form of nasty reaction in the human body. *Institut Pasteur* has certain protocols and I understand that the National Institute of Infectious Diseases in Japan has others. Doesn't mean anyone is wrong. We just need to compare our methods to make sure we use whatever approach is the most likely to yield results the fastest . . . Simon, I see my other call is coming. I'll talk to you later . . ."

Simon was encouraged indeed. One of the worries which he had not discussed too widely was the risk that they had not found all the bombs which terrorists might have planted in Israel. Any bomb that was discovered was no longer an issue; it had been made inoffensive, at least from the point of view of viral contamination and sarin gas poisoning. Yet, any bomb which they had not found could still wreak havoc. *The sooner we have a vaccine or a treatment, the more soundly I will sleep.*

■ ■ ■ ■ ■

Simon's phone rang: "Simon here . . ."

"Countess Renate . . . Simon, I think I have some useful news for you."

"Really, about what?"

"The Chinese fellow . . ."

"Already?"

Countess Renate did not reply to Simon's last comment. She went on:

"Well, my contact tells me he thinks the Chinese individual is Xi Qwan Ji. He believes he is a colonel in the Chinese army. He is not sure, but he believes that he is not part of the political leadership; I suspect it means he's not on the politburo. My contact doesn't know either whether he serves in the army or in the secret service. He'll check as much as he can and revert. At this point, he cannot confirm on which side the guy is—with the government or plotting against it. He hopes to find out more, but he doesn't want to draw attention."

"This is great. Frankly, you have me bluffed. I can't believe you could get that information faster. But I guess that's why you're in The Shadow Experts and not *Mossad* . . ."

"Very funny! I'll call you if I get more. Remember, my line's always open for you."

"I know. Thank you . . ."

CHAPTER.24

BERN, SWITZERLAND

Mark walked calmly from the apartment to his car, looking around casually to see if anybody was following him. He noted with a wry smile that a different car was starting its engine as he emerged from the building. From where he was, he could not see the faces of driver and passenger, but he thought: *I bet these are my guardian angels.* David had relayed to Mark the concerns of Simon, but both he and Mark believed that the risk was minimal for as long as there were briefcases yet to be dropped. Still, Mark heeded the warning and was paying more attention than usual.

He drove to the Chinese Embassy and found, coincidentally, a parking spot almost precisely where he had parked the previous time. Though he really wanted to, he avoided looking back at the embassy building as he was walking away. There were people who were observing all activity from the embassy and for him to look would have given out the fact that he knew he was spied on from there. This could have spoiled the whole thing. Better to let his colleagues do their jobs. David had in fact earlier asked Simon to dispatch more agents from neighboring countries to have a truly full complement of eyes; they would come in handy in this particular instance. Mark walked to the same bench he had used a few days ago and started to wait. He was wearing his earbud from the *Mossad* phone, so that David, Simon or anyone else could relay to him any important information. He ostensibly had his terrorist phone in his hand to ensure that any spy would see that he was ready for a call, should one come.

He did not have to wait long:

"Anwar?"

The voice at the end of the line was that of his "Asian friend." He sounded unhappy.

"Yes. Any problem?"

"How do you open the trunk on this car?"

"Just twist the VW sign on the lid . . ."

"Ah! Thank you. You can walk back to the car in five minutes."

"Thanks."

David's team had been able to take even better pictures of the man in the window of the embassy. It looked as if he was not alone. However, the man next to him was partially in the shadows. The lab would have to do its magic to try and see whether he could be identified. Both North Koreans appeared this time to be walking to the same car. It looked as if they were going to drive together to the North Korean Embassy.

When the five minutes had elapsed, Mark walked calmly back to the car. He checked the trunk and was delighted to see that there was a package indeed. Again, he checked that the only thing in the package was the set of three flasks. He allowed himself a casual glance at the embassy and saw that there was activity indeed in a back window. He assumed that it was his Chinese friend, but wasted no time trying to see more. He could explain some curiosity at what was happening in his direct surroundings, but he could not dedicate his sole focus to one element.

David on his side was going to have a lot of new information. His agents had, among others, a couple of relatively silent drones equipped with cameras. These had allowed the closest picture of the window in the embassy yet, but they also provided coverage of all comings and goings around it. Agents on foot and in cars were focused on the two North Koreans, who, indeed, went straight back to their own embassy. David noted that a car was pulling up to the Chinese Embassy as Mark was about to get to his car. Two people got into the car, including one who was ostensibly wearing a military uniform. David called his troops:

"To all agents, a car may be following Mark. Keep close to him and watch for anything suspect . . ."

The car left the embassy and drove virtually alongside Mark's car. It slowed down a bit as it was driving by. Mark got a glance of something through his left window and ducked. He had reacted quickly, but the menace was not what he thought. The occupants of the Chinese car were simply taking more pictures of him. They seemed also to be taking pictures of the car, but that was not a worry. The car would be returned to the rental agency within less than four hours. Mark would be driving a completely different car as he started on his way to Brussels and London.

David asked one of the cars that were following the North Koreans to return and drive as quickly as possible to create a second tail for the Chinese car. *Mossad* indeed hardly ever uses only one car during a surveillance. It is much better to have two cars alternate, one in closer contact, the other a safe distance away. It makes it much harder on the subject to pick up the tail. David described the black Mercedes S series to his agents. Within a minute, the two cars were in place. They were surprised when the Mercedes did not follow Mark. It took them seconds to realize that it was driving to the small regional Bern airport.

David immediately called Simon:

"It looks as if the Chinese contact is leaving Switzerland . . ."

"How?"

"Got to be a charter plane. There are virtually no scheduled international flights from there."

"Have your guys get me the plane's tail number. We'll put a watch on it. Bet you it's gonna go to London first . . ."

"Great. Thanks. Oh . . . By the way, we have new pictures, including from a man who was standing next to the Chinese commander. Could not see his face clearly, but I hope that enhancements will show us more . . ."

"Super. I'll forward anything you send me to Countess Renate."

■ ■ ■ ■ ■

Back at the apartment, Mark went through his "bomb-making" routine one last time. He was going to leave for Brussels the next morning early. So, he would have an early dinner and then go straight to bed, after his usual call to Debbie. He was to leave the flat with all keys inside, so that his handlers could close out the short-term lease.

Once the bombs were assembled, the briefcases placed back in the cellar and the traps set so that Mark could see whether anyone had come to spy on him, he drove to the car rental agency. He returned the Volkswagen. Using a rental agency, he had not used earlier, he went to pick up another car that would be returned in London, at the London City Airport. The choice was very limited, as renters do not like to have cars cross the English Channel. There was a limited market for cars with a left-hand drive in a country that drove on the left side of the road. The renter would have to wait until someone arrived somewhere in London and needed a car to go over to the Continent or ship it back without getting paid for it. He had to accept a turquoise, metallic Volkswagen Tiguan, a medium-sized SUV. It certainly neither performed nor had the comfort of his earlier choices, but, as he reminded himself, *I am doing this for work, not to have fun . . .*

He returned to the flat with his new car. He was surprised to note that the cellar had not been visited. *Do they trust me now?* More ominous thoughts came to his mind, but he rejected them all—*Why would they not wait until the last briefcase has been stored?* He went back up to the flat with the briefcases. He still needed to pack and to prepare himself for the trip he would take the next day. He opened the door and was surprised when he heard someone call his name from inside the apartment:

"Anwar?"

"What the hell is this?"

Mark was surprised to see a couple of men, looking like they were of Middle Eastern origin, calmly waiting for him in the living room as he opened the front door. He controlled himself and repressed the reflex of pulling his gun. He added in a loud enough voice:

"Who are you and what are you doing here?"

He was only partially reassured by the knowledge that his colleagues were hearing the whole conversation. They had bugged the flat earlier. One of the two intruders, who looked the oldest, said:

"This will be your last trip."

"That's correct, but you don't need to say this in such an ominous manner . . ."

"Oh . . . I see what you mean. I didn't mean anything nasty. We're here to give you your money. After all, you may want to keep it in Switzerland . . ."

Mark breathed a huge sigh of relief. They were not here to hurt him. They added:

"You've been a great help. Your role in the mission will surely be remembered."

"Any further bombs after this?"

"Don't know . . . It's up to Raqqa."

Raqqa is a Syrian town that the Califate had selected as its future capital. This was the first time that a terrorist conceded that there might be some sort of nerve center there.

"What about Ismail?"

"What about him?"

"Will he still be in Tel Aviv?"

"Why?"

"Remember . . . That's where I'm currently based . . . But that was for this mission . . . You don't believe I'm an Israeli resident, do you?"

"I see. Haven't heard anything. So, I guess you're going back there and wait."

The other Syrian nodded, but still was saying nothing. Mark smiled, took the envelope, opened it and pretended to verify its contents. Apparently satisfied, he placed it in his pocket. The two Syrians got up and proceeded toward the door. Mark's heart stopped when the second Syrian turned around, looked straight at Mark and pulled his gun out.

CHAPTER.25

TEL AVIV, ISRAEL AND AUSTRIA

Simon received a call from Countess Renate:

"I have further news on the Chinese officer, Simon."

"Go ahead."

"He is not in the army. He works in the secret service . . ." Simon let go a small whistle, saying:

"The Chinese secret service? Do we know what he does there?"

"Not yet. By the way, we still don't know whether he is official or rogue . . ."

"Ah . . ."

"Point is, we don't even know whether he was in Bern officially or on his own."

"What do you mean, Countess?"

"We've seen a case before where someone had started a rogue operation, all the while remaining in his official position."

"Seen that too . . . How can we find out?"

"At this point, my guess is we can't. Assume he is official, but don't do anything against the Chinese that you can't undo without leaving any trace."

"Thanks. Keep me posted if you find out more."

"I will."

Simon was looking at a message that an assistant had just slid before his eyes:

"Oh my God!"

He immediately called David:

"A couple of things we need to discuss."

"What?"

"Well, first, the guy who was with the Chinese army officer."

"So?"

"Well, he is known to us . . . and probably to others. It's Abdul-Aziz Abadi Ben Islam."

"Who is he?"

"A senior ISIS figure . . . He is number two or three, if they have anything like a formal hierarchy."

"Holly shit!"

"You said it. The other thing is that the Chinese officer works in the secret service."

"You mean that China is cooperating with ISIS?"

"We don't know that for a fact yet . . . But it is a possibility. We still don't know enough about Xi, the Chinese officer, to be definitive. However, we have to assume he is legit, until we find out for sure he is rogue."

"What does that mean?"

Simon went on to explain that the discovery had a number of implications. The first is that this may be the last series of bombs to be planted. That would explain the interest from the senior ISIS figure. He added:

"I'll take care of that. I need to talk to Countess Renate again. We've got to set up a trap and see what happens . . . The second is that Mark may be in real danger . . ."

■ ■ ■ ■ ■

David told Simon that Mark had gone back to the flat and that he had not heard anything since then. They agreed that they should be doubly careful. David asked:

"What happened to the plane the two guys from the Chinese Embassy took after it left Bern?"

"As expected, it landed in London. We had the time to have two guys there when they landed. The Chinese individual, Xi Qwan Ji, of whom we have increasingly good pictures by the way, took a cab to Heathrow terminal 4. China Eastern and China Southern leave from there. Safe to assume he's flying back to China. The other guy took another cab to Heathrow too. But it went to terminal 3. That's where you find Emirates, Middle Eastern Airlines and Royal Jordanian, among others. So, best guess is that they're returning "home," so to speak . . . We still keeping them under close surveillance. I'll update you when I know more . . ."

Simon was back on the phone to Countess Renate as soon as he hung up. Renate picked up after the first ring:

"Simon?"

"Yes, Countess, sorry to disturb you again . . ."

"You don't. What's new?"

"Well, we've identified the fellow that was with Xi, the Chinese officer . . ."

"Yes, so . . ."

"Senior ISIS figure . . ."

"Oh My . . ."

"We need to set up a trap . . ."

"What do you have in mind?"

Simon went on to explain his plan. He wanted ISIS to question whether the whole grid of bombs was functioning as it should. He hoped that it would lead someone to call Ismail. He added:

"To be sure to protect Mark, our guy, we cannot have any of the bombs in Europe appear to be malfunctioning. Those in the Middle

East are OK . . ."

"Let me talk to my guys, either Hai Chock or Raj. I'll get back to you . . ."

She was about to hand up when Simon added: "One other thing . . ."

"Yes?"

"Is there a way that your Swiss associate, Romain Switzer, could come back to Tel Aviv?"

"Why?"

"I'm concerned we haven't found all the bombs. I'd like to use a finer tooth comb to minimize the risk of one dirty bomb exploding, at least until we have a vaccine or a treatment for the virus . . ."

"Let me find out, but that shouldn't be a problem. How long do you think you'd need him?"

"Don't know for sure. I've got someone drawing a list of other possible sites. It could be as many as twenty."

"Throughout the country?"

"Yes, although there is a concentration in the Tel Aviv, Haifa and Jerusalem triangle."

"I'll get back to you on that as well. Anything else?"

"Well, now that you ask, a wild thought has crossed my mind. What if they have already placed the bombs in the U.S.?"

"You mean . . . They would have two teams at work on the same mission . . . Plausible. Tell you what; I need to talk to Hai Chock. The last time I talked to him, he was trying to penetrate their main computer. It's been almost a week. He hasn't called back. I'll let you know"

Simon was impressed how quickly Countess Renate had figured out his worry . . . *That would make last year's pandemic look like a clumsy dress rehearsal* . . . was all he could think of.

CHAPTER.26

BERN, SWITZERLAND, ACROSS BELGIUM AND THE UNITED KINGDOM

"Wait a minute . . . Why the gun?"

Upon hearing this, Mark's colleagues rushed out of their flat toward Mark's apartment. They were about to burst in when they heard:

"Just a warning, Anwar. You know a lot. We know how to get to you—anywhere. If we ever find out you're leaking anything, your life won't be worth a dime."

Mark decided he had to be very firm. He replied:

"OK, man . . . First of all, I know that. But let me return the compliment, my friend. You know almost as much as I do. You certainly know where all the bombs are and how they were put together. Your own guys got me into stupid trouble on the way from Barcelona to Madrid. Almost scuttled the mission. This has made my life quite a bit more complicated since then. Think of the number of times I've had to change cars, of the need to shave and disguise myself. Now this; I'm not sure how Ismail will react when I tell him of your antics."

The younger Syrian suddenly looked worried and contrite. The more senior of the two, the one who had been speaking earlier, looked at his associate somewhat askance. Mark concluded he had hit a nerve;

the Syrian's outburst was not planned. Ismail was probably more senior than these guys. The younger one either panicked or wanted to look big. It might well have worked if Mark had cowered. But his forceful response stunned both Syrians. *Good to know. I must be a senior figure after all.*

Mark's colleagues retreated quickly toward their apartment as the Syrians were ready to exit his flat. Mark went straight to the bathroom to discuss the issue with David:

"I think it's not a big deal. What concerns me is that this may show that nerves are frayed."

"You may be more right than you think, my friend. Was just talking to Simon . . ."

"And?"

"The fellow who was with the Chinese secret service officer . . ."

"Secret service?"

"Yes, wait . . . There's more. The other fellow . . . He was from ISIS near the very top!"

"Son of a bitch . . ."

"You said it. We wonder if this is the end of the part of the mission involving placing the bombs."

"But Ismail seemed to indicate that there were going to be bombs in the U.S."

"They may have had someone else place them."

"And build them?"

"Precisely. Anwar may not have been the sole bomb builder."

"This could be terrible. They could explode those."

"I know. I know. Simon tells me he has a plan, and that Countess Renate is working on it."

"Any different instruction for me?"

"No, do exactly as planned. I have doubled the number of people who are following you. This time, I'll have people following your car as well. Do not be surprised. They'll come onto your earbud to tell you what they drive."

"Sounds great."

"One quick thought: rather than going out to eat now, you might just get yourself some delivery and stay put in the flat until you leave tomorrow. I have someone watching your car; we'll know if they try anything on that front . . ."

"Thanks David . . . I guess I'll eat Chinese tonight . . . No pun intended."

■ ■ ■ ■ ■

Mark rose early the next day and, while in the bathroom, called his colleagues to tell them that he planned to leave at 7:30 a.m. latest. He asked them to warn David. Right on cue, he emerged from his flat with two suitcases. One contained all his personal items and the other the three briefcases which he would be dropping off over the next twelve hours or so. His luggage seemed lost in the cavernous trunk of his SUV.

He left Bern with a mixture of excitement as the end of the mission approached and of sadness as he had grown to enjoy a town which is both the national capital of Switzerland and yet a small town. To think that he was within shouting distance of actual bona fide agricultural fields when he went to pick up a set of flasks near the children's playground was striking for someone used to a sprawling agglomeration such as Tel Aviv.

He retraced the steps he had taken on his last trip all the way to Basel. There, he crossed into Alsace in France and drove through Colmar before hitting Luxembourg. The rest of the trip was through Belgium. The landscape was quite varied, and he enjoyed the wide variety of flowers and flowering trees he could see through the diverse areas he crossed: *It's amazing how Northern Europe is diverse,* he thought. In Brussels, he quickly found the Station Brussel-Noord, as it is known in its bilingual name. Its architecture is actually elegant, with its characteristic modern clock tower and a three-story concrete structure above which rises a glass and concrete, almost classical office building. He had no difficulty finding a parking spot despite its being the middle of the day. He walked into the locker room near a large waiting room off the corridor leading to the various train platforms. He repeated his well-oiled routine and walked away. He took advantage of the food complex to buy a couple of sandwiches and a big bottle of mineral water; being in Belgium, he could not resist treating himself to a small box of chocolates. Would he have the will power not to open it until he could give it to Debbie?

He returned to his car, speaking to his colleagues on his earbud. He told them that he was ready to go and would likely not stop until they all got to Calais to board the train to London. Everyone said they'd be ready within five minutes, as his colleagues had stepped out of their respective cars to grab a coffee. Mark started his stopwatch and got into his car. He killed some time eating his first sandwich, chicken and salad, as he had been careful again not to buy anything that might contain pork or pork products. He started his engine when the five minutes were up and was satisfied to see the two "friendly" cars follow him. He could not miss the one "unfriendly car" which had also followed him since Bern.

The two-hundred-and-fifty-mile trip to Calais was expected to take a bit longer than it should, as Mark was going to hit traffic most of the way. Plus, the trip would not be all on divided highways, including as it did a fair amount of two- or three-lane roads. But Mark was not worried; he had all the time he needed to connect with the train he would take into England.

Once in Calais, Mark and the two other *Mossad* cars went to the station where each car is loaded, with its passengers still in the car, into specially designed railcars that run in the Chunnel. They had bought their tickets ahead of time, as required, and found themselves more than an hour early. They quickly went through the custom and immigration procedures and were able to grab a cup of coffee and a piece of pizza. Twenty-five minutes before the departure of the train, each of the teams—including the handlers who probably had to scramble to get on the same train as Mark—returned to their cars. They were guided onto the train and were to stay in their respective vehicles for the thirty-five-minute duration of the trip. The almost totally windowless nature of the railcars made for a quiet, but potentially claustrophobic crossing. But Mark simply rested his eyeballs. Once in Folkestone, the disembarking was as orderly as the loading of the train.

The drive through London's suburbs was not terribly quick, but that did not matter much. Mark went straight to Victoria Station, where he found a parking place almost immediately. He quickly dropped the penultimate briefcase and, from there, went directly to London City Terminal. There, the process had been changed by David and Simon. He loitered a bit on his way to the locker hall. The point was to allow two *Mossad* colleagues to locate themselves, one each, at one of the two entrances to the hall. A single word in his earbud told him the setup was ready. He walked deliberately into the north entrance to the hall. At exactly the same time, his colleagues used a tranquilizer pin in a ring on their pinky to stun the two handlers who had been following Mark and had, ominously, not stayed together this time. They both fell asleep and would not remember anything when they woke up not more than fifteen minutes later. Mark let Hai Chock know that the baby had been placed in the crib. Hai Chock knew what to do: anyone looking at the global map would see that location light up if they were looking for it.

Mark was then quickly accompanied by two colleagues through customs and immigration procedures with his Israeli identity and in a matter of minutes found himself sitting in an unmarked Israeli Air Force private jet. It would fly him, and Simon, straight to Israel. Simon climbed the stairs of the aircraft and greeted Mark:

"Well done, my friend. And you're alive and well."

"Thanks for all the help, sir . . ."

"Your colleagues will return your car to the rental agency as planned. Your luggage has already been loaded onto the plane, although we've dispensed with the empty suitcase. May I offer you a decent drink?"

"With pleasure. I haven't had one for quite a while now."

"That's what I thought. Plus, it should help you sleep on the way. You must be dead tired."

"Not right now, but it's got to be the adrenaline rush."

Simon handed Mark a crystal tumbler with a generous helping of single malt Scotch. He added:

"Enjoy . . ."

The roar of the plane taking off covered their conversation. After lift-off, Mark was asleep within minutes.

CHAPTER.27

TEL AVIV, ISRAEL

Though he had slept on the flight, Mark was still allowing himself a bit more rest when the phone rang:

"Anwar."

"Yes . . . Wait a minute . . . Who is this? Ismail?"

"Yes, it's Ismail, your friend, Ismail. You have a lot of questions to answer, Anwar . . ."

"Hold it for a minute. I just woke up . . . What's going on?"

"For a start, why did you not fly to Geneva and take the corporate jet to return to Tel Aviv via Riyadh as planned?"

"Well, my friend, a few of your associates are not as pleasant or friendly as they seem. One of them pulled a gun on me in Bern . . ."

"What do you mean?"

He related the episode when the two Syrians paid him and then had one of then pull a gun and threaten him, adding:

"I was convinced they were planning to kill me before I took the plane to Geneva."

"What? That's crazy . . . What made you think that?"

"There've been a few occasions throughout this trip where it really looked as if the guys were not really on my side. First, the snafu on the road from Barcelona to Madrid."

"Was an accident . . ."

"That's what they said. But if they had tried to get me in trouble, that's exactly what they would've done. Then, there's the issue of the Chinese Embassy."

"The Chinese Embassy? Where?"

"In Bern."

"What happened there?"

"I'm not dumb, Ismail. I know I was watched from a window. I don't know who it was. But then, as I was getting ready to return to my apartment, after they had dropped the flasks in my trunk, a car drove out of the embassy. It went right next to my car and slowed down as it was driving by. I thought they were going to shoot me. OK, they didn't . . . They were just taking photos. But why did the Chinese want my picture? Plus, what have the Chinese to do with our plan?"

"You're asking a lot of questions . . ."

"I'm not finished . . . At London City Airport, why did my handlers, as I call them, split up with each of them covering an exit from the hall? They've never done that before and many of the halls we've visited had several entrances or exits?"

"Any more questions?"

"Not for now . . . Isn't that enough?"

"Honestly, I don't know about any of those, other than the snafu in Spain. And, by the way, I only know about it because you called me. No one has told me they were unhappy with your work."

"It may not be a question of being unhappy, Ismail . . . Maybe, I know too much now. And you know what?"

"What? What do you mean?"

"Well, if I know too much, so do you."

"What are you saying?"

"We may both have become expendable, my friend."

Anwar paused. Ismail did not reply immediately. Rather, he

seemed to be thinking for a few seconds, probably processing Mark's latest comment. Then he said:

"Impossible . . . They called me just this morning . . . Just before I called you."

"What did they want?"

"Seems like a couple of the bombs in Saudi Arabia and Dubai are sending funny signals."

Mark knew from an earlier conversation with David that Simon was going to work with Countess Renate to address a problem. More precisely, he knew that they were going to try and set up a trap. He did not know the nature of the trap that they were setting up. Yet, he immediately assumed that the two events might be connected. *Could they have managed to hack into their computer?* he thought to himself. He chose to play along:

"What's wrong with them?"

"Well, sometimes, they look as if they're switched on. But when the Raqqa computer tries to contact them, somehow, they switch off and become silent. In fact, I'm told they disappear from the map."

"Disappear? Really? And then what?"

"They come back on as soon as the Raqqa terminal breaks direct contact with them and moves to another bomb."

Mark paused and smiled: *They must have managed to hack into Raqqa . . . Let's see if we can get even more information . . .* He replied: "Hard to believe . . . Wait a minute. Just got a thought . . . Have you considered that the problem may be with the Raqqa terminal, not the bombs?"

"The Raqqa terminal? What?"

Ismail paused for a second and then continued:

"I don't know about that . . . I surely hadn't thought of it. What could be wrong with the Raqqa terminal?"

Mark saw the opening and pressed on:

"Well, if you like me to work on it with you, give me access to the map with the bombs. I will test them from a different, unknown terminal."

"What do you mean by unknown terminal, Anwar?"

"Just guessing."

Mark was thinking out loud, threading the story as he went. He added:

"Imagine that someone has gotten wind of the plan or a part of it . . ."

"Impossible . . ."

"Imagine, still. Someone who wants the plan to fail. What would they do? Well, they could have penetrated the terminals they know about . . . Come to think of it, that someone . . . It would have to be an inside job. Who else knows of the Raqqa terminal, Ismail?"

"Me and probably a couple of other senior leaders."

"Any one of them want to be the Calif?"

"Come on. What are you making up now?"

"Don't know. But, as you know, in this job, I've got to be careful. I never exclude any hypothesis, even if it seems crazy, initially at least."

"Anyway. Makes little sense. But keep on with your scenario."

"Imagine that they've penetrated the computer terminal. They could trigger a bomb even when the Calif doesn't want to. Or refuse to trigger it when ordered."

"Unbelievable. Yet, carry on."

"Now, very few people know me. I have another laptop which I bought without anyone knowing. For my personal use. Give me the access I need, and I'll be able to tell you whether I can work the bombs or not. If I can, it's their computer . . . If I can't, it's the bombs. Simple as that."

"Can't do that. Can't give you that information."

Ismail's reply was like a reflex. He had information that he knew he could not share. Yet, he was now thinking as quickly as he should. All of a sudden, Mark's suggestion made at least some sense, though he could not believe that anyone would betray the group from inside. Whoever it would be was bound to be found out. The punishment would be painful, immediate and definitive. Yet, he was in a real bind. If he did not do anything, the problem was going to persist. Would the Calif and other blame him? He could not see why they would. Yet, he knew there would have to be a scapegoat. Why not him?

On the other hand, Mark's suggestion could be a way, possibly, to become a hero in the eyes of the Calif. *What if there is a problem and I'm the one who brings it to their attention? They would trust me even more . . . What do I have to lose?* So, he added:

"Tell you what. You come here with your so-called unknown laptop. Then, we can do it together."

"When?"

"How quickly can you be here?"

"Where is here?"

"I'll tell you in a minute."

"Can't tell you how soon if I don't know how far . . . Come on, be reasonable, Ismail."

"OK, say, not far from where we met the last time."

"Give me a couple of hours . . ."

"Why so long?"

"You just woke me up. I need to get ready, eat something and all the rest."

Reluctantly, Ismail gave Mark the address where they were to meet and added:

"See you then."

■ ■ ■ ■ ■

Mark immediately called David. He needed a pair of the fancy video glasses in a hurry. He would explain later, though he did give David a short summary of his conversation with Ismail. David immediately understood and said he would have the glasses delivered to Mark's apartment, with all the required precautions so that no one could see anyone make contact with Mark. These glasses had video cameras that would record all that the wearer could see and store it in memory chips imbedded in the frames. They had other capabilities, but those would not be used in this case.

David still asked:

"Sure it's not a trap?"

"Thought about that. Can you have me tailed?"

"Of course, but we can't do much once you're in the place with him."

"Know that. I know that. But I'll wear a bug and my Kevlar jacket. Plus, instead of having my gun on my calf, I'll have it in a holster under my coat. Have someone follow me as close to the door as possible. Also, can you please let Simon know that I will be using the laptop that I had with me while in Europe. I am gonna need the chap from Singapore, you know, Countess Renate's guy, to hack into my computer."

David immediately organized the glasses to be delivered and called Simon. He related to him Mark's latest request. Simon was truly impressed in Mark's ability to think on his feet: *This could be a huge break,* he thought. He had indeed originally decided not to share with Mark the nature of the trap they were setting up. He wanted him to react with surprise. He could not have hoped for a smarter reaction on his part.

He immediately contacted Countess Renate, who in turn conferenced Hai Chock in. Simon got David on the line as well. They got as much of the story as possible from what David knew, as it was by then impossible to reach Mark, who, as Anwar, was getting to Ismail's office using public transportation, as Anwar would have. Hai Chock confirmed that he could easily hack into Mark's computer if Simon could send the IP. Mossad would thus have two different ways of getting into the overall ISIS plan. Mark's visual account would provide an unexpected shot at seeing where all the bombs were. While

Hai Chock's access would allow some control. With the penetration of Mark's computer, he thought he could bounce himself into both Ismail's and Raqqa's computers.

■ ■ ■ ■ ■

Mark knocked on Ismail's door. Ismail opened. A surprise awaited Mark: Ismail was not alone. *Could David be right? Is this a trap?*

CHAPTER.28

"Colonel Rabinowitz?"

"Yes."

"Colonel Kim, here . . ."

"Great to hear from you Colonel . . . What is new?"

Colonel Kim replied that his news was not earth shattering but deserved to be passed on. His services believed that they had identified the two North Koreans that delivered the flasks in Bern. They were indeed both agents in the North Korean secret service. More importantly, while one did not have much attached to his name, the one that went back once to the Chinese Embassy was somewhat senior, adding:

"Their ranks are not comparable to ours or yours, but I think he holds the title of Lieutenant Colonel. He's much more than a simple operative."

"What do you make of that?"

"I'd lean in the direction of thinking that North Korea's involvement is officially sanctioned. Lieutenant Colonel Chen, as that's his name, is at the same time not high enough to drive a rogue operation and too high to be a mere foot soldier."

"Where does that lead you vis-à-vis Choi, the scientist?"

"Got to think that the whole thing is planned within the security services. Now, I don't know whether or not Choi's original assignment to Wuhan was the first step in a long-term plan. Could just be that the plan was hatched when he returned to North Korea. Anyway, the one element which is still missing is whether there is a relationship with China . . ."

Colonel Kim explained that the assignment of a scientist like Choi to a Chinese laboratory, with the probable purpose of developing a biological weapon, was in itself a bit unusual, adding:

"I'm not saying it never happens. I'm just saying it's not commonplace. Further, for him to leave China in an apparently clandestine manner is even more surprising . . ."

Simon interrupted:

"Unless this circus is planned for your benefit and ours."

"True. But, if it is planned that way, then it's not a rogue operation within China. Or at least it's unlikely to be one. It would be a deliberate effort on the part of the Chinese to use North Korea in a nefarious manner. All the while being able to deny any involvement if the North Korean connection was ever found."

Simon agreed and took the logic further. It would have to mean that the developments between the U.S. and North Korea over the prior several years were also a sham, particularly to the extent that China was suggesting they were trying to control North Korea. He paused for a minute and then asked:

"Does that tell us that something in fact went wrong in the Chinese-North Korean relationship? Could North Korea have recalled Choi when they found out he had reached some success just because they did not want China to find out?"

"You know, I am no fan of the Chinese, as I do not always understand what they do. Yet, unless you go all the way to the pandemic scenario broached by the Hong Kong defector, Dr. Li, that Covid-19 was deliberately created and released . . . Unless you think that, I much prefer the thought that Covid-19 was an accident and that the North Koreans are playing both sides against the middle."

Simon conceded that the other scenario was so frightening that he preferred to believe that the Chinese had global goals, but were still not prepared to go to the extreme to achieve them, adding:

"They're too big, too powerful to take that risk . . ." Colonel Kim agreed, though he added:

"Unless that's what they want us to believe. Remember, Colonel Rabinowitz, the Russians are masters at chess. The Chinese are masters at Go. A lot more different possibilities . . ."

He asked Simon to keep him in the loop on any further development. Simon asked him in turn to try and learn as much as he could about Choi, as Simon could envisage some action but needed more detail. He added:

"By the way, have you been able to confirm the location of the lab?"

"Yes, we're pretty sure it's the one we identified at the outset . . ."

"Accessibility?"

"Extremely risky. Hard to do it in a covert action. No agent of mine could take that risk. It'd be almost like a suicide mission . . . And with virtually no chance of success."

"Do we know how the virus is bottled and sent to the field?"

"We don't but the diplomatic pouch would be the most logical in terms of how it leaves the country and is delivered."

Simon opined:

"Would make the official involvement more probable . . ."

"Indeed, though not totally clear. I know of instances where rogue diplomats used the pouch. Obviously, it would be easier for him if he is official."

Returning to Choi, Simon asked:

"Understood. Do you think other people know much about Choi's work?"

"As of now, my guess . . . my *educated* guess is that he heads up a group of scientists. The group's focus has to be viral research. I suspect that everyone in the group knows the manipulations they conduct. Yet, I'm not sure anyone knows the whole story. What makes me feel that way are the few early deaths . . . I bet you the dead were people who worked with him; either they weren't told of the risk or they did not follow the rules to protect themselves. Now, they should all have learned a lot by now."

"This has been very helpful, Colonel Kim. I'll speak to you soon. Thanks again."

"Most welcome."

CHAPTER.29

TEL AVIV, ISRAEL

"Ismail, we're not gonna be alone?"

"No, Anwar. Meet Farouk Abboud ben Malouf, one of my close associates . . ."

"Why the change? You didn't say anything about him on the phone."

"Farouk goes to Raqqa often. He's here to observe and possibly report our findings. We're all on the same side."

"OK. Suit yourself. I'm only trying to help . . ."

"Take off your coat . . ."

"Don't mind if I don't. Caught a bug in Europe. Small fever and sinus headache. I need to stay warm, even too warm."

"OK. Hope you'll get better soon. Good thing you don't need to travel soon . . . Unless you find that the bombs that don't work need to be switched."

Mark smiled meekly. He then took his Dell laptop from his briefcase and asked for a plug to keep it fully charged. Turning it on, he started asking for a number of specific details, names of files, passwords and the like. He needed them to connect to the network to which Ismail's own computer was connected. Before leaving his apartment, Mark had

had a conversation with Hai Chock of Renate's network to brief him on what he needed to do. So, he started with one of the questions he'd been told to ask:

"Do I have to go through your computer, or can I connect directly to Raqqa?"

"Why do you ask?"

"Simple. Assume that both Raqqa and your computer have been identified. If I reach Raqqa through yours, I'll probably be flagged. If I reach Raqqa directly, I'm one of many internet surfers and I may be able to go through without getting infected myself."

"Infected?"

"Yes, the assumption has to be that there's a virus, a worm or something like that somewhere in the system."

"A virus? A worm?"

"Yes, computer virus or worm. That's how hackers manage to creep into unwitting computers . . ."

"I see. I see. I'm no computer wizard. I got confused with the virus with which we're working . . ."

"Totally different. Anyway, can you help me connect directly?"

Ismail reluctantly and after having exchanged glances with Farouk agreed. Mark pulled out his glasses from his pocket and donned them. Ismail asked:

"Why the glasses?"

"Need them when I work on any screen. It helps me see better and avoids straining my eyes."

Ismail bought the line. He then coached Mark through the steps he had to take to connect to the Raqqa computer.

"Victory! Here we are . . . Now, how do I get to the map?"

"What map?"

"The one we looked at together once. The one that shows where the bombs are . . . I need that to be able to pick one or two bombs and see if I can talk to them without them going silent."

Ismail continued to guide Mark through the various motions, without knowing that a quarter of a world away, Hai Chock was replicating each and every move Mark was making. That would give him access to a part of the Raqqa computer he had not broken into yet. He had found a way to interfere in the transmission from the Raqqa computer to any one of the bombs, but he was doing it without knowing which bomb was being contacted.

"OK. I see that the picture has changed since we last looked at it, Ismail."

"How so?"

"Well, there were no bombs in the U.S. the last time."

"Good point. They've had someone else plant them while you and I were concentrating on Europe after the Middle East."

"We must be close to our goal now."

"That, I don't know, but we're surely closer than before."

"Understood. Can't believe they'd bother with South America or Africa . . . Come to think of it, I only see a bomb in Africa, in South Africa in fact . . . Logical, little else to do there. Also, nothing in the Communist block or in China . . ."

"These are friendly countries."

"You don't consider Saudi Arabia or the Emirates as friends?"

"They are . . . But the bombs are insurance against them not doing what they're asked."

"Quite smart. I assume all of this comes from the Calif. He's definitely smart . . . Very smart . . ."

Ismail and Farouk smiled looking at each other. Mark had trouble keeping from laughing. He now knew that *Mossad* and the members of The Shadow Experts knew at that very moment where all the bombs were. That was a huge win. However, he still needed to make believe that the Raqqa computer was bugged, thinking to himself: *It was only partially bugged then, but now it's completely bugged . . . How ironic.*

He told his two acolytes that he would then start to work on a couple of bombs: "Pick one . . ."

They picked one in Eilat, in the south of the country. David and Simon noted that they had not known about that one. Mark went through the process that Hai Chock had taught him. He connected to the bomb by keying a number which appeared on the screen next to the point on the map corresponding to the bomb. The light on the map changed from yellow to green. He turned to his friends:

"Well, I can do two things now. I can explode it; I assume the light will turn red, and all hell will break loose there. On the other hand, I can disconnect, and everything will get back to where it was before."

"Don't trigger it. What does this mean?"

"I'd say that the Raqqa computer is bugged. There's a virus in it. Someone has managed to get into it."

"Should we try another bomb, just in case?"

"Sure. Which one?"

Ismail picked the bomb in King Khalid International Airport in Riyadh. Mark repeated the same exercise, with the same results as with the bomb in Eilat. He added in a deadpan tone of voice:

"Seems pretty clear. Don't you think? It's Raqqa, not the bombs."

"What can we do?"

"Well, that I don't know. I'm no computer expert. My guess is that you should look for the bug. Now, should we repeat the experience, but this time going through your computer, Ismail?"

"Why?"

"To find out if you're bugged too . . ."

"Oh. Sure . . ."

Ismail guided Mark to help him connect through his computer, totally oblivious to the fact that he was in effect helping Mark and The Shadow Experts get control of his own computer as well. Once that was done, Mark repeated the experience with another bomb. This time, they picked Lod, another city which had not been flagged earlier. Mark showed them that he could not give instructions to the bomb; the light went on briefly and then the bomb disappeared. Ismail exclaimed:

"That's exactly what Raqqa says is happening there . . ."

"Well, my friend, I'd say that yours is bugged as well." Mark added:

"I would look carefully at the inside of the organization. Someone knew enough to target two very important computers. Now, again, I can't tell you if other computers have been targeted or not, but whoever is doing this knows what they're doing. Farouk, do you access the site?"

"What site?"

Understanding that Mark was referring to the site with the map, he added:

"Well . . . No."

"OK, so I can't test your computer unless Ismail wants to give you the key to the map."

"Not necessary" was all that Ismail could reply, after having again exchanged glances with Farouk. Mark turned to Ismail:

"Can we speak privately for a minute?"

"I have no secrets for Farouk."

"Sorry, it's private."

Farouk moved to another room, ostensibly because he had to, not because he wanted to. Mark looked Ismail straight in the eyes and said:

"From what I see, unless you have duties that are way beyond what I know, you're just like me, my friend."

"What do you mean?"

"We're both expendable. They don't need us anymore. They've got their bombs. The world map looks well covered. They can go ahead and trigger whatever mayhem they plan to trigger. They won't tell us about it, because we're not part of that plan."

"Can't believe that . . ."

"Imagine for a minute you're the Calif. Would you like two people you don't control be able to access the bomb constellation or talk about it?"

"To whom?"

"To some secret service. I'm sure *Mossad* would love to hear what I know or what you know."

"But, if I did that or you did that, we'd be tracked down and killed without mercy . . ."

"Unless you or I've been able to get a new identity in exchange for the information."

"Wait a minute. How do you know all that?"

"Come on Ismail. Everybody knows that. Just type one or two key words on your computer and you'll find dozens of posts on the topic. Think about it. They might get to you and kill you or me or both of us for that matter, but some info would have leaked. Killing us now removes that risk."

Mark could see that his narrative was getting to Ismail. He could not take it further as Farouk came back in the room, asking:

"Finished?"

They could both only nod. Mark thought: *and what if that Farouk is some sort of executioner?* Knowing that he was wearing a bug, he added for the benefit of whomever was listening:

"Farouk nice to have met you. I hope we see each other again in equally pleasant circumstances."

Farouk muttered a few incomprehensible words. Mark said his goodbyes and left the flat. As soon as he was sure he was far enough that they could not hear him even with a long-distance mike, he spoke into his bug:

"Need to remove the other bombs in Israel as soon as possible . . . Also, tail both Farouk and Ismail. No idea where that'll lead us, but I have a hunch that Farouk is not straight . . ."

"Okeydokey!" was all that he heard in his earpiece.

CHAPTER.30

After viewing the tape from Mark's glasses and hearing his report in person, Simon first called Countess Renate:

"Countess, this is getting quite serious. We have discovered the location of most if not all the bombs . . ."

"How?"

Simon explained to her Mark's latest mission. She whistled and only said:

"Mighty impressive, sir. Congratulations . . ."

"We're proud of him, but he couldn't have done it without Hai Chock . . ."

"Glad to be of help . . ."

"But now we'll need you, Romain Switzer and your two computer geniuses to help us retrieve all the bombs we're still missing. Since there are a few more here, would you be able to join us here?"

"I'll be there tomorrow by midday. I'll send you the details. Should I land at Ben Gurion or Palmachim?"

"Wait a tick. We would need Romain Switzer and his tool as well."

"Can you get him the same jet you got him last time?"

"Can't he fly with you?"

"Nope. I'm very private and I could be interrupted by a client while in the air . . . Also, you may need him longer than I need to stay."

"I see. So, what do you propose?"

"I'll get his availability. I'll let you know. Then, you organize a jet to get him to Palmachim and I'll get myself there as well at about the same time."

"Fine . . . I'll wait for your call."

Simon was thinking: *She does not joke with secrecy . . . I guess that's got to be good, but it's also an expensive luxury . . .*

■ ■ ■ ■ ■

His next phone call was to Jack Turnbull, his opposite number at the Central Intelligence Agency, on a secure line. After talking to Ariel Landau, his boss, he was convinced that he needed to bring the Americans into the loop. After all, there were bombs on their territory and *Mossad* was not going to conduct covert operations in the U.S. He explained the situation in as few words as possible, including the fact that he was working with an outside consultant whom he would not name. Jack was a bit surprised at that, but he knew Simon well and never doubted the seriousness of his work. Jack's initial reaction was simply unprintable. He was furious. But Simon calmly brought him back to earth telling him that he believed that they had control over many of the bombs, though not those in the U.S. yet. Also, they had hired a couple of specialists that could help deactivate the bombs in the U.S. and thus get control over these as well.

"That's good news . . . What do you need from me, Simon?"

"Simply total secrecy and your OK to operate on the U.S. territory without anyone knowing. By the way, I'm happy to bring one of your agents with us, but it has to be absolutely top secret."

"Should not be a problem . . . When do you want to work?"

"I'm waiting for availability from our consultant. Then, I've got a few more bombs to take care of here in Israel. After that, we can move to the U.S. We'll have one loose end, Johannesburg, South Africa. We can address it on our way back to Israel from the U.S."

"What's gonna be involved?"

"Permissions to land an Israeli Air Force private jet in a few U.S. airports; custom clearance for all on board; logistical help at each location and discrete clearance with local authorities."

"Minor issues." Jack said laughing out loud. He agreed to set up the various clearances Simon needed and would be awaiting further instructions. He added:

"What's with these bombs?"

"That's the top-secret thing, my friend. Let me just tell you that they contain both sarin gas and a new virus which makes Covid-19 look like minor leagues."

"Damn it! What are you doing about those?"

"Well, that's where the outside consultant is most crucial. They've already identified the virus. They've discovered two antibodies which they have begun testing. The process will be a lot slower now: drug testing takes a lot of time."

"Who's doing all that?"

"The French and the Japanese . . ."

"No U.S. firm or lab?"

"Guess not . . ."

"Couldn't we get the liquid containing the virus to start our own work?"

"Afraid not. That's one of the conditions of the deal with the consultant . . ."

"Why do we need them now?"

"First because I've given my word. Second, because they have equipment which we do not have to find the bombs. Third because they have the specialists to deactivate the bombs, hack into the terrorists' computers and thus gain control. Do you need any more? . . ."

"Tell me, Simon, your consultant . . . Wouldn't be Countess Renate and The Shadow Experts, by any chance?"

"Why are you asking?"

"Just a hunch. We've never partnered with them, but we know people here who have. Secrecy, efficiency and effectiveness. Sounds a bit familiar . . ."

"You may well be right, my friend . . . But I won't confirm. I can't . . ."

Jack got the message and stopped asking questions. He was thinking that he would love to be able to meet Countess Renate. He was professionally interested in her work. Jack was one of those political appointees who was in fact as truly apolitical as one could be. He was concerned with the welfare of his country and held its core values in high regard. At the time, with these values under attack from certain parts of the political spectrum, he naturally tended to lean in the opposite direction. But he was well aware that neither side of the political spectrum had a monopoly on hypocrisy or self-interest. Someone like Countess Renate, who seemed to be only interested in helping those unjustly attacked, would seem a kindred spirit to him. He hoped that this venture would provide him with an opportunity to meet her and made a note to discuss this privately with Simon when appropriate.

■ ■ ■ ■ ■

Simon was at Palmachim Air Base to greet both Countess Renate and Romain Switzer. They arrived on different planes, but at roughly the same time. They immediately proceeded to the four towns which had not been identified in the earlier bomb search. Simon had arranged a helicopter to save time, although they used an Israeli jet to go to and from Eilat, at the tip of the gulf of Aqaba; a jet would be a lot faster given the distance. They found the bomb in the locker hall at the airport there. With the help of Hai Chock who was on the phone, they deactivated the bomb and simply removed the bomb and the flask. They did not feel there was any need to replace them with an inoffensive briefcase. That ship had sailed. Hai Chock ensured that the bomb still appeared on the ISIS map, which he could then see on his own computer thanks to the work done by Mark.

From there they flew back to Palmachim where they boarded a helicopter to Tiberias, then Nazareth and finally Lod, before returning to Palmachim. In all three locations, the terrorists had chosen the locker halls at the railway station. Because of the proximity to many people, they decided to remove those bombs altogether and, with Hai Chock's help, ensured that the bombs showed up on the screen on their original locations despite their no longer being there, as they had just done in Eilat.

The whole effort took less than five hours, including the two-hour roundtrip to Eilat. When back at Palmachim, they focused on the next steps, which were to occur in the U.S. and, eventually, in Johannesburg. With Countess Renate's permission, Simon conferenced Jack Turnbull in. He wanted to plan the execution of the bomb disposal in as much detail as possible so that the process took as little time as possible on the ground. Further, given the time difference between Singapore and the U.S., they wanted to avoid having Hai Chock working at crazy hours. Unfortunately, as they did not have the IPs of the surface-pro tablets in each of the bombs, they could not pre-emptively set their coordinates on the ISIS computer. They would have to do that at each location once they had deactivated the bombs and Hai Chock had been able to lock into the tablets. Poor Hai Chock would not spend a great night over the two days that the group expected the bomb disposal to take.

Jack expressed the desire at some point to meet Countess Renate. She said she would welcome it, although she had no plans to travel to the U.S. They exchanged a few additional pleasantries, and the conference call was terminated.

Countess Renate left almost immediately to fly back to Austria.

Simon drove Romain Switzer to the Sheraton hotel in Tel Aviv, with a beach and sea view. They would leave the next day for the U.S.

■ ■ ■ ■ ■

In all, there were a dozen bombs in the U.S. spread around nine cities: New York, Washington, Atlanta, Dallas, Los Angeles, San Francisco, Seattle, Chicago and Boston. New York, Chicago and Washington each got two bombs, while the other six cities had only one. Thankfully, the terrorists had not demonstrated a great deal of originality; they chose to plant all their bombs at airports. At one point, Simon had smiled noting that Grand Central Station in New York would have been a much better location than John F. Kennedy airport; the airport is spread over six terminals, while there is just one massive hall at Grand Central. Plus, during rush hour, a good number of senior executives use the train to go back to their suburban homes. *Talk about hitting the right people*, he thought.

The team comprised David Heller, Romain Switzer and Mark Levi, if only because of his familiarity with the bombs. They did not need either Countess Renate or Simon, while Jack Turnbull had elected to let the team do their jobs. His trust in Simon was complete. Hai Chock, from Singapore, would join by Wi-Fi at each location. The earlier communication between Jack Turnbull and Simon had ensured that the team had received all the appropriate landing rights in each of the airports where they landed.

At each location, the routine was the same: land and park the plane at the private terminal or on the spot on the tarmac where private planes were directed; go with Romain Switzer to look for the bomb. This involved several different stops, for those airports which had several terminals. Yet, after having found the first bomb at the International terminal at JFK Airport in New York, the team went first to the International terminal at all other airports, if there was one. Clearly, the terrorists lacked imagination; they did not vary their targets much. *It almost looked,* Mark thought, *as if they were trying to drop off their bombs as quickly as they could, if necessary, eschewing efficiency.* Once they had located the bomb with Romain's help, they would deactivate it, contact Hai Chock to trick the bomb into broadcasting the current location even though it was removed, and then take these bombs away with them. As the bombs would be on the plane, they were very careful to disassociate the detonator from the explosive, initially with Raj's help, though Mark learned quickly how to do it and no longer needed Raj, after the third bomb was neutralized. After they had located and disposed of the first bomb, at JFK, in the early afternoon, they took a helicopter provided by the CIA to get to Newark Airport across the Hudson River. They found the bomb there, again, in Terminal B, which serves most of the international flights. The helicopter took them back to JFK, where they boarded the jet to fly to Washington Dulles Airport. They had to travel to Washington National to deal with the second Washington bomb; they did that trip by CIA helicopter as well. Jack Turnbull had offered to host the group for dinner and took them back to an airport hotel where they would spend the night.

The next morning saw them fly to Atlanta, then to Dallas, to Los Angeles and finally to San Francisco. They spent the night there. They were shaken during the night by a small earthquake. It produced no damage of note, but it was a first for the three men who had never experienced any earth tremor before. The next morning, they flew to Seattle and then to Chicago, where they had to deal with both O'Hare and Midway airports, with the now well-oiled help of the CIA helicopter shuttle. They stayed at the Hilton Hotel at O'Hare Airport and flew the next morning to finish the U.S. part of the mission in Boston. They completed their work in Boston in time to fly to Johannesburg, with a refueling stop in Tel Aviv. One day later, they were all back in Tel Aviv, with the firm conviction that all the bombs were now either removed or duds. The one at Johannesburg's Tambo International Airport, the busiest in the country, was in the locker hall of Terminal B, which serves domestic flights. They left a dud there as an insurance policy.

CHAPTER.31

TEL AVIV, ISRAEL AND AUSTRIA

"Countess Renate?"

"Yes Simon, good to hear from you. Romain tells me that the trip to the U.S. and South Africa was a success."

"It certainly was . . . Now let's hope that the terrorists do not have any other bomb that would be hidden even on their own system."

"Everything is possible, Simon. Yet, given the direct access we have to their systems, you'd have to think that any other threat would be different. Wouldn't be with these same bombs."

"Let's hope . . . I'm calling you because I think it is time to "flush" out Mr. Choi, Mr. Chen and Mr. Xi."

"Flush out . . . What a wonderful image . . . What do you have in in mind?"

Simon conceded that he did not have a formal plan yet. He outlined an initial undeveloped thought and asked Renate whether this was something with which she could help. She offered both her help and the practical solution:

"If you all provide the funds, I can arrange to have accounts opened in their names in some third country and have money deposited in them. Our next step would be for the bank to reach out to them at their addresses in North Korea for Choi and Chen and in China for Xi, asking them for investment instructions."

"What an ingenious scheme . . . How would you do that?"

"Simon . . . Simon . . . I can't tell you everything. Let's just postulate that one of our associates is in the right position in a bank to have this done."

"What area does your network NOT cover, Countess?"

"Fewer and fewer as time passes, Simon . . ."

They agreed that Simon would get the local addresses of the three targets and forward them to Renate. She would call him when everything was set up and Mossad would organize the money transfers. Simon liked Renate's idea because it would surely work well in North Korea. The paranoia within the regime was bound to lead to Choi being placed under surveillance. Learning of a large amount of money in a secret foreign account had to lead to action. Any lack of action would indicate that his research has not reached total fruition. Yet, someone would be placed next to him to learn from him and eventually take over. That was the best possible scenario for Choi. Anything else involved him facing an untimely death.

For the two members of the secret service, Xi in China and Chen in North Korea, the scheme would allow Simon and Renate to determine whether the roles they played were official or not. If official, chances were that neither would suffer from anything, other than possibly being asked to bring the money back respectively to China and North Korea where it belonged. They would be asked why the money arrived and they would probably deny they knew anything. They would talk of entrapment and would probably spontaneously offer to give it to the Party. If either or both were rogue in any way, the regimes would probably get rid of them, after having tried to get them to speak.

In a way, this was exactly the kind of flushing out that Simon needed. As a matter of common curtesy among secret services, it was an unspoken rule that junior double agents or traitors were discretely denounced to the "other side." On the other hand, no such understanding existed when it came to senior spies. Thus, the treatment of Xi and Chen by their respective superiors would definitely identify their roles and indicate how important their positions were.

With respect to Choi, Simon would have preferred to find out more from Colonel Kim. But, in his latest phone conversation, it was quite clear that Colonel Kim had reached some sort of a dead end. No one in the lab was willing to talk to Kim's contacts. The option of destroying the lab was only feasible if one assumed a covert sabotage, which was deemed something that was beyond the reach of South Korea. Turning to Xi in China, Simon would eventually discuss it with the CIA, but his hope was that he was rogue and that China would be willing to help in exchange of Xi being uncovered.

■ ■ ■ ■ ■

"Simon here . . ."

"Simon, this is Countess Renate . . ."

"Hey . . . How are you . . . Great to hear your voice . . . Anything new?"

"Yes. The trap is set. We now need to fund it."

"How do we do that?"

Renate explained that the accounts had been set up so that they were in each of the individuals' names, though the bank retained a form of power of attorney. Thus, as she noted:

"We do not need to wire the money. We'll just use a line of credit at the bank. They will credit the accounts, but the money will be removed from any of these accounts, if there is an attempt to draw on it."

"Nice scheme, but is it legal?"

"Totally legal in Austria, which is where the bank is located."

She further told Simon that the bank officer would organize express letters to be sent by courier to each of the three individuals asking for instructions for how to handle the funds.

"Could he get in trouble?"

"Unlikely . . . He is way up in the hierarchy . . . Can't tell you anything more."

"Understood Countess. You have your ways, and your ways seem to be working."

Simon added that he would wait about two days before having leaks planted in both North Korea and China, concluding:

"That's when we will see who they really are. Shouldn't take more than a week, I guess."

Simon did not have to wait the full week he expected. The third day, after the letter was sent, Hans Koerig, the senior bank officer, in fact the head of the bank, received a call from North Korea. He had provided his direct phone line together with his email address on the letter he had sent:

"Mr. Koerig?"

"Yes . . ."

"Choi Jae-Jin here. What is this story about the million-dollar deposit on my account at your bank?"

"Let me check Mr. Choi. How do you spell your last name, with a 'y' or an 'i'?"

"An 'i' . . ."

He paused for a few seconds, pretending to key some data into his computer.

"Yes, you are correct, I see that a deposit was made by wire. It comes from another bank but does not mention the origin of the money. It just mentions "from one of our clients . . ."

"Well, this must be a mistake. I do not have any relation with anyone who would want to give me one million dollars."

"I don't doubt it, Mr. Choi, but what can I do? I received the money; they asked that it be credited to your account; and we have an account in your name."

"I do not want the money. By the way, I never opened an account at your bank. I didn't even know your bank existed until I received your letter . . ."

"Odd. Quite odd. Let me see . . ."

Hans Koerig pretended to busy himself a while again and explained that he had documents that bore the signature of a Mr. Choi which instructed the bank to open an account in his name, and named the bank as having a power of attorney. It also instructed the bank to contact him as soon as funds were wired. Choi Jae-Jin could not believe his ears. He, naturally, had no idea of what these documents were. At the same time, one could almost feel that he was also a bit tempted by the size of the honey pot. He certainly would not say it on a telephone line that he, correctly as it turns out, assumed was bugged. He kept protesting:

"This must be a hoax. Can you please send me copy of these documents?"

"Certainly, sir. If you provide me your email address, I can even send you copies of them by email. You would get them in the next hour or less."

Choi may have been a solid scientist, but he was not a spy, or someone used to those kinds of tricks. He immediately provided his email address to Hans Koerig who promised to send him the information as soon as he could.

▮ ▮ ▰ ▮ ▮

Hans hung up and called Countess Renate:

"Hans Koerig here . . ."

"Yes, Hans, any news?"

"Yes, Choi called me. He does not recognize the account."

"Didn't expect him to call. Must seem urgent to him. What language did he speak?"

"English. Not great, but understandable. Remember, I'm no fluent English speaker myself . . ."

"I know. You prefer Austrian. Anyway, what happened?"

"Well, as planned, I offered to send him copies of the account opening documents by email."

"And he agreed?" She said with her voice rising a bit.

"He did."

"Well, send me the documents first. I will forward them to one of our associates to have him imbed worms and viruses in them. I'll forward them to you when I get them back. Under no circumstance should you open them then. Your computer, and any server to which it is connected, would immediately be bugged. When you get the document from us after we have "enhanced" them, simply send them to Choi. Before you do, call me. I'll provide you with specific instructions so that you can do that without saving the documents but also without leaving any trace of how you got them."

Hans who had dealt with Countess Renate several times in the past as an associate in her network did not need to hear more. This would not be the first time that The Shadow Experts used a simple and almost routine request by someone to introduce a computer virus into their system and to gain some or even total control of their client's server.

CHAPTER.32

TEL AVIV, ISRAEL AND AUSTRIA

"Simon?"

"Yes . . ."

"Countess Renate, here . . . I have important news . . ."

"Wonderful . . . Go right ahead."

"One of the three traps has produced results, although not the one we expected."

"What?"

Renate went on to recapitulate the phone call she had had with her banking associate. Simon could not believe the punch line:

"We're going to get some control over Choi's server . . ."

Simon was predictably elated, although he threw some cold water on the excitement:

"This is great, provided he sent his work email address. We have little interest in his personal server, do we?"

"Who knows, my friend? We have a good shot at finding out how close to the government he is. Assume he is only moderately cooperative with them. In that case, would it not be reasonable to assume that a lot of the sensitive material on the virus is kept on a private server?"

"Countess, you are a genius. Didn't think of that. If he is part of the government, everything will be on the government server. Hopefully, he's using the correct server for his emails."

"Darn right."

"Let me know when you have further news . . . Can hardly wait."

"While we're on the phone, Simon, anything new at your end?"

Simon replied that nothing as dramatic as what she had relayed. However, they were working on Ismail to see whether he could be flipped to the "Good Side," as he put it. He explained that Mark Levi, aka Anwar, was trying to scare him with words and ideas at present. His next step would be to interfere with his computer to lock him out of some of what he currently sees. It would be made to appear to originate from Raqqa, although it was in truth the work of cyber specialists with *Mossad*. He added:

"The connection created by Hai Chock is breathtakingly efficient."

"Good to hear. Anything else?"

"Not at present. Although Ismail has been talking of the possibility of more bombs being placed in particular in Israel. We're monitoring that like hawks . . ."

"Understood."

■ ■ ■ ■ ■

"Colonel Rabinowitz?"

"Yes . . ."

"Colonel Kim here. I wanted to bring you some news . . ."

"Excellent, what is it?"

Colonel Kim explained to Simon that noise, and he insisted it was just noise, made his services suspect that the role of Lieutenant Colonel Chen Hei Woo looked to be official. He indeed argued that sources with access to the government were talking of a plot to implicate Chen in a bribery scheme. He added:

"We've even heard that he had said he would willingly turn the money over to the state if there was any truth to him having a foreign bank account."

Kim noted that none of what he was reporting was definite, but he said that it looked as if Chen was being protected or at least allowed to protect himself. This, to Kim, suggested that whatever mission he was on was likely to have official sanction. Simon expressed some disappointment, as it seemed to mean that the North Koreans were in this mess up to their eyeballs. If that were true, it would, in Simon's words "be a clear case of state-sponsored terrorism." Kim replied that he would not be surprised, because his services have long observed instances of state sponsored terrorism on the part of North Korea. Simon countered:

"Sure . . . But this time, bombs were planted almost around the globe. They can be seen as direct attacks on virtually every developed country whose political system they despise. Sanctions could be quite severe and it's hard to imagine any of the targeted countries voting against them at the U.N."

"You're correct, Colonel Rabinowitz, but do not forget the potential veto from either China or Russia or both."

"How could they openly side with such criminal activity?"

"One way would be to blame North Korea for procuring the weapon, but then argue that the real guilty party is ISIS who chose the locations . . . North Korea could plead innocence in terms of where the bombs were going to be planted, except on Israeli territory."

Simon conceded that, officially, the argument could be made. Yet, as he immediately corrected:

"We know that Chen was involved in the latest delivery of the deadly virus. How could he claim that he was not aware of what was being done?"

"That's unfortunately correct. We have pictures of Chen going to the Chinese Embassy. We suspect he was there to meet with the Chinese Colonel . . ."

"Colonel Xi."

"That's right. But, on the other hand, we have nothing that links them both to the delivery. The pictures we have in the car are of Colonel Xi and Abdul-Aziz Abadi Ben Islam, the senior ISIS figure. I'm sure we can link Chen to Bern, but nothing much more than that. But we have nothing linking Chen to Xi."

Simon had to accept that the scenario just painted by Colonel Kim was entirely plausible. He reflected for a moment and blurted out:

"We need to find out how Xi reacts to his sudden wealth . . ."

He speculated indeed that a key to the quandary was whether Xi was an official member of the Chinese Secret Service or a rogue officer in that secret service. Colonel Kim added that discovering that Xi was acting in an official capacity would be nothing short of a catastrophe. Simon simply replied:

"Would we ever find out? Knowing how the Chinese behave, I can imagine that he would appear to be sacrificed on the altar of geopolitics. Doesn't mean he would be executed publicly, but he could well go on some extended vacation, and possibly even come back with a different name. Otherwise, how could China support someone who seems to have been caught red-handed doing something that the world would condemn without doubt?"

"I do not share your optimism, Colonel Rabinowitz, I worry that China is involved in some way, though I can accept the hypothesis that they are using North Korea as a way of distancing themselves. I'm waiting for some serious disinformation campaign to start."

"Well, if you are correct, Colonel Kim, it's time we jumped into action on the ISIS front. If any of this comes to their ears, one must assume that a logical response would be to explode a bomb in a place that would not be a massive threat to the world, but could still be used to show they are serious . . ."

Simon at that point was obviously thinking of Johannesburg, the bomb they had left, without the biological or nerve agents, as their "insurance." He knew that ISIS did not know that the bombs had been deactivated. Yet, he had to organize some distraction so that, if it did explode, a few of the signs that it had been successful could be reported both to the Calif and through the press.

He called Countess Renate to share with her the scheme he had just concocted . . .

CHAPTER.33

As was expected by Simon and by Colonel Kim, a bomb did explode in Johannesburg. ISIS, hearing unpleasant rumors concerning Choi and Xi at the very least, was mulling over the idea of making an example. They were thinking of showing they were serious, without directly confronting major developed countries. Yet, they never had the time to execute their plan. Simon executed it for them. ISIS could not explain how it happened, and it only increased both their frustration and their worries that some mole was operating within their network. The one scenario they never considered was that *Mossad* had exploded the bomb. Armand Duchemin immediately flew to Johannesburg, mandated by Countess Renate, at Simon's request. He had with him a large number of doses of a supposed medication. That the little glass bottles he carried with him were filled with physiological serum, an inoffensive mix of sterile water and mineral salts, would not be known by anyone, but him, Countess Renate and Simon.

Countess Renate had called the South African Secret Service as soon as news of the explosion came out. She could not reasonably call earlier, even though she was in the loop. She told Jason McMillon, the head of the agency, that she knew the explosion involved some deadly virus. He was initially surprised, but she calmed him with the explanation that many of these bombs had been set and that nobody could let the news out for fear of starting a true panic. Further, they needed to be able to go back up the tree, so to speak, to ensure they could get to the culprits. She mentioned that some fingers pointed to ISIS, but also argued that there might well be some rogue country behind the plan:

"Do you know who, Countess?"

"Wish we did" she lied at least partially.

At any rate, she explained that the *Institut Pasteur* in France had developed a drug which would kill the virus. She added:

"All I need is for you to keep everything under wraps, except for allowing the news of the bomb to come out, which I guess is done by now, and for letting someone from the *Institut Pasteur* fly to Johannesburg and deliver the drugs. He will be happy to help inoculate everyone who has been exposed."

"It goes without saying, Countess."

He had hardly finished his sentence when Countess Renate wanted to correct her earlier statement:

"By the way, please maintain anyone who has been exposed in some quarantine at the airport until Professor Duchemin arrives . . ." Having already implicitly accepted the offer, Mr. McMillon could hardly refuse the request. He was sure that he could avoid having to explain the quarantine decision until it was safe for him to do it, after Professor Duchemin had worked his miracle. He was not totally on board with Renate's explanation, but he could see the disastrous consequences of not going along. He ordered the quarantine as requested and added a complete lock down of the airport area, including the closing of the airport, except for the rescue flight which would arrive within less than twelve hours. All other flights were to be redirected to Cape Town, the country's second largest airport.

Armand had taken advantage of a corporate jet loaned by a friendly supporter of The Shadow Experts. He had no one with him on the aircraft, other than the crew of two, because of the weight of the nearly three thousand doses he was carrying. McMillon had organized for a few volunteer doctors and nurses to dress up in the same kind of protective clothing they had used for the Covid-19 pandemic. They had originally been used to help the people who thought they might have been in contact with the viral gas and needed medical attention as well as quarantine. They would also be available to help with the inoculation of the people who had been exposed to the explosion. The fast action of Renate, who was warned by Hai Chock within seconds of the bomb being triggered, meant that the number of potential victims was somewhere between one and two thousand.

Upon landing, Armand was greeted with cheers and taken to the tent where the inoculation would take place. He was initially quite pleased that the number of people potentially affected was somewhat small. He obviously did not worry that anyone else could have been affected, because, in fact, no one had been affected. The deadly flask had been replaced by an inoffensive one. He was delighted still that very few people had been hurt by the explosion itself. That was indeed the biggest risk to the people of South Africa. Ostensibly, the locker hall was reasonably empty when the ISIS bomb was triggered.

People were lined up and moved one at a time to one of the five tables where they received an intramuscular injection of the so-called drug in the shoulder. The most they would feel, beside a little prick at the time of the injection, would be a mildly sore shoulder for a day. The scene was fascinating to see as a study in human behavior. Before they walked to the place where they would be injected, people seemed to drag their feet and suffer in some way; the minute after they received the injection, they were happy and did not seem to have any of the symptoms they thought they had before. Armand smiled at the subterfuge but knew how crucial it was for ISIS to believe a bomb had been triggered and released its poison. ISIS must have wondered how *Institut Pasteur* had developed an antidote.

■ ■ ■ ■ ■

When the senior terrorists learned of a rumor that linked Professor Choi to a secret bank account, they became convinced that he had double-crossed them. They had picked up the rumor from the North Korean secret service agents that were in contact with them. ISIS immediately thought that Choi had shared his formula with someone else, probably for money. That would be consistent with the rumor. They postulated that the someone who gained access to the formula or a live vial of the virus itself would have started to work months ago. Depending upon when Choi had shared his formula, they might have been at work on the antidote for as long as Choi had been back in North Korea. In other words, someone was working on a cure while Choi and his lab were manufacturing the virus. That drug, which had been somewhat publicized after the inoculation of victims in South Africa was complete, was the reason why the virus did not work.

They were furious that Choi might have thus benefited both from being praised as a great biologist by his regime at the same time as he was earning bribe money that would allow him to defect in due course. They had implicitly concluded that Choi had played both sides against the middle and had used them. They imagined all sorts of punishments he might be subject to. They were sure that Lieutenant Colonel Chen would take care of that.

The one thing they could not explain with respect to the Johannesburg blast was why the sarin gas seemed to have no effect. They were indeed expecting that people in the vicinity of the explosion would suffer from the sarin gas and die the painful death associated with chemical weapons. The point was to incapacitate them and thus prevent them from trying to control the other agent. The biological element of the weapon, the virus, was expected to be released in the air and contaminate anyone coming to the help of the chemical victims or coming in contact with them. With their perpetual paranoia, they again assumed immediately that North Korea had played a trick on them. Obviously, they assumed that Choi had something to do with it, but they could not take it to the logical extreme.

Choi's lab was not involved either in the production of the Sarin gas or even in the manufacturing of the flasks. ISIS had always been told that Choi would be given the empty flasks, fill them with the viral liquid and seal that part of the flask with sufficient care that no one else could possibly be affected as they manipulated the flasks. So, in their understanding, someone else, beside Choi, would add the liquid sarin gas to the flask before placing the final seal and delivering them to their bomb maker. ISIS began to wonder whether the North Koreans had sold them inoffensive gas in place of Sarin or diluted it to the point it was no longer effective. They could not explain how a state would do that to them.

They decided that they would have to test the one flask which was left after the planting of the bombs in the U.S. The team that planted the bombs in the U.S. had indeed decided at the last minute to ignore Boston's central train station, their last target. The team was indeed considerably less seasoned than the one ISIS thought they had at work with Anwar. They had become frightened, panicked might be a better word, when someone looked at them with more than casual attention as they were placing the bomb at Logan Airport in Boston. They had then decided to dismantle the last bomb and bring the components back with them to Syria. Needless to say, the senior terrorists had been quite disappointed, but they conceded that, if the risk of being discovered was real—and nobody knew whether it was or not—escaping the country as quickly as possible might have been the best solution indeed.

There was a small refugee camp near Raqqa that would provide the terrorists the wherewithal to test the flask they had. They decided to explode a bomb there, after they had reconstituted it. They placed it in the middle of the camp, near the latrines. They did not hide it too diligently, as they knew that they would explode it as soon as those placing the bomb would be out of arms way. Sadly, they did not seem to care who these refugees were, or even whether they were supporters or detractors of ISIS. They coldly figured they would be wonderful guinea pigs.

The explosion was powerful, though, sadly, there was not a lot of physical damage—given the nature of a refugee camp. There were not that many permanent structures that could be destroyed. On the other hand, the death toll in the camp was significant within less than three days. More importantly, analysis carried out on the bodies demonstrated both that the gas had worked and that there was a viral infection. They buried all the victims in the Muslim custom—this must be done, if possible, within twenty-four hours of death. As is unfortunately at times the case, press coverage of the accident was minimal, as Syria did not want yet another disclosure that chemical weapons might have been used on its territory.

Satisfied with the outcome of the explosion, the terrorists concluded that the bomb that exploded in South Africa was probably not defective, though some suspicion remained. They assumed that the problem in South Africa had to be that the bomb was exploded at the wrong time of day and that victims had been treated too quickly. Their suspicions of Choi remained as high as ever; there was no question that someone had an antidote, so someone had to have shared the specifics of the virus with someone else. Who could it be if not Choi?

■ ■ ■ ■ ■

Simon eventually got wind, through Anwar and Ismail, of the suspicions of ISIS. He called Renate and shared the information with her. They both had a good laugh and agreed that their first wave of disinformation had accomplished its goal. Yet, there was still quite a bit more to do. Simultaneously, they felt terribly sorry for all the victims in the refugee camp.

CHAPTER.34

Hans Koerig was surprised when he opened his email account, as he always did, first thing each morning when he got to the office. Among a variety of useless correspondence, one of the emails contained instructions to wire the funds in the account of Xi Qwan Ji to another account, in Aruba, in the name of ZG Reserves.

Hans immediately called Countess Renate to seek instructions, though he knew that the transfer order was in good form.

"Countess?"

"Yes, Hans. What's up?"

"I have instructions to transfer the funds in Xi's account to another account, under the name of ZG Reserves in a bank in Aruba."

"Can you hold off for an hour or so?"

"I'll hold off for longer than that. Normal procedures call for me first to ask the sender to authenticate the request. That could take a while. Though I might also get it by return email."

"Great. I'll call you back . . ."

Renate's next call was to Wong Hai Chock in Singapore.

"Hey, how are you?"

"A bit sleepy . . ."

"Sorry. The Shadow Experts know no hour, day or night . . ."

"I know. I know. Yet, you asked, so I replied . . ."

"Fair point. Tell me, can you hack into a bank account, if you know the bank, the account's name and it number?"

"Usually, it's possible, but it really depends on their cyber security precautions. Where's the bank?"

"Aruba . . ."

"Ah. Good news. They're good at preserving the identity of their customers, but they aren't so good when it comes to cyber security. What's up?"

Renate explained to Hai Chock the key points of the operations that involved flushing three individuals whom they suspected of working with terrorists. Money had been sent to three accounts opened in their names, to the usual bank in Austria. One of them had requested the money to be transferred to a different account. She added:

"We'd like to know what's in the account. Our suspicion is that the individual just seeks to move to money where he already has his hidden stash, but there may be other possibilities . . . Eventually, if appropriate, we might want to confiscate some of that money."

"Just send me a secure email with the information and I'll get to work . . ."

Countess Renate then called Simon:

"Simon, Renate here . . ."

"Hey, great to hear from you. What's new?"

"There's movement in Mr. Xi's account."

"What sort of movement?"

"He's asking for the money to be transferred to another account, in Aruba."

"Same name?"

"Nope. The new one is called ZG Reserves . . ."

Simon reflected for a second and then started laughing. Renate asked:

"What's so funny, Simon?"

"Well, Countess, I'm pretty sure the account's name bears no direct relationship to Mr. Xi."

"Wait a minute . . . How can you be sure?"

"Well, might I suggest that ZG could well mean Zhōngguó Gòngchǎndǎng, the pinyin translation of the traditional Chinese for 'Chinese Communist Party.' You may have stumbled on one of their reserve bank accounts . . ."

Countess Renate replied in a mix of admiration and dejection: "How in the world would you know that Simon?"

"I assure you that I do not know everything. But I stumbled on that myself a few months ago. I simply made a mental note of it. Who knows why we remember certain things and forget others?"

"Getting philosophical on me, Simon?"

"Never while on the job. So, unless Xi is among the leaders of the Communist Party of China, I imagine that he does not have much of a claim to whatever finds its way into that account."

They traded another couple of jokes and concluded the conversation with the agreement that hacking into the account was a top priority. Simon however added:

"If we're right and it's an official Chinese account, the key will be to know whether the instructions that came from Mr. Xi were given willingly or under duress. If willingly, the Chinese secret service are in on the operation; they may not have known about the money, but they're prepared to grab it anyway. If under duress, he was probably rogue and is being forced to cough up the money; and that's probably a prelude to even more unpleasant things for him. At any rate, I'll put our agents on notice. I want to hear everything they can on the fate of Mr. Xi . . ."

Within minutes, Renate was back on the phone with Hans Koerig.

She wanted to know how the verification of the instructions was going. His answer did not surprise her:

"So far, no reply . . . But they may still be asleep . . ."

"Well, let me know when you have anything please."

Back on the phone with Hai Chock, Renate agreed with him that he should try to hack into the account but be sure not to leave any trace at the outset. She wanted to gain control over the account. Yet, she had to ensure that no one could see that there had been an intrusion. Hai Chock replied:

"Not a problem. I'm just going to give myself access . . . Could be quick . . . Could take time . . . Time will tell."

He spent the next several hours at work. His main challenge was to find the password that the Chinese might have used to control access to the account. Indeed, getting to the bank and to the home page for the account was easy with the information he had. Yet, the difficulty, in Aruba as in any other place, was to find a way into the bank account. That's where a password was needed.

Though there are passwords that use Chinese characters, he assumed that it was unlikely that such characters would be accepted by a computer in a country which operated in Dutch and English. A special computer keyboard would be needed, or they would have to use topological graphic passwords. These are a new type of cryptography as they consist of two parts: one is a graph and the other one is a set of discrete elements. He simply assumed that this is much too new a concept to have been accepted by a bank in Aruba.

He connected his random password generator to the target account. The generator would produce and enter many randomly selected "words" made of numbers, letters and symbols; when the generator stumbled on the actual password, the account would be available. Hai Chock smiled when the first three and then the first ten numbers were generated, and nothing happened: *at least they don't have a system which shuts you out if you do not get the password the first few times.* As he was bouncing his instructions around at least a dozen servers around the world, the servers of The Shadow Experts, being shut off would have simply made the task more complicated, not impossible. He would have had to repeat the operation with a different combination of server routings.

It took him a full six hours, and literally billions of tries to get into the account. His main challenge was that he did not know how many characters the password would have. Neither did he know whether the password would or would not include solely letters or solely digits; it could be a mix of both, or all of either. A more sophisticated variant, which he was ready to use if the first efforts did not work, would have included all symbols available on a regular computer keyboard. Eventually, he stumbled on "110Mao49." He kicked himself. *You idiot, you could have saved yourself a lot of time. Mao Zedong declared the creation of the People's Republic of China on October 1, 1949. Why didn't you try that first?*

He took a brief look around the account and whistled when he discovered that the account showed a balance of nearly nine hundred million dollars. He thought: *I need to contact Countess Renate immediately.*

■ ■ ■ ■ ■

"Countess Renate?"

"Yes, Hai Chock . . . What's new?"

"Got into the account . . ."

"Super . . ."

"Not a big one . . ."

"Really?" she said with some disappointment in her voice. Hai Chock laughed out loud and came clean. He said:

"Yeah . . . Just short of a billion bucks."

"Oh. My God . . ."

They both laughed. Countess Renate added:

"Let's not do anything quite yet. But could you prepare an attack to get some of that money out of the account in the near term? I'd love for us to be able to act quite quickly when we're ready to pull the trigger."

"Sure. I'll first have to figure out what transaction level arouses suspicion there. In particular, is there some automatic mechanism? Whatever we do, we surely don't want to trigger that. Once I know what to avoid, I'll write a program to generate transactions just below that threshold. I'll route them all through multiple channels to the account in Austria . . . It'll take them forever to figure out where the money went."

"The account we use to donate to charities, obviously, not ours . . ."

"Obviously."

"Wouldn't it be ironic if a part of the hidden reserves of the Chinese Communist Party went to help the International Red Cross and the Red Crescent, and Malteser International . . . To me, they're the only relief agencies that truly don't mix politics in their work."

Renate was referring to two large organizations. Both organizations work without concern for race, religion or political affiliation; their point is to help those who need it most. The International Red Cross and Red Crescent Movement are quite well known, with nearly one hundred million people working or volunteering for it. The red cross or red crescent on a white background are internationally recognized symbols. Malteser International may be less well-known, though it is still quite an active organization. It is the worldwide humanitarian relief agency of the Sovereign Order of Malta. Countess Renate always added Malteser when thinking of charities dedicated to disaster relief, as her family had a long tradition of supporting the work and the charism of the Order through the centuries.

Countess Renate then called Simon to brief him on the development. He replied:

"Excellent, Countess. What are your plans now?"

"We'll draw monies out of the account and give them to charity . . ."

Simon did not reply right away. He paused for a minute. . . He hesitated, but then told the Countess that he was not sure that her idea was "quite right," adding:

"We may disagree with their political system, but we can't steal their money . . . Can we?"

Countess Renate agreed and reassured Simon that it was never her intention to steal any money, adding:

"The point is to compromise Xi further . . ."

"Well, either he's rogue, and he may already be dead, or he is official . . . In that case, we would be punishing the Chinese for an inhuman act of terrorism."

"I see your point, Countess, but there's a pretty thin line there . . . Anyway, it's not my responsibility . . . I'd rather never know what happened to the money."

"Understood, Simon."

CHAPTER.35

TEL AVIV, ISRAEL

Mark Levi finally believed that his role in this adventure had come to an end. In fact, a pause in the action might have been a better phrase. David had allowed him to move back to his own apartment from the one that he occupied as Anwar. And life was starting to look normal again.

Ever since his return from the overseas part of the mission, his relationship with Debbie had moved dramatically forward. Realizing that he was as much of a *Mossad* agent as she had been, if not in fact more directly implicated in dangerous actions, Debbie opened up some more about her past. In particular, she had shared with Mark that she had been a deep-cover *Mossad* agent in Iran. He was stunned:

"You, a spy?"

"Yes, darling. A spy. An undercover spy, but a spy, nevertheless. My last mission worked out very well, but it killed the love of my life . . ."

Mark winced as he heard these words. He thought: *Does it mean I am not?* Yet, he refrained from interrupting her. She continued:

"Until I met you . . ."

Mark breathed a big sigh of relief. She explained the circumstances of her loss without attaching all the blame to Farid. She clearly felt she could have prevented his treason and suicide, if she only had known and talked to him. At the same time, she had to concede that she was not the one who had chosen a national loyalty over his loyalty to his fiancée. Mark was very supportive and tried to make her feel more comfortable:

"Eventually, you need to let go of that guilt. Otherwise, it will eat you up."

He further suggested that they should let bygones be bygones and focus on the future. Debbie asked:

"Does Simon know about me?"

"I assume you mean you and me. Certainly not from me."

"Well, you know, it would be fun to reconnect. Who knows, I might be helpful again."

■ ■ ■ ■ ■

The phone rang. It was David Heller calling Mark:

"Hey, sorry to bother you, but I have an important question for you."

"Shoot . . ."

"How do you read Ismail?"

"What do you mean? I could write a volume on him . . ."

"I know, poorly phrased question. Sorry. Where does he stand? Could he come across or is he really one of them?"

"Why does it matter? We have access to his computer and to theirs. Why do we need him?"

"An indicator . . . Eventually, we're going to bomb Raqqa. Want to hit as much of the ISIS leadership as we can . . . By the way, have you heard of the bombing of the refugee camp?"

"What bombing?"

David went on to relate what he knew had happened in Raqqa. Though *Mossad* had only limited knowledge, they had been told that people had died both of Sarin gas contamination and of infection with some unknown virus. "What the hell is that?"

"Well, Mark, we have been thinking about that for quite a while. In the end, the most likely explanation is that they started doubting Choi and the North Koreans when the bomb that exploded in Johannesburg resulted in no reported deaths. We assume that they believed that Choi had to have shared his virus with someone else and that the someone had found the antibodies. Also, they wondered whether the North Koreans gave them flasks with fake sarin gas as well. So, the only way to be sure was to explode a bomb and see what happened . . ."

"Got to accept that it might make sense from their twisted perspective, but still. All those innocent people . . ."

"Nothing surprises me from these butchers."

"Same here, I thought. But they just did. By the way, David, you were going to make a point when we diverged onto the refugee camp . . ."

"Yes . . . About Ismail, Sorry; got lost in the refugee camp disaster. We need someone inside ISIS to tell us when all or at least most of the bigwigs are there. Also, they keep changing location within Raqqa, or at least that's what we hear. We could use someone to flag the exact time and the exact location . . ."

Mark explained that he viewed Ismail as a loyal member of the group. At the same time, he thought that Ismail was also prone to fear. He had seen it in his eyes when they recently had discussed the idea that both he and Mark were expendable. He concluded:

"I think that he needs a real scare if we want to even consider bringing him onside . . ."

"Any thought?"

Mark suggested that this might be the right time to produce the real Anwar's body. He knew that *Mossad* had partially embalmed it and placed it in a coffin. Yet, he had not been buried. He thought that it might be a good thing for an anonymous phone call to tell Ismail that someone would drop the body of Anwar by his apartment. In fact,

Ismail might suggest a better drop off place. Mark added:

"But, at any rate, the idea that Anwar was dead might remind him of the conversation he had with me. I had told him we were both expendable. Now he is told I am dead. Might scare him silly. A phone call to offer to talk to him after that shock would be a good way to test then whether he was ready or not . . ."

"Who should call him?"

"Obviously, it can't be me. How could I be dead and on the phone at the same time?"

David asked:

"What do you suggest?"

"Well, I shouldn't be the one that calls about Anwar's body. It's got to be someone else. We'll see how he reacts. My guess is that he'll panic."

"But who, if not you?"

"You or anybody else. It doesn't matter. Well, wait a tick. Probably best that it isn't you. Whoever you pick from the team can do it."

"Fine. Then what?"

Mark thought for a short while and said. The next phone call after he has disposed of Anwar's coffin could be from you."

"Why me? Well, you could say that you would like to help him . . ."

"You know . . . I like the beginning of your plan, but not the end. Assume it's not me, but you that makes the second call."

"But I'm dead . . ."

"No. You're not. Because you come out and tell him that we played him all along."

"Think about it. He would have to be mad at the manipulation, but that could well make him fear even more any form of retaliation."

"I see . . . You think that he would now fear even more for his life, if we leaked to ISIS that he screwed up the mission, then he would really be deep in it . . . Am I close?"

"Not close . . . Right on target my friend."

"Well, OK. Makes sense. I could do it. But Debbie and I are on a week off. Any chance I can enjoy that holiday?"

"You should enjoy it. Being disturbed by one phone call would not be the end of the world . . . Would it?"

Mark grudgingly agreed that he would do it.

■ ■ ■ ■ ■

Mark and Debbie's relationship had progressed to the point where they were spending quite a bit of free time together. While they had not yet moved into a common apartment, they were quite intimate. When David called, they were booked into a hotel in the Negev desert. They hoped to catch up on the time they had missed while Mark was traveling through Europe, and ever earlier while he was in the Jaffa Mossad apartment playing the role of Anwar. They could not see each other then, and the short phone call from Mark's toilets did not do the trick. They were enjoying their time together.

The prior evening, in fact, they had found themselves reminiscing of their first night together. Both agreed that neither had planned for something to happen that particular night. It just did. They were celebrating the six months since they had met. They had had a great dinner at Kukiza; one of the highest rated, traditional, Israeli food restaurants in Tel Aviv. That it was a bit more expensive that many others did not seem to matter. After all, it was meant to be a celebration. They ate, drunk and had a wonderful time. Minoo invited Mark to have a night cap at her apartment, adding:

"I don't have a lot of choice, but I am sure I have some arak."

Arak is an omnipresent drink through the Middle East. It is traditionally made of only two ingredients, grapes and aniseed. Aniseeds are the seeds of the anise plant, and when crushed, their oil provides Arak with a slight licorice taste. In truth, however, one could argue that variants on the theme are present throughout the Mediterranean Basin, including the famous Pastis liquor in France,

Sambuca in Italy or Ouzo in Greece to name but a few.

They had enjoyed that drink sitting on Minoo's couch, facing her television set in the living room. One thing led to another and they found themselves first on the floor on the living room rug, and a while later sharing the same bed. Both had not had sex, since they had lost their erstwhile partners. The wine at dinner, the Arak afterwards and the growing love which they clearly shared had chased away inhibitions. Possibly for the first time, they were finally free from the past and ready to contemplate the future together.

■ ■ ■ ■ ■

Back in their resort room in the Negev, Mark's phone rang:

"Mark, David here . . . Anwar's body was delivered. Ismail was all over the place. We told him the coffin was closed and he could not look inside. He believes it's you. He seemed quite worried . . . In fact, he was indeed more worried than sad, or at least that's what Dan, the person who called him and delivered the coffin said. Maybe, it's time for you to call him."

Mark agreed. He spoke with Debbie about the call and she helped him prepare himself. Then, he called Ismail, using Anwar's phone.

"Ismail here . . ."

"Well, my friend, it's me, but I'm not who you thought I was."

"Anwar what is this. They've told me you're dead. We've buried you yesterday."

"Well, that's the point Ismail. You did bury Anwar . . . But I never was Anwar."

"But . . . Who are you then?"

"Hold onto your seat and prepare to be surprised. I work for *Mossad*. Your friend Anwar has been dead for a while. That's probably why they must have told you that the coffin could not be opened."

Ismail replied with a weak voice:

"They did."

Mark continued:

"We caught him as he dropped the bomb at Ben Gurion Airport."

"How can this be? You placed a whole bunch of bombs for us."

"True, but what you do not know is that we exchanged the dangerous flasks for inoffensive ones. Many of the bombs are there, but they can hardly do any damage. Plus, a few of the bombs are not even where the computer says they are."

"Don't believe it."

Mark said a few words in Hebrew, giving an additional couple of details to Ismail. Ismail was speechless. His mind was racing. In fact, he was thinking of what the consequences would be if it was discovered that the bombs were inoffensive and that he, Ismail, had helped *Mossad* play that trick. What could he do to Mark to keep him quiet? A few seconds later, he was smiling interiorly, thinking Mark could not see it. Mark then added:

"By the way, I would strongly advise you against sharing any of this with anyone."

Ismail replied:

"I won't. But one piece of advice calls for another one. While on the mission in Bern . . . Remember, you called your girlfriend once from a place where we were able to listen in. Better yet, we were able to trace the call. You would not want anything bad to happen to Deborah Massler or her father Maximillian, would you? I suggest we meet and talk about the future together."

Mark suddenly felt his blood freeze in his body. The idyll with Debbie was going very well. Now, it could be upended. He told Ismail that they should meet to discuss. Ismail promised to call him soon with the details.

CHAPTER.36

AUSTRIA, SINGAPORE AND TEL AVIV, ISRAEL

Countess Renate had called a video conference to discuss the next steps in North Korea. Present on the call were Hai Chock, Simon, David and herself. She opened the conversation:

"As we all know, we've been able to penetrate Choi Jae-Jin's computer. The email address he had given to Hans Koerig was his personal address, suggesting that he was already planning—or at least considering—to double cross his employers, given the right offer."

Hai Chock added:

"Yes. It's unfortunate it did not give me direct access to his office files. Yet, he was sufficiently imprudent to send emails back and forth between his office and personal addresses. So, in the end, I am able to work in both spaces . . ."

"Wonderful work, Hai Chock."

"Hey, all in a day's work, Countess."

Simon saw the opening for him to discuss what he was hoping could next be done. He explained that it was probably not feasible to access anything in Choi's lab from a physical standpoint, given what Colonel Kim of the South Korean secret services had told him. Thus, he could only think of one route, explaining it thus:

"We need to find a way both to discredit him and to make the North Korean believe that his work was worthless . . ."

Countess Renate countered:

"Wait a second, Simon. They know that the virus is deadly, don't they? They've had people die there, correct?"

"Absolutely, Countess. I misspoke. We need to make the North Korean think that whatever is left in files or even in the lab is worthless . . ."

"Now I understand. How do you think we should move?"

Simon explained that, in his view, and, giving credit to David, whose idea it originally was, he could imagine three different threads. The first involved a systematic cleaning of all files that could be accessed both on the personal and the office server. Hai Chock reacted:

"That should not be too hard, but I'm going to need some outside help."

Countess Renate asked him why, and he replied that the names of the files would probably be in Korean; he surely did not speak the language. Countess Renate volunteered to bring Armand and his friend Dr. Park in the loop, adding:

"I hope North and South Koreans speak the same language." David surprised everyone, Simon included,

"They do and they don't. In written form, the differences are minor, though North Korea officially used the Munhwaŏ dialect, while the South Korean stuck to standard Korean. Where the differences are greater is in terms of pronunciation. The South Korean standard pronunciation is based on the dialect as spoken in Seoul. The North Korean standard pronunciation is based on the dialect as spoken in Pyongyang."

"How in the world did you learn that, David?"

"Don't know. I recently looked it up on the Internet. Don't know why, but it stuck with me."

"You never cease to amaze me, my friend."

Countess Renate cut to the chase:

"Well that settles the point. Dr. Park or someone else agreeable to Armand can help. So, what's the plan?"

Before replying to the question, Simon felt he needed to add an important point:

"With respect, Countess, shouldn't we spend a bit more time on this? Armand is indeed an obvious solution. Yet, I can think of at least a couple of other alternatives. First, *Mossad* has Korean speakers. We could use one of these people, couldn't we?"

"Great suggestion, Simon . . . Anyone else?"

"Well, yes. What about Kim Dae Jung. I have been in contact with him directly, thanks to Armand and Dr. Park."

They went around for a while and eventually settled on the solution of using one of *Mossad*'s own agents. It surely allowed the operation to remain as secret as it should be. More importantly, as Simon added:

"Do we really want Armand to feel that he has helped sign a guy's death warrant? He's a scientist, not a secret agent . . ."

Countess Renate conceded. With that agreed, Simon replied to Renate's earlier question on the plan. He would start wiping out files on the office server, suggesting:

"I would bet that Choi is the principal user of these files. I can't believe he would ring the alarm bell right away. Then, we should move to his home server . . ."

He argued that the goal would be to remove anything that was in any way related to Choi's research work, adding,

"Wouldn't mind it, if copies were made before erasing the files."

"Obviously," was all Countess Renate could add, while Hai Chock confirmed that it would not be difficult at all.

Simon described a second step which would require Hai Chock to manage to send an email to Choi's office email from some fake overseas address. He suggested that anywhere he would be expected to seek asylum would be possible, though he would shy away from the

U.S. for the obvious reasons and from China as they still did not know what role Xi was playing. He added:

"We've got to assume that his email is bugged. This should reinforce the initial North Korean suspicion triggered by Hans Koerig's initial request for instructions."

He paused and asked Renate:

"By the way, do we know whether Choi ever replied to Koerig, after he had received the documents "proving" that he had opened an account?"

"Actually, I do not. Let me make a note to call him . . ."

Simon went on to outline the third and final step:

"Finally, could Hai Chock manage for Choi's server to send a reply to the email he would just have sent him? In that email, Choi would say to his supposed overseas contact that everything is in order; that he had erased all files on his server and on the office's. It should also add that whatever is left in the lab is worthless and fake; it is aimed at pointing people in the wrong direction . . ."

Renate could not contain herself:

"Simon, that's Machiavellian . . . The poor guy's death sentence."

Simon had to concede that this would likely be the outcome. He in fact surprised everyone with his next comment:

"My only worry is that they are careless in disposing of what is left in the lab. In fact, it would still contain the deadly virus. Many people could be infected and die."

Countess Renate noted that the thought was kind, but that people who work in those laboratories and manufacture the kind of biological weapons they do shouldn't expect nor ask for a lot of leniency.

Countess Renate's next call was to Hans Koerig who confirmed that he had not heard from Choi since he had sent the email.

Renate paused and mused:

"Wonder what this means."

Hans Koerig had no useful answer, leaving Renate to ask whether he was sure that the email had been received. Hans replied that he had not flagged it and could therefore not be sure. They agreed that Hans would resend the email and, this time, flag it so that they could know whether or not the email had been read. They know that no one is forced to allow the sender to see that an email had been accessed, but flagging it increases the chances.

The one worry in Countess Renate's mind was that Choi might already have been arrested. She was concerned that the plan they just agreed with Simon, David and Hock Chai was based on the critical assumption that Choi could freely send an email. Without that, who would believe the last email which Simon had indicated could have been sent by Choi, if he was already dead or at least in prison?

She called Simon back right away:

"Simon, just thought of one possible problem."

"Yes?"

"What if Choi has already been arrested?"

"Holy Moly, darn right! That destroys the disinformation part of the effort. How can we find out?"

"I've got two ways. The first is in train: Hans will resend the earlier email providing the account opening documents. But, this time, he will flag it. With any luck, Choi, if he is alive and receives it, may agree to send a receipt. Even better, he might even reply . . ."

"And if he doesn't?"

"Well, the ball is now in your court."

"My court? What do you mean?"

"You did say that you had a relationship with Colonel Kim Dae Jung, right?"

"Right."

"Well, any chance you could ask him to find out?"

"We can always try. But I'm not sure how they would do it . . . I'll get back to you."

Simon's next call was to Colonel Kim who, thankfully, was working late that evening, his time:

"Colonel Kim, Simon Rabinowitz here . . ."

"Ah. Colonel Rabinowitz. How can I help?"

"We really need to know whether Choi has been arrested or not."

"Why is that important, my friend?"

"We are planning to plant some disinformation through him, but the effort is worthless if he is already in jail."

"Don't understand. Can you tell me more?"

"Let me just say that we need for people to believe that he sent an email. We assume that he would not have access to email in jail."

"Got it. Don't know how successful we'll be, but we surely can try. How long do I have? When do you need an answer?"

"Yesterday."

"I see. I see. Well, I'll get right to it. I'll call you as soon as I have anything . . .

CHAPTER.37

The first thing Mark did after talking to Ismail was to discuss the situation with Debbie, aka Minoo. In many ways, he was delighted that she had shared about her past, as he was sure that they could review the situation calmly and professionally.

Debbie's first reaction was to think of her father: "Could we find a way to relocate him temporarily?"

"I'm pretty sure we can, but that will have to involve Simon."

"Well, I was telling you I would like to see him again. Didn't think it would come that quickly . . ."

They went around the major questions they needed to be ready to discuss and then called David, asking him to organize an urgent call with them that would include Simon. David asked:

"What's up Mark? Did you talk to Ismail?"

"I did and the news has some very worrisome components. Can we get Simon on the line; it'll save me having to repeat myself."

David was surprised at Mark's reaction. He was clearly a bit flustered and that was not in his make-up. He called Simon who made himself immediately available.

"Mark? Simon here? What's up?"

"Well, let me first bring someone on the picture."

As the call was using Zoom, Simon could suddenly see Minoo's face in the picture. He exclaimed:

"Minoo? Or should I say Debbie?"

"Either will work, Simon. Good to see you . . ."

"OK, guys, let me assume that you haven't called to tell me you're getting married."

Mark and Debbie had a good chuckle, though the look on their faces told Simon he might not be terribly far from reality. Mark added: "No. You're right. I'm bringing up Debbie because Ismail threatened to hurt her and her father if I did not cooperate."

"How can that be?"

"Well, it turns out that one of the calls I made to Debbie while I was in Europe was picked up and traced . . ."

"Oh. Shit. How?"

"Honestly? Don't know. It can't have been in the apartment as I only spoke from the toilets. If they had picked it up there, they would also have found out about all our calls with you, with David and even with other colleagues."

"That's good. I follow. But from where?"

"I've got to assume that they had a way of listening in when I was in a hotel room, or in the car. Can't imagine how. But I only called Debbie from the car once and otherwise from hotel rooms."

"I've got to assume it was from your car. You picked your hotels at the last minute, didn't you?"

"Sure did . . ."

"So, they wouldn't have had the opportunity to bug the room. Plus, if they had bugged a room, they would know more. Back to your earlier argument with respect to the apartment. So, it's got to be from the car."

"That would be when I gassed the car up in Bordeaux. I made a quick call from the outside of the car while the pump was going."

"Look no further. Well, that's a tough lesson, but it's a good one." Simon then asked David what precautions were currently in place.

He replied that nothing was in place at present.

"Mark, any problem if we put you under surveillance?"

"Here? In the middle of the Negev desert?"

"Is that where you are?"

"Yep, not too far from Beersheba in fact."

"Having fun . . . Not too hot?"

Without waiting for an answer, he added:

"Any problem with a discrete tail?"

"I guess we don't have a choice" Mark replied after having looked at Debbie and seen her nodding. Yet, he added:

"We worry about Max, Debbie's father . . ."

"Debbie, can we contact him directly?"

"Sure. Why?"

"Can we ask him to allow us to move him for a short while?"

"He will ask why . . ."

"Can we say?"

"Not the whole bit. Tell him we have heard of an Iranian plot and want to move him to a safe place until we see what they have in mind."

"He'll be frightened."

"Probably, but less so than if you tell him the truth."

"Can see that."

They then discussed the obvious next steps. Simon would arrange for Debbie and Max to receive new cell phones, with their respective numbers on quick dial. She should not use hers nor should Max. Also, Mark would get another phone as well, but he should keep the old one, so that Ismail could still contact him. He asked:

"When are you coming back to Tel Aviv?"

"We were planning on next Sunday."

"OK. Let me find you a new place. I gather that you do not need multiple bedrooms at this point."

Mark objected and Minoo's face told Simon that she agreed with Mark, adding:

"Simon, that's personal . . ."

"Sorry, Minoo, I'm just being practical. I'm not prodding."

Simon had not hung up for more than a few minutes that he called Mark straight back:

"Do you know Ismail's number by heart?"

"Simon, why would you ask?"

"Tell you in a second . . . Do you?"

"Sure . . ."

"Good, mark it down and then smash Anwar's cell phone to pieces."

"Why?"

"Geolocation my friend. Geolocation. By the way, now look in the pieces of Anwar's cell phone. Anything abnormal?"

"Truth to tell, Simon, I've never looked at the insides of a cell phone . . . What do you mean?"

"Don't have the time now. Place the whole thing in a plastic bag and bring it back. Now, how did you get to Beersheba?"

"Drove my car."

"OK. I'm sending a helicopter to get you and Debbie. Someone will drive your car back. We'll bring you first to headquarters and then we'll find a place where you can continue your holiday. Where are you now, exactly?"

"We are at Desert Rose, a hotel near Ben Gurion's tomb."

The graves of David Ben Gurion and his wife Paula face the Tsin canyon and the Avdat highlands in the heart of the Negev. The views are simply breathtaking. Some people actually call the site the Israeli Grand Canyon, although, size-wise, they really do not compare. Less depth, fewer twists and turns and arguably fewer colors. Yet, it is hard not to think of the Grand Canyon when standing near the balustrade less than a hundred feet from the two tombstones. Near the site is the desert home which the former Prime Minister built in 1953. It remains a great tourist attraction.

Simon added:

"Please, do not ask any more questions. I suspect that you are already a target. They've traced you with Anwar's phone. Whether they plan to kill or kidnap you, they could already be on the way."

■ ■ ■ ■ ■

Mark and Debbie were escorted to Simon's office straight from the helicopter pad. Max, Debbie's father was there already.

"Good to see you safe and sound. All three of you." Mark could not resist:

"Simon, what took you?"

"The more I thought about it, the more I came to believe that the story of having caught one of your phone calls did not sound right."

"What do you mean?"

"It makes no sense Mark. First, you made other phone calls from your car, even if only one was made from outside. Second, if they wanted to use Debbie, sorry Minoo, as a hostage, they would have simply picked her up. Her name and picture are on the University Webpage . . . Plus, we didn't think you were tailed in Bordeaux."

He continued explaining that there was a much better explanation but added that it was one that Ismail could not reveal without making it useless looking forward. Mark had to ask:

"What are you talking about?"

"Well, remember Anwar's phone. Imagine that it has a geolocation feature. They could trace all your steps since you've been back. It's a good thing you did not come to the office with it . . ."

David interrupted:

"And it's a good thing that your initial monitoring was from a location away from headquarters . . ."

Mark could only say: "Oh My God . . ."

"You can say that again. Now, remember what you did prior to leaving for your shortened vacation?"

"Simple. I drove to Debbie's place. I picked her up and we both went to say goodbye to her dad."

"Look no further, my friend. They could easily have tracked you there. Then, they would have looked on the building directory . . . How many apartments do you believe have owners two of whom sharing the same name?"

Mark blurted out:

"That's why he did not know that she goes by Debbie and that her father by Max. Ismail used the names on the directory; she appears as Deborah Massler and Cyrus as Maximillian Massler. Bastards . . ."

Simon calmed his associates and, pointing to all three of them added:

"We need to find a different environment for you all. Debbie and Max, I am deeply sorry that *Mossad* is again causing you trouble, but it has to be done."

Debbie replied:

"I understand Simon. And I'm sure that Papa does as well. Now what do you mean by a different environment?"

Simon conceded that he had not thought that far. He offered the hospitality of *Mossad* in one of their few discrete apartments with permanent guards outside the door and down in the street, as a short-term measure, adding:

"By the way, I know this stinks. You two were looking for a holiday and Max was living in peace . . . Now you've got to live in a prison, a golden prison, but a prison nevertheless."

He explained that he wanted to keep them in Israel for a little while longer. Turning to Mark, he argued:

"I need you to be here to be able to get a phone call from Ismail. I'm hoping that he'll become more amenable to "discussions" once that contact is established and you have made it clear to him that he cannot do anything against you, Debbie or Max and you have explained that we can do a lot to hurt him. Should become docile as a little puppy."

He told Mark that he should send a message to Ismail telling him that he had lost Anwar's phone and giving him an alternative number on which he, Ismail, should call. Simon explained that the new number would be manned 24/7 by an agent located in *Mossad* headquarters. Any technique they could use to geolocate the phone, based on the number, would invariably point to the same address, *Mossad* headquarters, adding:

"And I bet they won't want to attack this building . . ."

He went on to explain that the agent had the facility to conference in Mark without anyone outside of him knowing Mark's number. Debbie beat Mark to the finish:

"Pretty smart, Simon. But then, so what?"

"Mark, am I correct believing that you do not have any living close relative in Israel?"

"Unfortunately, yes . . ."

"Well, I think we should probably buy you a year away from Israel unless you choose to make it permanent. Mark, we'll put you on a leave of absence with full salary. Debbie and Max, you unfortunately know the drill already . . ."

"We do" they said in unison.

CHAPTER.38

TEL AVIV, ISRAEL

Mark's new cell phone rang:

"Mark here . . ."

"So, your real name is Mark?"

"Well, hello, Ismail. What can I do for you?"

"Well, remember, we need to meet."

Mark had rehearsed this conversation with both David and Simon and then again with Debbie. They covered every possible angle they could conceive. He was ready to go from practice to performance.

"Well, Ismail. I remember that you told me we should meet. I'm simply not sure I want to meet you . . ."

"You wouldn't want any harm to come to Deborah or Maximillian, would you?"

"I certainly would not. But how are you going to find them?"

"We know where they live."

"I hate to correct you, Ismail. But the only thing you know is where they used to live . . ."

"Used to live?"

"Yes, my friend. Next time you want to use hostages, you need to take them before issuing the threat. As we speak, they are very safely hidden . . . In fact, I'm not even sure you could ever find them . . . You'd need to comb the globe."

"Bastard . . ."

Mark calmly explained to Ismail that *Mossad*'s reputation was well justified. He simply said:

"Simply look at what you did. Not what you told me you did. What you really did, including looking up the two names on the building directory . . ."

"Bastard . . ."

"You keep saying this, my friend. Let me tell you: it's tedious. Anyway, *Mossad* has figured out your game. And we've played the only counter move we could in the circumstances."

Ominously, for Ismail at least, he added:

"There is only one card left in our, *Mossad*'s, hand, and in your hand . . ."

"What do you mean?"

"Simple my friend. You help us and we'll protect you as well as we can. You don't and we'll let ISIS know what has actually happened with the bombs and all the rest . . . Then, goodbye Ismail, and for good."

Ismail hung up. Mark was not overly surprised. He would never have expected Ismail to go from what he thought was a position in which he held all the trump cards to one where he was at the short end of an ultimatum. He was sure that Ismail would call back, sooner or later.

Debbie, who had watched the conversation unfold, though she only heard one side of it was laughing:

"What a turn? He must be chafing like mad . . ."

"I'm pretty sure you're correct, honey. But this is still not a game. I want it resolved for good."

She could not disagree. Mark's next move was to call Simon to brief him. David happened to be in Simon's office at the time. Simon put Mark on the speakerphone. They congratulated Mark for having played the role as well as he did. They did argue that he should stick around for another day or two, just to be able to catch Ismail should he call. Simon added:

"Have you all thought of where you want to go?"

Mark gave a few thoughts which the three of them had agreed upon, but in the end added:

"We hope we can be somewhere that is safe and can allow at least Debbie and possibly me as well to work. A one-year vacation is way too long . . ."

"Not to worry. We already have a few ideas. The real difficulty will be for you, Mark. We do not want to expose you to any harm. Yet, at the same time, we would not want you to reveal anything about our operations . . ."

"How would I do that?"

"We've got to work on your profile to be sure that nobody can track whoever you will be back to Mark Levi . . ."

"Oh. I see. Good thinking, Simon. I guess I selfishly did not think of those risks. Maybe a desk job?"

"Quite possible, though harder in foreign locations. Call me when you have more that is if Ismail calls before you all take off."

■ ■ ■ ■ ■

Ismail did wait a full twenty-four hours before calling back. The agent at headquarters conferenced Mark in. Ismail was dismayed that he could still not get any trace of where Mark was other than at *Mossad* headquarters.

"So, Mark. What's the deal?"

"Well, Ismail, I would be happy to introduce you to a friend of mine. You still have the same cell phone number?"

"Yes."

"Can he call you?"

"Who is it?"

"Do you really care? Don't assume he'll give you his real name . . . And don't assume as well that he will use WhatsApp."

"What do you think he'll want?"

"Information, my friend. Information."

"About what?"

"I don't know. About the organization . . . who is where and who does what to whom? Honestly, Ismail, the list is endless."

"How can I be sure they'll protect me?"

"Hate to tell you that, but do you really have a choice?"

"Bastard . . ." was the last word Mark heard before Ismail hung up again.

■ ■ ■ ■ ■

David Heller called Ismail:

"Hello. You must be Ismail. I am a friend of Mark, the one you knew as Anwar . . ."

"That bastard . . ."

"Was only doing his job . . ."

"OK. So, hello. What can you do for me?"

"Funny, I was about to ask you the same question . . ."

David explained to Ismail that his situation was somewhere between catastrophic and hopeless. He therefore should accept the role of informer, providing *Mossad* with information on ISIS. At this point, he told him that the most interesting information concerned the whereabouts of the Calif and his immediate associates.

"Why would you want to know that? By the time I know and tell you, I'll bet he will have moved to another place."

"Well, Ismail, this is a beginning. So, the Calif moves often . . ."

"Sure does. There are so many hiding places there . . ."

"Where is there?"

Ismail stopped dead in his tracks. He realized that he was giving information away without getting anything in exchange and said so to David. David told Ismail that, at the outset, he did not need to worry, unless he thought he was already burned, which David argued he did not think he was. Ismail conceded that he was still on firm footing, although "losing" Anwar, aka Mark, would be viewed as a failure. David agreed that it might be if it was known, but asked:

"Does it have to be known?"

Ismail was lost for an instant. He could not follow the dialog. He knew he had lost track of Mark. How could that remain a secret was the top question on his mind. David explained, starting with a question:

"What did you expect from Mark, in exchange for leaving alone Deborah and Maximillian?"

David was careful to use the "official names" of Debbie and Max, thinking *we might still have some use for their usual names remaining secret a while longer.* Ismail replied:

"We wanted to know how he was able to fool us. Who had helped him? What he really knew? In short, we wanted to learn whether any part of our plan could still work . . ."

"Well, why can't I give you a few answers that you can pass onto whomever you must? . . ."

"They'll kill me if they find out . . ."

"Frankly, Ismail, they'll want to kill you anyway at some point. That's where we can help and protect you."

He added:

"But I am pretty sure that unless you goof up, they don't need to know the truth for a while. You are therefore safe until then . . ."

David could tell that Ismail was on the fence. He was clearly worried. The extent of his failure was becoming clearer as time passed and he found more snippets along the way. At the same time, he was equally frightened to "move to the other side." He blurted out:

"And if they don't get to me, they'll get to my wives and children. I have two sons. They're too young to be in the group, but I was grooming them."

"My friend, I know that this is hard. But let's be honest. You have some time. Use it wisely. You can relocate or at least send those people you absolutely want to protect on some trip. We can help you there, if that's what you need."

Ismail sounded more and more confused. In the end, David thought he needed a shock; so, he said:

"Tell you what. Call me on the number on which you used to call Mark. The operator will always know how to reach me. I can't make the decision for you. You've got to make it yourself. Good luck."

And he hung up. Ismail was left three-quarters broken to ponder his future. At this time, everything looked bleak to him. Could it really be that the only possible future had to include *Mossad*?

■ ■ ■ ■ ■

David called Simon with the diagnostic that Ismail was not a slam dunk. He might come around, but he seemed totally confused. David added that he could not tell where his loyalty or motivation were, though he did express some surprise that he thought of his family, particularly his sons. Simon replied that some additional pressure needed to be applied. He suggested that he would contact Countess Renate and revert to David when he had news.

"Countess Renate? Simon here . . ."

"Great to hear from you, Simon. What's up?"

"I think we need your help, more specifically, Hai Chock's help."

"To do what?"

Simon explained that he felt that some pressure needed to be placed on Ismail and that the way to do it was to have a few files disappear from his computer and from Raqqa's, adding:

"We do not need complete pandemonium. We need for him to see a few computer files disappear from his desktop or his server, whatever. I've got to bet that he will call some higher up to find out what's happening. The higher up will be surprised and tell him he would look into it. Looking into it, the higher up would find out that a few files had also disappeared from their own server . . ."

"I can imagine the rest, Simon. There are going to be a few nasty phone conversations between Ismail and headquarters . . ."

"He may even be asked to Raqqa . . ."

Countess Renate conceded that the plan was brilliant. Though she doubted, rightly as it turned out, that Ismail could be tailed deep into Syrian territory, there were many ways he could be put under surveillance. Simon was indeed betting that Ismail would make a call to David as soon as he had noticed the file problem on his computer. The balance of the scenario was absolutely obvious. David would organize an innocuous meeting; would give Ismail a phone on which he could call him directly; and that phone would have a geolocation feature which would point out precisely where he went in Raqqa. Renate objected:

"Simon, you told me that this is how they tracked Mark. Don't you believe they'll look for that?"

"Possible. But my bet is that he'll be so disoriented and frightened that he will not think of it. After all, we would love to see where he goes, but we're not ready to strike yet. So, knowing where the hierarchy is now is not our primary concern. This would only be a useful dry run . . ."

"Smart, Simon. Smart."

■ ■ ■ ■ ■

David's and Simon's plan turned out to work exactly as expected, at least with respect to Ismail. He did notice that a dozen files had disappeared, one of which was the file that allowed him to see the world map with the location of the bombs he now knew were inoffensive. He called Raqqa and asked why they had removed the files from his computer. His associates were dumbfounded when confronted with the question, having played no part in the disappearance. They promised to investigate.

Ismail then called David and told him of the problem. David feigned total ignorance and agreed to meet Ismail in front of the building where Mark used to live. David was careful both to wear a Kevlar jacket and to have reinforcements around him if he needed them. Ismail seemingly came alone. He was in a state of near panic. David calmed him and offered to give him a phone with direct access to him. The phone would still go through Mossad headquarters, but there would be no operator, allowing Ismail to believe that it was a direct line to David, who had introduced himself as Moshe Felder. Ismail did not seem to think of the possible trap and took the phone.

He used it less than two hours later to tell Moshe, aka David, that he had been recalled to headquarters, adding:

"They, too, have lost files. They want to discuss the whole thing . . ."

"Would not worry about it, Ismail. Remember that Mark had told you that both yours and Raqqa's computers had been hacked. It's the hackers at work in my view. Simply agree with them to trash the two servers and replace them with two others. Just make sure you transfer all files before you switch to the new ones. You would not want to lose everything?"

For the first time, Ismail allowed himself to smile. He truly believed that Moshe was trying to help him. Little did he know that the process recommended by David would simply transfer the files and the viruses from the old to the new computers. Hai Chock would retain control of those servers, but Ismail might look like a local hero.

CHAPTER.39

TEL AVIV, ISRAEL, AUSTRIA AND SEOUL, SOUTH KOREA

"Colonel Rabinowitz? Kim here."

"Great to hear your voice. So, what's the news on Choi?"

"Well, by all accounts I could get, he is still a free man . . . He's been seen by at least one person we know."

"Wonderful. Thank you very much. By the way, while I've got you on the line, where do we stand on Chen?"

"Ah. Well, there is every indication that Chen is acting from an official position. Nobody has picked up any sign that he has been sidelined. In fact, someone noted that he was standing closer to the Supreme Leader in a recent ceremony. So, I would assume that he is judged to have carried out the mission well."

"OK, excellent. Thanks a million."

Simon's next call was to Countess Renate. He had two messages and a question for her.

The first message was to tell her that Choi had seemingly not been arrested. The original plan stood, and it was time to start the execution. She asked Simon to hold. She called Hai Chock right away and instructed him to start the process. Returning to the line with

Simon, she asked for the next piece of news. Simon brought her up to date regarding Chen Hei Woo. Renate was not surprised:

"That's what we expected all along, wasn't it?"

"Can't say I disagree with you . . . But I find it truly disgusting that a regime such as that one could do that. Really . . ."

Simon paused but Countess Renate did not take the opportunity to add anything. Simon then turned to his question:

"Have we found out anything more on Xi Quan Ji?"

Renate had to concede that she had not heard from her contact in China. She promised to call him as soon as the time zones worked and to talk to Simon afterwards.

The next morning, Countess Renate was on the phone to Simon again:

"Well, the news on Xi is not totally clear. But indications are not great for his future . . ."

"You mean he was rogue?"

"Not totally sure. My friend tells me that he has not been seen or heard of, since the news of the money on the Austrian bank account came out. I told him of the request to move money to a different account. He calmly and gently explained to me that anyone in a position of power could have sent the email. In fact, he argued that he was not even sure that Xi was still alive."

Simon asked whether Hans had ever gotten a reply from Xi. Renate chided him:

"Simon, my friend, the last time we had that conversation you told me you did not want to know. Why do you want to know now?"

"*Touché*, Countess. I do not need to know, do I?"

"No, you don't."

CHAPTER.40

TEL AVIV, ISRAEL, AUSTRIA, TOKYO, JAPAN AND PARIS, FRANCE

"Armand-san, Oshima here . . ."

"Great to hear from you, Oshima-san. I have great news to report."

"Well, so do I, Armand-San."

Armand was so excited that he did not pick up on Oshima-san's opening. He wanted to discuss the latest results of the human testing of the antibodies. The test had proven both that a cocktail of the two antibodies worked better than either taken individually and that there were so far no adverse reactions on humans. He concluded:

"We may have both a vaccine and a therapy for those already infected . . . But we are far from completing all the tests and getting the required regulatory approvals. Until that time, we should not say anything."

"Totally agreed. This is wonderful. You must know that our own work is producing virtually the same results. We have noted that mixing antibody A with antibody B in a 40/60 percent proportion generates optimal results."

"What do you gain?"

"Faster reactions to the infection and fewer side effects . . ."

"Interesting, we only worked with 50/50 cocktails here . . . Which side-effects have you neutralized?

"Nausea which occurs in about one in five victims. Also, we found that the incidence of migraine headaches is also significantly reduced."

"Quite interesting. These two have different causes and affect different parts of the human system."

"True, but migraine headaches are known to cause vomiting or nausea . . . So, there could well be a link."

"This is powerful stuff. Have you tried all possible combinations?"

"Frankly not. One, we have to try it on humans and we really do not have enough double-blind experiments to try more than a couple of proportions. Second, we really want to understand, technically and chemically, what is causing the improvement. Once we know that, we might use mathematical models to seek the optimal combination, and then, finally, test it. Lots of work to do still . . ."

"Totally agree. Should we discuss how our two labs can work together on that?"

"I can't see why not. I'll bring Tomioka-San. You probably will need one of the two colleagues you introduced me to."

"Sure."

Oshima-san added:

"By the way, Armand-San, we are now associates . . ."

"How?"

Armand paused a minute and beamed:

"In The Shadow Experts? Really? This is wonderful news, Oshima-San. I hope we will get to work together often."

CHAPTER.41

TEL AVIV, ISRAEL

Ismail called Moshe, aka David, on his safe line as soon as he was back from Raqqa. He explained to him that the questioning he had undergone there was not very pleasant, though, in the end, it turned out OK. As he put it:

"At the outset, the senior leaders I met seemed convinced that I was part of a plot. I asked them why and how. They replied that I was the only other person whose computer was being bugged."

"Did you tell them you had warned them?"

"Yes, I did. I reminded them of the problem which Anwar, I mean Mark, had showed we had. I even reminded them that Farouk Abboud ben Malouf, one of them, was with me when Anwar demonstrated that there was a problem."

"What did they say?"

"Farouk was there, so they asked him. He could only confirm what I just said."

"They still don't know that Anwar was not Anwar?"

"No. No. Absolutely not."

"So, what happened next?"

"They shifted their stance and asked what I thought could be done . . ."

"Excellent. Did you tell them what we'd agreed?"

"Yes."

"And?"

"They agreed that it would make sense."

"So?"

"We have other servers in the Raqqa area. So someone brought two new ones. They looked as we transferred the files from the old to the new . . ."

"And?"

"They also asked me to do the same with my server, which I had brought with me."

"Good. Good. Then?"

"They launched the servers. Clearly, the files that were lost were lost, but all the others are still there."

"So, they let you drive back to Tel Aviv."

"Well, they did, but my mission is to shut this office down and move to Damascus."

"Why Damascus?"

"They don't want everyone in Raqqa . . ."

Ismail added that he was able to stop by his village and see his family. He told them to pack their things and move to Damascus, to the address that the senior leaders had given him. David asked:

"So, your family is safe?"

"Well, safe for as long as I am safe. But they all know where to find them and me. So, we'll need to find some other solution."

"Understood, Ismail. Now, I need you to tell me where the three or four major hiding places in Raqqa are located."

"Here it comes . . ."

"Hey, wasn't that part of the bargain?"

"Yes. But how can I be sure?"

"You can't, but you can trust me. I've helped you deal with the computer problem, didn't I?"

"You did."

They agreed to meet later that afternoon in a safe location which David had chosen. Ismail was worried that he might be under surveillance. David told him that there was no need to worry. The place he had chosen had a discrete exit where he would be picked up and driven to *Mossad* headquarters. Nobody could possibly follow him. He would be brought back to the initial location when the meeting was over, adding:

"Nobody will know that you didn't stay there the whole time."

"What if I am confronted?"

"I'll give you a story. Don't worry." David paused. He then casually asked:

"How many cell phones do you have?"

"Well, two. The one I'm calling you on and which you gave me, and my other one . . ."

"Do not take your other phone with you when you come to meet me."

"Why?"

"I'd bet that it is bugged and that they can see where you are . . ."

"I'd forgotten about that. Funny, that's what we did with Mark and it didn't occur to me that they could do the same thing to me. You're really trying to be my friend, aren't you Moshe."

■ ■ ■ ■ ■

David had in fact slightly changed the plans when Ismail arrived at the agreed upon shop. He had decided against having Ismail come to *Mossad* headquarters. The risk was too high, in his mind, that Ismail carried some other bug which might give the whole plan away. Rather, he arrived with a driver and a bodyguard in a black Mercedes minibus, with heavily tinted glasses in the rear compartment. It sat four people, with the middle row of seats, among the three generally available, being used as a kind of a table.

He showed Ismail a few recent satellite pictures of the Raqqa area and asked him to point out the locations of interest. Ismail was initially surprised that the bus was not moving. David explained to him why he had made the decision to stay there and suggested to him, when he returned to his apartment, to undress totally and check each piece of clothing quite carefully, adding:

"Let me know if you find anything that shouldn't be there . . ."

Ismail looked quite concerned, but David simply told him that the precautions might not be needed. Yet, as he put it:

"Our job is to imagine the imaginable. Staying one step ahead of the enemy is much easier than having to confront it with guns blazing." Ismail pointed to four locations that he knew were routinely used.

David whistled when he looked at them on the map. First, they looked totally innocuous. And second, they were almost always located near people concentrations, commenting:

"It's not a joke. These guys use civilians as shields. Talk of cowards."

Ismail did not respond. The issue simply had never occurred to him. He was probably beginning to have second thoughts about the leaders and the revolution he was supporting. Yet, deeper in his head, was the combination of strong religious faith and fear of reprisals which had hitherto kept him totally committed.

Minutes after having helped Ismail out of the minibus and back into the shop, David was on the phone to Simon.

"We have the information we needed. These bastards are hiding near places where civilians congregate. We knew it was the case, but I, for one, always hoped that was not totally true."

"You know, David, we do not fight the way they do. They're what they are. Let's not allow them to get into our heads. Harboring any sort of judgment about them is like giving them rent-free space in our brains. Let's do what we need to do?"

"So, what do you have in mind?"

Simon explained the plan to David, at least in its broad strokes, telling him that more would be forthcoming when they were face-to-face.

Simon next called Jack Turnbull from the CIA. He told him that Mossad needed their help to strike a blow, which hopefully would be the final one on ISIS.

"I'll see what I can do . . ."

■■■■■

Within twenty-four hours, the CIA had focused two geosynchronous satellites on the Raqqa area and set up a special focus on the four sites which Ismail had identified. Three days later:

"Simon, Frank here."

"What's up?"

"Don't know if those are the only sites, but there seems to be regular traffic among them."

"Any recurring pattern?"

"Not really. Well . . . Maybe one. Most of the time, it's a single car shuttling between two posts. Occasionally, you have a convoy."

"Ah. Very interesting. Always at around the same time?"

"Well, yes and no. Usually either morning or evening. Rarely during the day."

"Could it be when one or several bigwigs move for or from the night?"

"Exactly what I assumed, but we don't have enough data points to draw that conclusion yet . . ."

Simon thanked Jack and asked to be kept up to date. On his side, he said he would be coordinating a couple of drone missions which would be used to trigger the bombing. Simon, with Ariel's and the War Cabinet's concurrence, had indeed decided that the bombing would be done surreptitiously and with no direct attribution to Israel. Ostensibly, suspicions would directly point to Israel, but Simon and the Israeli government wanted to ensure that nothing could be traced to them through photos or any other form of reporting.

His idea was to use very high-flying, Kovesh drones, which were RQ-170 Sentinel drones Israel had bought from the U.S. and enhanced, in part with features that made then stealthy. They would drop laser guided bombs. Guidance would be provided by Eitan drones that would be shining a laser beam onto the target or targets. Eventually, the bombs dropped from fifty-thousand feet by the Koveshes that were not more than twenty yards in width and thus not visible from the ground unless one knew exactly where to look, would lock onto the laser beams and follow them down to the target.

Further, in order to avoid civilian casualties to the maximum possible extent, Simon was planning for the bombing to occur at night, when the bulk of the population was asleep and thus away from places such as schools or markets. This, combined with the inherent precision of the bombs themselves, should ensure that casualties would only be recorded within the one structure they were targeting with each bomb.

■ ■ ■ ■ ■

As he was completing the review of his plan, Simon all of a sudden had a major doubt. He needed David to find out one more crucial piece of information from Ismail.

CHAPTER.42

TEL AVIV, ISRAEL, SEOUL, SOUTH
KOREA AND AUSTRIA

Renate called Simon with an important piece of news:

"Simon? I just heard from my friend in China. It does look like Xi was in fact arrested and is about to be tried in what they call an open court."

"Ah. That's important. It is bound to be picked up by the press . . ."

"And they will reveal the plot . . ."

"You're right. I'm pretty sure they had him thoroughly "questioned" and therefore know the North Korean connection . . ."

"More importantly, they know of the virus."

Countess Renate and Simon felt that they needed to speed up their campaign. From Renate's standpoint, this involved making sure that the public was not unduly alarmed. Armand and his colleagues would need to make some sort of announcement. From Simon's point of view, it meant that he could no longer wait for the absolutely ideal moment to hit ISIS headquarters in Raqqa. They agreed to carry out their respective missions and to keep in as close touch as possible to ensure perfect coordination.

■ ■ ■ ■ ■

"Armand? Countess Renate here?"

"Wonderful to hear from you. What can I do for you?"

Countess Renate explained the situation to Armand, with the plea that some sort of announcement be carried out with respect to dealing with the virus. They discussed a few options in great detail and agreed that Armand was going to take care of the work. He congratulated Countess Renate on hiring Oshima-San, to which she replied:

"Thank you for the introduction, Armand."

Armand had a lengthy conference call with Tomioka-san and Oshima-san. They agreed that they would not disclose the original discovery made by the Japanese team and focus solely on their joint response to the discovery of the deadly virus in a flask. They secured the permission of the management of both institutes and called a global, video press conference. All three scientists would speak, and the discovery would be presented as a joint effort.

Armand started with some history:

"A while back, we were presented by the secret service of a friendly country . . ."

Several reporters tried to interrupt to ask for more details.

"Please, ladies and gentlemen, do not interrupt. When we are finished you will perceive the enormity of the issue. Hopefully, you will then understand that we are not at liberty to say much more. In fact, you should believe us when we say that, often, we do not know more than we are revealing . . . Others may know more, but they have not shared it with us."

He continued:

"We were presented with a flask with a clear liquid in it. We quickly determined that the liquid was a solution containing a highly infectious virus. With the help of Professor Dominique Dubreuil of the National Veterinary School of Alford, we were able to identify it as being a man-altered variant of a virus that occurs naturally in felines. This one apparently came from the lion family."

Oshima-San continued after having apologized for speaking in Japanese with simultaneous translation:

"Professor Dubreuil told us that viruses that occur in one genus, here felines, generally were found in one form or another in other species within the same genus. We found antibodies in the blood of common house cats and from that were able to discover both a possible vaccine and a possible treatment."

Tomioka-San took over and added, still in Japanese:

"Obviously, our work is not complete. We have experimental solutions which we could deploy in an emergency if such emergency developed. Yet, it will take more testing and more detailed work before we are ready to apply for and get regulatory approval."

Armand concluded:

"We have been told that a terrorist plot was to explode bombs around the world that would release the virus and cause a pandemic which would have made last year's Covid-19 challenge look like a training exercise. Who the terrorists are and what they were trying to accomplish has not been shared with us . . ."

The room was getting a bit rowdy. Armand calmed it down:

"What we have been told, however, is that all the bombs were discovered and disabled. The virus does not represent a risk at this point for the world's population."

■ ■ ■ ■ ■

At almost that very moment, Countess Renate fielded a call from Simon:

"Countess, just got a call from Colonel Kim . . ."

"And?"

"Well, it seems that the situation in North Korea is resolving itself . . . But with a nasty twist."

"Choi is dead?"

"Probably is, but that is not the nasty twist I'm talking about . . ."

"What is it then?"

"Well, there are reports of numerous deaths around the lab where he used to work . . ."

"Don't tell me that they seem to be caused by the virus . . ."

"Got it in one. My fears seem to have come to pass, if I can say it that way. I would bet that they disposed of all the material remaining in the lab, believing as our email allegedly from Choi intimated that everything was inoffensive. Cultures were flushed down drainpipes and contaminated the immediate area."

"What are we to do?"

"I've talked to Ariel Landau, my boss, and the Israeli government is informing everyone to quarantine anyone who comes out of North Korea . . ."

"Hope this works. Thankfully, we have emergency medications, but we don't want to stretch our luck too far. We're not ready for prime time . . ."

"I know. I know. Will you let Professor Duchemin know. And ask them to inform their contacts in Asia?"

"Sure will."

"Thanks."

"Simon, David here . . ."

■ ■ ■ ■ ■

"Do you have the information we need?"

"Yes. Ismail had to be convinced, but he came through in the end."

"Good. So?"

"There are bunkers below the locations in Raqqa, but they are not typically used for sleeping. They are only used when there is a bomb scare."

"Great. Thanks, David. We can go on with the plan, now."

CHAPTER.43

TEL AVIV, ISRAEL AND RAQQA, SYRIA

Four bombs exploded almost at the same time in Raqqa. The damage to the targets was absolutely lethal, though collateral damage was minimal. Speculation was rampant as to what might have caused the simultaneous blasts, though there was no tell-tale sign that anyone could point to. Ostensibly, Israel was immediately blamed, but no one was able to point to Israeli aircraft being anywhere near the targets. In fact, Syria prided itself that its anti-aircraft defenses would have detected the planes and shot them down. Nobody referred to drones being sighted either, though six of them were involved in the operation: two Sentinels which dropped the bombs and four Eitan to guide each bomb to its target.

Being forced to act sooner than he would have liked had convinced Simon that the risk of the detection of extra drones was worth it, given the fact that the news was about to break that terrorists had attempted to blackmail the world into submission to its ideology.

■ ■ ■ ■ ■

David Heller was helping Ismail pack his gear when the door of Ismail's apartment was flung wide open. It was Farouk Abboud ben Malouf. He was carrying a gun. Without any word, he shot at both

Ismail and David. Ismail did not have the time to say anything. He dropped to the floor like a stone. David too.

Farouk's luck, however, was totally different than David's. *Mossad* had in fact created a Kevlar combination as an improvement on the traditional Kevlar jacket. David's combination started right behind his shirt collar and extended to mid-thighs. It also covered his shoulders and the top of his arms. Farouk's two bullets struck David, one in the torso and the other near the left shoulder. They were stopped without fail by the combination, the new design preventing the second from hitting arteries near the brachial plexus. His gun, which he had in a holster on his left side, was out in a flash and the one shot he fired hit Farouk straight in or near the heart. He probably never realized what hit him. David was sorry for Ismail who had come to the "good" side in good faith, in the hope of being protected. Yet, he could not blame himself or anybody else in *Mossad* for not having anticipated that Farouk was the executioner whom Mark had suspected. The news of the bombing had hit him like a ton of bricks. Farouk assumed right away that the only person who could have helped was Ismail and he knew where to get him.

EPILOGUE

In truth, I hesitated long and hard before writing this story. Indeed, though I briefly appear in it, I am really there in a peripheral role. Yet, in the end, two things got me over the decision line. The first was the admiration which I have developed for Countess Renate and her team. I was able to see or hear of all these experts at work, and it reminded me a bit of activities that I had had, at a considerably more junior level, in years past. The second is that the abject extremes to which certain terrorist organizations or totalitarian regimes will allow themselves to go must be revealed. Without this book, I doubt very much that more than a minor part of the story would have come to light. If more books like this one were written, it is my hope that the repulsion which these terrorist activities provoke in me would also be shared by more people.

I must thank all the people who participated directly in the story for sharing a lot of their memories with me. I was very touched by Countess Renate who gave me a lot more time than I ever hoped would be available. Obviously, I am solely responsible if the dialogs do not exactly reflect what was said. Yet, I will promise my readers that I never made a change to what they told me for the purpose of making the story or anyone in it look better or worse.

I recently heard the sad news that Lee Han Soon had been found dead in his apartment in Hong Kong. The note that he left clearly states that he felt in part responsible for not having been more forceful in revealing what he knew both about Covid-19 and the most recent virus. I suspect that Professor Duchemin's judgment was correct: Han Soon became a participant in a cover-up scheme, although he probably did not do it out of conviction but out of fear for his job, or, worse, his life.

My husband and I—yes Mark and I did get married—are now safely relocated to a country where terrorists will have a hard time finding us. My appearance has had to undergo yet another change, as I am teaching at the local university. Thus, my picture appears on its website and it cannot be the same as that appeared on the site of the University of Tel Aviv. Mark remains at home currently, as he is still in a position where he could both hurt himself and any mission in which he played a role, should he be uncovered. He occasionally helps Simon with broad planning issues, but I sense that he will need some real activity soon. This will not be a big issue in the short term, as he is about to become a father. He will have time to help take care of baby when he or she is born.

Countess Renate has kindly asked me to become one of her associates, although probably more junior than others, on nuclear matters. I am delighted to serve in that role, for as long as I can do it without endangering my husband and our child to be born.

The only sad news that I must report is that my father did not deal too well with the need to move yet another time. He became depressed and eventually cut back on his food intake to the point that he had to be placed in hospital. Sadly, that is where he died less than a couple months ago. Naturally, I miss him a lot. But my biggest pain is that he will never know his first grandchild and *vice versa*. Mark and I are pretty much in agreement that somehow, if our baby is a boy, Cyrus will be featured somewhere in his name.

I am not sure what name I should use to sign this story. I still feel like Minoo and I still call my husband Mark. Maybe, one day, we will be able to be Mark and Minoo Levi and live in peace . . .

www.ingramcontent.com/pod-product-compliance
Lightning Source LLC
Chambersburg PA
CBHW051142030726
47504CB00004B/1005